PRAISE FOR

CHASING EDEN

Chasing
EDEN

S. L. Linnea

St. Martin's Paperbacks

This is a work of fiction. All of the characters, organizations, and events portrayed in this novel are either products of the author's imagination or are used fictitiously.

CHASING EDEN

Copyright © 2006 by Sharon Linnéa and B.K. Sherer.

Excerpt from *Beyond Eden* copyright © 2007 by Sharon Linnéa and B.K. Sherer.

Map by Christian Fünfhausen

ISBN: 0-312-94961-8
EAN: 978031294961-7

Printed in the United States of America

St. Martin's Paperbacks edition / June 2007

St. Martin's Paperbacks are published by St. Martin's Press, 175 Fifth Avenue, New York, NY 10010.

10 9 8 7 6 5 4 3 2 1

CONTENTS

FACTUAL NOTES

During the fall of Baghdad in April 2003, the National Museum of Iraq in Baghdad, along with its satellite in Mosul, were looted nearly simultaneously. The first wave of theft was orchestrated by professionals who knew exactly what they were looking for. They worked with precision and efficiency.

While many items initially reported missing were later found hidden for safekeeping in off-site vaults, the theft remains one of the great archeological tragedies of the age. Among the items taken from Mosul were certain ancient atlases and cuneiform tablets. Among the items originally reported missing from the central Iraq museum are the Dagger and sheath of Ur, crafted of gold and lapis lazuli, made in 2400 B.C.E.

All major troop movements and place descriptions in this narrative are accurate, based on publicly available information about the operation. Characters in the narrative are fictitious, and any resemblance to real persons is unintentional. The views presented in this book are those of the authors and do not necessarily represent the views of the Department of Defense or its components.

Descriptions of places and historic sites are accurate as of the date of the story.

PROLOGUE

April 8, 2003, 4:05 A.M.
10 kilometers south of Tallil
Southern Iraq

Adara Dunbar opened her eyes to find herself floating in a world gone brown. The air shimmered and folded in on itself in constantly moving circles. Nothing stayed solid. Where was she?

She clawed at thoughts to catch hold of them, but they, too, darted past her, spinning out of control. It was disconcerting, the effort needed to lay claim to some shred of her identity, of her surroundings.

Then she moved slightly and with the tearing pain in her abdomen came a shock of lucidity. She had been shot. She had been captured. She was on a cot, in a tent.

There had been a man in the black robes of the Fedayeen, Saddam Hussein's trained assassins. He had a sharp nose and a black beard, shaved close. But his eyes were what she remembered. They were violet. In a woman, they might have been beautiful. In his face, they blazed hatred. He had asked her questions. He had delighted in causing her pain.

She stirred again, and the tent walls seemed to fall in on her. She closed her eyes quickly, but the world did not stop spinning. And her stomach lurched as well, vomit rising in her throat. Suddenly her nausea and confusion made sense.

She had been drugged. That was the only answer.

For the first time, she panicked.

What had she said?

Adara opened her eyes again to see where the guards were. She was alone in this tent with the cot, but she could see shadows against the walls of the larger tent adjoining hers. How many were there? Four? Six? She could hear low mutterings in Arabic.

"God, help me," she whispered. "Give me wisdom. Give me strength."

She was a messenger, delivering the most important information of her life. It concerned safeguarding the secret that had shaped humankind for millennia—and, most likely, the real reason for the war that had started days before.

How had these men found her? Where had their information come from? How had they gotten this close?

She reached under the black *hijab,* the head scarf that also covered her neck. With great relief, she felt the small silver chain still there, the pendant still intact.

There was no question. She had to deliver the message.

Her hand was sticky, and as she held it up, she saw it dripping with blood. She tried to move, to ascertain the extent of her injuries, but the pain of even a small shift caused a sharp intake of breath. She did not want to call attention to the fact that she was conscious. Why was no guard left here with her?

She forced herself up, pushed the wine-colored fabric of the robe from her right side—and she knew. She had been left for dead.

From outside, a new voice was heard, shockingly loud, strikingly nonchalant.

"Muleskinner One Two, this is Rock Three November. Over."

The American accent was dead-on. He repeated, "Muleskinner One Two, this is Rock Three November. Over."

The response came over the crackle of a radio: "Rock Three November, this is Muleskinner One Two. Over."

The new voice was female. It was familiar.

"I have been tasked to relay the following message from Muleskinner Six. Break. Be advised, a ROM site has been established along MSR Falcon. Break. Are you prepared to copy grids? Over."

"Ready to copy."

And with those three words, Adara knew. She had given them the name of her backup.

The man outside her tent continued. "Proceed along MSR Falcon to grid Papa Victor 17771667. Turn left onto dirt road and continue for two hundred meters. ROM site located at Papa Victor 17751660. How copy? Over."

"I copy Lima Charlie. Thanks for the relay. If you are in contact with Muleskinner Five, tell him we should arrive in about three zero mikes. Over."

It was Jaime. The sound of her voice sent Adara reeling back into Dr. Hayden's History of World Religions class. An unusually hot September day in Princeton, Professor Hayden's hair flaring from his head like leaping sunspots. The two women sat next to each other. They had formed a bond the first day of class, the only students actually paying attention in what was obviously a beyond-boring required course for the majority of their classmates.

"Muleskinner One Two, Rock Three November. Wilco. Out."

She had led them to Jaime Richards. She had as good as arranged the ambush; she had signed Jaime's death certificate.

With an incredible act of will, Adara held up her right arm. It was bare; the bracelet was gone. Hot tears crowded her eyes.

Short of a miracle, her mission had failed completely.

If there was one thing she had learned in her short life, it was that there was little use in waiting for miracles. Sometimes you had to create them yourself.

—PART ONE—

Tallil/Ur

The first sign of trouble was a jolt to the Humvee. The vehicle continued another few paces, but it was slightly rocking, like a man with a limp. Chaplain (Major) Jaime Richards hit the brake and pushed the gear stick into park. "What now?" she muttered.

Before the question was completed, her chaplain assistant, Staff Sergeant Alejandro Ramon Benito Rodriguez, was on the ground, searching for the cause of the problem. The other five vehicles in their small convoy saw their predicament and rolled to a halt in the darkness of the barren landscape.

Jaime got out as Sergeant Moore, a tall black man—a good six feet to her five foot seven—climbed out of the lead vehicle and joined them. "What happened?"

"It looks like we ran over a small bale of concertina buried in the dust," Rodriguez said as he grabbed a battery-powered work light from the back of the Humvee. Concertina was the Army's improved version of barbed wire. It was stronger, with razorlike barbs that could easily slice through clothes—or flesh.

"Damn," said Sergeant Moore, sighting the left rear tire.

"That's wound around that wheel tighter than a ball of yarn!"

Jaime pushed at the Kevlar helmet over her plaited blond hair and stifled a sigh. So what else could go wrong? She was in the headquarters of the 57th Corps Support Group, whose mission it was to support units in the Fifth (V) Corps with essential supplies such as water, ammunition, and fuel. V Corps had entered Iraq first and had already secured camps in Tallil and other towns that dotted the way to Baghdad.

Jaime was with the CSG Headquarters, which had headed out at noon yesterday, April 7.

Everything had gone well until one of the Humvees in her unit had broken down and the mechanics had tried to fix it so that it could move under its own power. All fine and good, but that had meant they'd been stuck on the side of the road for hours. Once they'd started moving again, a sandstorm had kicked up, slowing their pace at times to a crawl.

The little six-vehicle convoy had no way of locating the rest of their unit until they received the radio message twenty minutes earlier. They must be within radio range, and that was good news.

It seemed they'd been out of the sandstorm and moving with purpose for an entire five minutes before they hit concertina. What else could go wrong?

Rodriguez crawled under the Humvee on his back, switched on the work light, and started pushing against the wire with his boots. Moore shook his head. "You'll never get that off by yourself."

But the compact staff sergeant was absorbed in his task. Jaime could see in an instant that Moore was right. There was good reason the soldiers referred to concertina as barbed wire on steroids. It was thick and nasty and could have fallen off any passing tank. "We'll need help," she said. "Why don't you continue to the ROM site with the rest of the convoy and see if they have a wrecker there? We're only one klick from the turnoff point."

A Refuel On the Move site, or ROM, was the Army's version of a mobile gas station. According to the transmission, they were less than one mile from the turnoff for the ROM established by their own soldiers.

"Yes, ma'am. But we should leave another vehicle here with you." Sergeant Moore thought for a second. "Specialist Houghton has an automatic weapon, so I'll leave his vehicle, Headquarters 15, here with you, and the rest of us will head for the refuel site."

"Here. Take my GPS. I have the ROM site programmed in." Jaime offered him her personal handheld global positioning system. It was the only one in their convoy.

Moore took it gratefully. "What about you?"

"You're sending a vehicle back, right? We'll be fine."

"OK. Keep a guard posted at all times. There are still pockets of resistance in Tallil."

"Already done . . . look." She pointed toward Private First Class Patterson, an 18-year-old white female from Kentucky, who had hitched a ride in their Humvee. She stood five meters from them, intently scanning the countryside, her weapon ready to fire.

Even as the chaplain pointed, she noticed that Patterson's silhouette on the dark desert landscape was losing definition. Another sandstorm was kicking up. Just what they needed.

When will I learn? she chided herself. *Never, but never, wonder what else can go wrong. You'll invariably get the answer.*

Sergeant Moore was moving back up the line, instructing drivers as he went. Headquarters 15, Specialist Houghton's vehicle, pulled out of line and circled back toward them. The other four, three Humvees and an ambulance, roared forward on the road.

"Any luck?" Jaime asked, squatting down by Rodriguez. What he lacked in height he easily made up for in muscle and sheer determination. He didn't answer but kept resolutely kicking at the encumbering wire. Jaime opened

her door and found her work gloves. She squinted at the
wire and gingerly tried to find a handhold from above. It
wasn't easy. Concertina would slice through ordinary work
gloves like a steak knife through watermelon. But she continued to try. There was little chance they could actually
free the wheel without a wrecker, but it was better to give
an effort than just wait.

Rodriguez shifted back out from below the vehicle. "I
think I saw some wire cutters," he said, and shifted his
search to the back of the Humvee. He turned around with a
small pair of cutters and a grin on his face.

They squatted together and he tried to come up under
the concertina with the tool, but there was no way the small
clamps could even make a dent. "I guess that's what makes
this stuff so effective," he sighed.

Suddenly the sound of gunshots—small-arms fire—
tore through the darkness. As they leapt to their feet, the
sky erupted in light as flares exploded over a hill about two
hundred meters away. Another round of shooting was answered, this time with something larger.

"Tallil?" asked Rodriguez.

"No, it's too close for Tallil."

Jaime strode to Private Patterson, also fully alert,
watching the flares set off by the military to reveal the attackers in the distance. The young soldier held her rifle
with a combination of enthusiasm and nerves.

"I'm ready, ma'am," she said.

The chaplain turned and stalked toward their second vehicle. "Houghton?" she asked.

Specialist Randy Houghton was on the ground, his automatic weapon in position. "I see it, Chaplain. It doesn't
sound like they're heading this way. Yet."

"I hope you're right."

The next round of flares illuminated an ever-thicker
swirl of sand. Jaime knew her immediate objective was to
get out of any potential line of fire. As a noncombatant, she
wasn't even carrying a sidearm. She did, however, have her

own security detail in the person of her chaplain assistant. She came behind the truck and was startled to find Rodriguez on his feet, looking off into the desert in the opposite direction.

"Chaplain?" he said.

She squinted, dismayed by the quickening intensity of the sandstorm. The whistle of the wind was picking up as well. What was he looking at? Why wasn't his weapon drawn?

Then she saw it—a shape moving in the darkness. She turned to make certain that Rodriguez had his weapon ready and was shocked to find him moving off into the sand instead. She grabbed her night-vision goggles from the driver's seat. Was it a person? The movement was not fluid—neither a walk nor a crawl. But it was advancing. It had to be a person. What was Rodriguez doing? It could be a trap. *Damn! You don't just go walking up to an unknown person in the dark!*

"Patterson!" she called, and the young soldier turned, saw the situation, and used her weapon to cover the receding form of Rodriguez. They both watched, dumbstruck, as he fought his way over— and through—the sand to the figure. It collapsed into his arms. Jaime moved forward to meet him. It was slow going, each step hard-won. Finally she reached Rodriguez as he plowed forward, carrying the person in his arms.

"What . . . ?" started Jaime, shouting to be heard.

"She's injured!" answered the staff sergeant, not breaking his labored stride. He laid the form down gently on the sand behind the truck. Chaplain Richards was still startled by his actions, but before she could respond, a female voice spoke.

"Jaime," it said.

The chaplain dropped onto her knees in the sand. She moved the dark scarf from the woman's face. Jaime had never been more shocked in her life. The features were familiar, but so completely out of context she couldn't make

the connection. They were streaked with mud, the head
scarf unwound to reveal thick black hair plastered with
sand and sweat.

And then Jaime's mind found a circuitous route to
recognition.

Princeton Seminary. Her year getting a master's in
world religions. The school library. The scent of wood. An
open map of the possible dwelling places of Abraham, patriarch of three major faiths. The Tigris and Euphrates
rivers. Ur of the Chaldeans. And Adara, studying with her.
Now here they were, halfway around the world, in the middle of a sandstorm in Iraq, outside Tallil, a stone's throw
from Ur. They were here.

"Adara?" she said.

"Listen." The younger woman's voice was urgent
through parched lips. "Message. So . . . important. You
must deliver it."

"What are you talking about? Message for whom?
From who?"

"In four hours. 0800. 3057 4606."

Out of habit, Jaime reached into the cargo pocket of her
pants and pulled out a small green notebook she carried
with her everywhere. She wrote down the numbers.

"I don't understand. 0800 is the time. But what are the
other numbers?"

"The Fourth Sister," Adara whispered. "You must find it!

"Here," she said, and she had to struggle for another
breath. From beneath the folds of crimson material she
withdrew a delicate chain. A finely crafted silver pendant,
less than an inch long, hung from it. The pendant looked
like a flattened cylinder—barely wide enough to contain
something very small. "Must bring home the lost sword."

"Adara! What are you telling me? I don't understand.
Are you hurt?"

"Yes," she said. "Not important. Please, promise me.
The message. Leave it there. 3057 4606. Where the Sister
points."

"The Fourth Sister."

A faint nod.

This was all too baffling.

"Where are you hurt? We're traveling with an ambulance—medics. As soon as we can free our wheel, we'll catch up to them."

"They've gone? No! The radio call . . . ambush. Don't go."

"It's OK," Jaime said. "It was one of our guys. Had to be—our transmissions change frequencies every second. No one who isn't U.S. military can listen—let alone talk to us."

Ambush, mouthed Adara, and Jaime gingerly moved what remained of Adara's tattered robe from her side. Even in the darkness, Jaime could see her friend was in serious trouble.

"Rodriguez," Jaime called, and he appeared beside her.

"Look what they were carrying in Headquarters 15," he said, brandishing a pair of bolt cutters.

The gunfire that split the night this time was heavier caliber. More gunfire, and an explosion. Jaime and Rodriguez scrambled to their feet. "That's not the hill," said Rodriguez. "That's further ahead up the road."

"Ambush," whispered Adara again, urgently.

Jaime's assistant handed her the light, and she knelt to hold it by the tire, keeping it as hidden as possible. These wire cutters worked like a charm. Eight snips and Jaime was able to grab the concertina wire carefully with her gloved hands and peel it back.

Sergeant Rodriguez already had Adara in his arms and was placing her carefully into the transport.

"Get her settled!" Jaime yelled at him. "I'll tell Houghton we're going to proceed. We've got to assist the rest of the convoy! They're being ambushed! They don't know it was a bogus call. They think we've got friendly forces just ahead!"

"Due respect, ma'am, but I'm not driving you into a known ambush!"

"OK, it's noted you've argued the security crap. Let's move!"

"But ma'am!"

She clearly saw the dilemma reflected in his eyes. His job was to keep her out of harm's way. But they also needed to help the vehicles up ahead.

"Are you driving, or am I?" The question painted him into a corner. Since she had no weapon, the safest setup would put her in back, Rodriguez driving, Patterson riding shotgun. But Rodriguez couldn't stop her from driving, or from heading straight into the ambush.

Richards and Rodriguez squared off, eyes blazing. "You don't have a choice, Sergeant," Jaime said, for once underscoring his rank. "Get Patterson." And she ran to instruct Headquarters 15.

Gerik Schroeder liked the black robes. He had never worn robes before, never gravitated to the color black, but he enjoyed the appropriateness of wearing the time-honored symbol of the bad guy. Fedayeen. Hitler's SS. Darth Vader. Black was understated. Powerful. Slimming. He smiled to himself.

He did enjoy his work.

Gerik wondered who had chosen black for the SS. He'd never really thought about the importance of the statement made by uniforms. Besides the basic black of the Fedayeen, the uniforms for this war were a complete fizzle. No power behind them at all. Unlike the sleek, wasplike uniforms of the SS skull and crossbones. Swastika. Red on black.

So few people realized that the SS had not just been an elite fighting unit. It was a priesthood, the High Priesthood of the Blood. Each member had the correct family background, hair and eye color, and skull shape. But beyond that, each was brilliant and educated. They were taught by the greatest scientific minds of the century, the scientists of the Armanenschaft.

They could read the great secrets of the Runes; they

knew of the seven Root Races. They knew that if they
could just return the Aryan race to its pure-blooded state,
they would become god-men again. But although they had
searched the world, they had not found the one necessary
missing element. And so their attempt had met with failure.

Luckily for Gerik.

The Western world should know by now that you might
be able to defeat an army, but you can't destroy a true religion by killing its prophet. The SS might be gone, Himm-
ler might be gone, but the Ancestral Heritage Society had
never died. For 60 years, they had grown stronger, and,
quietly, the search had continued. The world had changed,
and the Society had indeed forged strange alliances. Together, they'd finally traced down the missing element.
They'd found it, right here in Iraq. And Gerik, now the
highest leader of the Society, the *Grosskomtur,* would be
present for the victory.

As it turned out, the Arab girl they'd captured did not
know the location of the final link. But she knew the identity of one who did: Chaplain Jaime Richards.

A sandstorm was brewing. Perfect. Limited visibility
would make his job that much easier.

"Vehicles approaching," said a voice, low but distinct in
his earpiece. Indeed, outlines of American Humvees were
emerging from the sandy darkness of the road.

His adrenaline surged. "Stay out of sight until they're
all engaged. I don't think they'll have time to set up defen-
sive positions. If they do, your target should be in the center. If not, target will almost certainly be in the back, low,
behind the vehicles. I'll keep you advised."

You talk too much, thought Gerik. *If I didn't already
know everything you just told me, we'd both be in serious
trouble.*

The gunfire began. As hoped, the convoy was taken by
complete surprise. The vehicles squealed to a stop as they
realized their way was blocked. They were unable to exit
the kill zone. Gerik heard shouts and watched the soldiers

ascertain the direction from which the attack came. They scrambled behind their vehicles to find fields of fire.

"There are only four vehicles!" hissed the voice in his ear. "Dammit!"

Gerik was well hidden to the side of the road south of the assailants who had opened fire. He found himself across from the last vehicle to arrive, an ambulance. Even though he knew where the Commander was, he could barely see him hidden on the hill across the road and to the west of their location. The Commander held binoculars, with which he was reading the occupants' names that the military so helpfully displayed on the front windshields.

"The chaplain's transport isn't here!" he muttered. "Stay down!"

How could the chaplain not be here? Gerik felt his disappointment morphing into rage. This was his moment. His whole body was poised, his mind prepared to bring in his target. And his target hadn't showed!

The American soldiers were returning fire. What now? How long would they engage?

The smell of gunpowder surrounded him like an old friend. *Hang on, Commander. Give it time. This is our one chance.*

And then, once again, patience paid off.

He heard motors approaching from down the road. The final two vehicles were racing to join their friends. The chaplain cometh. Hallelujah, amen.

The two Humvees roared into sight.

"Wait for my I.D.," spoke the Commander's voice in his earpiece.

The new arrivals obviously knew they were entering a situation. They pulled up just short of the kill zone and arrayed themselves in herringbone formation, the first splayed to the right, the second to the left. The occupants exited on the side away from the enemy fire.

Oh yes, it's the enemy, thought Gerik. *You just don't know which one.*

"Chaplain, last vehicle!" came the voice. "She's out. She seems to be arguing with her assistant. The assistant is moving forward. Now! Go! Go! Go!"

Gerik again wanted to punch the Commander. He despised the way he talked down to his team, and especially to Gerik, who was his equal. Granted, the Commander was their man inside the U.S. forces, but Gerik still despised his habit of not only stating but also repeating the obvious. Gerik disengaged the earpiece and slid down the small berm, slipping easily into the darkness behind the convoy.

Everyone was occupied, facing the other direction. They thought this was an attack. Not a kidnapping.

It was clear that there was only one soldier who did not have a weapon drawn. She was alone, down low, behind the rear left wheel of her transport. Her chaplain assistant was nowhere to be seen. Gerik knew a moment of disappointment. The chaplain must be taken alive. There were no such limitations on the handling of the assistant.

As Gerik made his move, a sudden recurring blast of ammunition joined the engagement. One of the new arrivals had an automatic weapon. That set the stakes higher, the clock running faster.

Gerik took two strides from the back of the Humvee to where Jaime was crouched. He reached down and grabbed her, pinioning her arms behind her back.

He stood and was surprised at how light his target was. "Rodriguez!" the chaplain shouted. She was tall and lean, with high cheekbones, flashing hazel eyes. Even covered with dirt and sand like everyone else, she had potential, he could tell.

She was also a wildcat.

It was fortunate for him that her desert boots were so much softer than black leather Army boots, or she would be inflicting noticeable injury even now. It was clear she had self-defense training. It didn't matter. His training far outweighed hers.

Her flak jacket made things more difficult. It was heavy,

coming up too high on her neck to let him get a good hold. She also had something unwieldy at her waist—a chemical mask. He almost had her, though. She broke one arm free and took a fierce bite out of the second and third fingers on his right hand.

He grabbed for her arm, knowing that once he had her elbow, he could easily dislocate her shoulder—assuming the flak jacket didn't get too much in the way. Then it would be a simple matter of pulling her back over the small hill, zip-tying her wrists, taping her mouth, and waiting for a ride.

But in one orchestrated movement, she managed to slice her elbow into his solar plexus and wheel around. He bent slightly and whipped back to grab her. As he did, he felt something drop from an inside pocket of his outer robe. Not taking time to find it, he was able to knee her in the back. He'd spun her around, ready to punch her face, when a bolt of pain shot through the top of his head. His vision swam and he fell to his knees.

Someone else had joined the fray. Feigning more dizziness than he felt, Gerik leaned closer to the ground, turned, and grabbed the ankles of the new person standing behind him. He pulled her forward, and the person fell with a thud.

The complete shock Gerik's mind registered at seeing her face made him lose a valuable second. "You!" he hissed.

Adara didn't even look at him. Instead, she released the tent peg with which she'd just whacked him, grabbed an object from the sand beneath him, and flung it forward toward the truck ahead. It landed at the feet of the chaplain assistant, who was returning from his errand toward the front of the convoy. But Rodriguez didn't pick it up. He had only one objective: the safety of Chaplain Richards. "Chaplain!" he called, gun drawn.

The moment Jaime had her freedom, she'd disengaged and run several yards before turning back around. When she did, she stood, aghast.

Gerik stood near the rear wheel of the last Humvee, holding Adara in front of him with an iron grip. Adara looked at her. There was no fear in her eyes. "The sisters," she said.

"Release her and step back!" Rodriguez yelled, the muzzle of his weapon pointed at Gerik's head.

Ahead in the convoy, an engine gunned to life. One of the first Humvees was turning around. Bursts of fire from the squad automatic weapon kept the enemy on the hill occupied while, one after another, soldiers were boarding their transports and turning around.

The stupid little staff sergeant must have told them it was a trap, there were no friendly forces to offer assistance, turn around.

Some nonverbal communication was happening between Gerik's prisoner and the chaplain.

He realized he had to abort his mission if he was not to be captured or killed. There would be another chance. They had until the precise hour of the quarter moon: April 9, 11:00 P.M. Tomorrow night.

But as for now, his intended target wasn't even looking at him. He'd fix that.

"Jaime," he said calmly.

She looked up. His violet eyes locked with hers. He felt like he could bore inside her. He was leaving a worm of fear. A worm that would live inside her forever. He smiled at her. And with a swift, practiced move, he broke his prisoner's neck.

Adara slumped to the ground. The man in black turned and ran. Rodriguez fired three shots after him into the dark.

As Gerik turned the corner into the vast darkness, he heard a cry of anguish. He knew it was Jaime Richards. He smiled. His message had been received.

Jean St. Germain stepped out of the small car and turned once to make sure the driver still remained, waiting silently in the dark.

"This way, Mr. St. Germain," said the businesslike voice beside him.

They walked quickly around the freestanding garage, toward the rear of the museum. The city was in chaos. No one in his right mind was out.

An old flatbed truck was pulled in behind them, its headlights extinguished. Half a dozen men jumped down. Jean did not even look at them.

"We have an agreement, yes?" he asked, afraid his nerves were showing. "If anything happens to me, you know there will be very serious consequences."

"We have an agreement," the man beside him replied, not breaking his stride. "You needn't worry. We're not murderers. We're art collectors."

"Yes, well."

The museum sat, quiet and dark. There was no electricity. Whether it had been cut or was simply out like most of the city's, he did not know. All he knew was that he'd been promised there'd be no alarms. Although who would answer alarms tonight?

The single door they stood before was in the dark. The gentleman next to him produced a key ring and undid a series of locks.

The door swung open. The small group went silently inside. The museum was a modern building of glass and cream-colored bricks. In the dark, it all flattened to gray. St. Germain's guide knew his way. They walked briskly down parquet floors heading in the opposite direction of the main galleries. Jean had studied a hand-sketched map of the museum and had expected to stop at the ramp to the basement. Instead, they continued on down the long, empty hallway. His confidence began to grow. Six million American dollars had bought him entry to the museum and two specific items. It also bought him a ride back to the safe house.

He dared wonder if the portly Iranian art collector beside him was slightly amused by "Jean St. Germain," the Frenchman whose French was less than perfect.

Who cared? The collector had his cash. For weeks the museum staff both here and in Mosul had been working frantically to move many of the most precious antiquities in the world out of war's way, to keep these irreplaceable artifacts out of the hands of looters. Oh, well.

The collector finally stopped at the door to the only room that opened off this corridor: the Restoration Room. Jean's heart began to accelerate as they stood before the door and he realized how close he was. How many decades of work and risk and planning were about to pay off. The lives that it had cost. The lives that it would change.

The keys once again appeared in the hands of the collector. The door swung open. Jean stepped inside. For the first time, he turned on the flashlight he carried. The collector put a hand on Jean's shoulder and motioned toward a single table in the middle of the room. On it sat nine items, each in its own burlap sack.

"I believe the items you seek are on the right-hand side."

"And the others?" Jean asked.

"Other items that have been pre-purchased." The portly man chuckled. "However, you are getting the best bargain, by far. The others will all have hefty delivery charges. You are the only 'will call.'" The collector found this inordinately funny.

Jean stepped forward to the table. He lifted the first item, removed it from its sack, inspected it briefly, and put it into a large velvet pouch inside his burlap bag. He repeated the process with the adjacent sack.

"You are pleased?"

"Yes."

"Your car is waiting outside. The cash is no longer in it."

"As agreed."

"Merci. A pleasure. My associate will show you to the nearest exit."

Jean walked with renewed confidence back down the hall and stood for a moment, looking through the tall glass windows, where Baghdad was falling and the world burned.

He tested the weight of the ancient items in his bag.

"The war is over, gentlemen," he said, although the hallway was empty except for him. "You can all go home now."

From this moment forward, it didn't matter how many tyrants were dislodged, how many empires rose and fell. It was all rearranging those proverbial deck chairs. It was good to know who was really in control. "Another gift for you, Eulogia," he said.

He walked back out into the sultry Iraqi night that was curiously devoid of American guards and hurried into the darkened car with motor idling. As it pulled away, he knew that history had just taken a sharp turn and there was no looking back.

April 8, 2003, 5:42 A.M.
Logbase Rock
Tallil Airfield
Southern Iraq

Jaime would always be grateful that, even under fire, Staff Sergeant Rodriguez had treated Adara with care and respect. Jaime didn't know the protocol for dealing with civilian corpses during a gun battle in wartime, but as the transport in front of them had turned around to flee, Rodriguez had come to where she knelt over her friend. "Chaplain, you need to get into the vehicle," he said. And without asking, he had picked up Adara's body and laid it carefully in the back of the Humvee.

Adara.

The day that kept replaying in Jaime's mind was a December Monday in 1998. She and Adara sat at a rickety wooden table, watching snow swirl outside the front windows of Hoagie Haven in Princeton. They had books open in front of them. The hoagie they'd split (#23, the Katharine Hepburn, no onions) was gone, but each still nursed a drink. They were allegedly studying for the next day's test, but they were mostly amusing themselves by writing each other witty notes in Akkadian.

Two of their female classmates, considerably younger than they, had arrived and gone up to the counter to order from, and argue with, the two brothers who owned the place. "No peppers?" one was saying, "How come you want hoagie, no peppers?" Once the young women had finished sparring with the heavyset brother about the presence of vinegar and oil on the requested sandwiches, they returned to what had obviously been a very serious conversation about the charms and assumed sexual prowess of one of their professors. Adara and Jaime, each in the grip of inspiration, started writing symbol-laden notes about the matter.

▷▭⧄⟨ ◁⟨⟨ ▷▱⧄ , said Adara's.

"Compensate for what?" asked Jaime with a grin when the younger women had paid for their take-out orders and left. "His lack of *vigor*?"

"You've got it," said Adara. "I think you'll ace the test." She took a sip of her drink. "So, have you ever had a crush on a professor?"

By that point, Jaime's emotional armor was so thoroughly second nature that the question bounced off, unnoticed. Instead, she found herself studying Adara, the soft curls of her long black hair, flawless skin the color of gingerbread, her large brown eyes naturally accented by thick lashes. Jaime was certain that a number of professors had taken note of her friend. Whereas physical training had made Jaime thin and muscular, Adara, while not carrying an extra pound, had naturally rounded curves—apparent even though she wore neither her jeans nor her peach-colored sweater tight.

"You didn't answer my question," said Adara.

"Why?" asked Jaime. "Have you ever had a crush on one?"

"I've always wanted to," Adara replied. "I guess I've just never been assigned the right classes. And you're dodging."

Jaime's next words shocked even herself. She hadn't intended to say them. "I fell in love with one of my seminary professors," she said. "That's why I'm here."

"Wow, really? What was he like?"

"Dr. Atwood. Assistant professor. Taught Bible history. Felt his mission, beyond teaching, was to understand the causes and daily crises faced by the peoples in the Middle East, particularly Israel and Palestine, and try to wrest the peace process from control of the extremists. Every year, he took a group of his students to Israel to visit schools and kibbutzim, and to visit whatever Palestinian settlements were safe enough. I went my second year. What can I say? I'm a pushover for a man with nobility of spirit."

"So, were all his female students in love with him?"

"Seemed that way," said Jaime. Her heartbeat had accelerated, and her breathing was getting jagged. "The fact that he was completely committed to his work and didn't seem to notice the opposite sex at all only made him more attractive."

"He was attractive?"

"If you saw him in a movie, I'm sure he'd look pretty skinny and average. Nice thick hair, though. Brown. Always meant to switch to contacts, but at least wore wire rims."

"OK, I don't get it. You graduated from seminary, obviously, and this Professor Atwood isn't here. So, what's the connection that brings you here?"

"I did graduate from seminary," said Jaime. "It's funny, I'd thought Paul—that was his first name—was attracted to me, too, though of course he couldn't admit it when I was a student. But I sort of hoped, after I graduated . . . but, no, he seemed more than happy to let me go. I was called to an assistant pastorate at a church in Springfield, Missouri, and chose to go on active duty soon after that. Met lots of guys, but nobody like Paul. There was nobody like Paul.

"We met completely by chance in the airport in Rome three years after I became an Army chaplain. He was on a busman's holiday, and I was supposed to join my brother and his fiancée in Florence that week. But we each had unscheduled time, and he offered to show me the historic sites of Rome. . . ."

"Yes?" asked Adara.

Jaime finished her drink. "Yesterday would have been our eighteenth-month wedding anniversary," she said.

She saw Adara glance down at her left hand, where there was neither engagement nor wedding band. "He . . . ?" She didn't know how to frame the question.

"He died," said Jaime. "A year ago September. We'd been married three months. The Army brass asked if I'd like some time away from full-time duties, and I accepted this assignment. I'm becoming a specialist in world religions. I'll go down and teach at the chaplain school when I'm done here, before being reassigned."

"Oh," said Adara. She reached across and put her hand over Jaime's. The wedding ring that Jaime now wore on a chain around her neck suddenly felt heavy. But she left it hidden.

They sat for a moment before Jaime sat up. "OK, come on," she said. "I translated your note! Your turn."

That had been the only time during the year at Princeton Seminary that she had talked about Paul. It said a lot about her high regard for Adara that she had. Adara had been a special friend.

"Chaplain?"

Jaime blinked and tried to corral her thoughts.

"Chaplain Richards?" Rodriguez was speaking to her from up front where he was driving, Private Patterson riding shotgun.

"Hunh?" came Jaime's eloquent reply.

"Do you have the challenge and password? It changed at oh three hundred."

"Lemme check. . . ." She fumbled through her cargo pocket and pulled out her green notebook. Enough light was encroaching outside that she could make out the words. "The challenge should be 'wastebasket' and the password is 'dinosaur.' "

Even as she spoke, they came in sight of the entrance to the base at Tallil Airfield. One guard was posted out front, and concertina wire was strung across the road to limit access. Back another 10 meters was a second guard by a .50-caliber machine gun mounted on a tripod.

The closer guard, wearing a flak vest and Kevlar helmet and carrying an M-16, approached their Humvee.

"Do you have a wastebasket in there?" he asked.

"No, but my son has one with a stupid purple dinosaur on it," answered Rodriguez.

The young guard laughed. "That's a good one. Are all these vehicles with you?"

"Yes, all six are from one convoy."

Jaime leaned forward. "How do we find the 57th CSG TOC?" The Tactical Operations Center was the hub of activity for the unit. Jaime knew that word of the ambush had been radioed ahead of their arrival at Tallil, but there was no telling how the facts had become twisted in the relay. She'd better head there first and set the record straight.

"Straight down this road, ma'am, about one hundred meters."

He strode back, pulled the concertina out of the way, and motioned them through.

Inside, once they'd parked their vehicles and the others dispersed, Rodriguez waited for Jaime to disembark.

"Chaplain," he said softly, "you all right?"

Jaime was oddly moved by his tone of concern. Her former assistant had opted out of the Army when his term expired at the beginning of the year. When large numbers of troops began deploying to the Middle East, there was suddenly such a huge need for deployable chaplains—and chaplain assistants—that she had already been in Kuwait when she'd gotten word that a new assistant had been cross-leveled to her corps support group. A further miracle was that they had been able to find each other in between Camp New York in Kuwait and crossing the berm into Iraq. Desert hookups had not been running smoothly.

But Rodriguez had jumped into the job. Despite his retort with the password, he was not married and had no chil-

dren. When Jaime had asked about his parents, his answer
had been a simple, "The Army is my family." She had not
pressed further. The two of them had a natural rapport.
Even as he stood awaiting a reply, she felt the irony. It was
supposed to be her asking the question. It was not supposed to be her having seen a friend deliberately murdered.

She willed herself to give him an honest answer. "I have
no idea how I am," she said. "But waiting won't make it
any easier to face Jenkins."

"Yes, ma'am," Rodriguez agreed.

Together they walked to the Muleskinner TOC and
pushed aside the double door flap on the tent, which kept
any light inside from spilling out. A young private sat behind a small table at the entry. He was bleary-eyed, obviously nearing the end of a long night shift and looking
forward to climbing into his bunk. He looked up, nodded
recognition, and went back to the novel he was reading.

The night shift battle captain saw them enter and came
over. His name was Adam Whittaker, and both his commanding height and his chiseled features served to make
him easily one of the most handsome officers in the CSG.
He also knew what he was doing. Jaime liked and re-
spected him. But his words were neither unexpected nor
welcome.

"Chaplain, the XO wants to see you ASAP."

The executive officer, Lieutenant Colonel Ray Jenkins,
was across the tent, his back to them, studying a large map
on the sidewall. Jaime's teeth clenched at the sight of him.
He was her height, five foot seven, with a slight build, his
brown hair cut short into the ever popular high and tight.
As the XO, he was second in command of the unit, being
outranked only by the group commander, Colonel Abraham, "Abe," Derry. Jenkins's mission was to ensure all
staff administrative functions moved smoothly and effi-
ciently, so his colonel could focus on more important
things. Unfortunately for the staff, Jenkins was a flamer—
he blew his top at the slightest provocation. He was also a

control freak, wanting to have his hands in every detail of the staff operations and demanding his staff get his OK before every move.

Which was why Jaime drove him nuts. As the executive officer, he was her immediate supervisor. However, as chaplain, she had direct access to the CSG commander with issues that concerned the unit. Jenkins hated that she didn't need his permission.

Jenkins heard the captain addressing her, and he turned and stalked across the tent. *Let's see,* thought Jaime, *what would be an appropriate opening? How about "Are you OK?" or, "Sit down; tell me what happened."*

"Chaplain. What the hell were you doing sending the convoy into an ambush?" he spat, the artery in his neck pulsing madly.

"I didn't know—"

"And why the fuck did you leave the highway?"

"Sir . . ." She took a breath, trying to maintain her composure, to keep from crying or yelling, or both. "We received message traffic from Rock diverting us to a ROM site at that location."

"There was no ROM site along that road! Who sent the message?"

"An NCO from company operations. His call sign was Rock Three November."

"There is no such person!"

Jaime swallowed hard. "I've figured that out, now."

She had never seen Jenkins in such a fury, but he kept his voice low. "So you're telling me the enemy had access to a SINGARS radio with the proper security fill and knew the right call sign to use. They guided you to a bogus ROM site and were waiting with an ambush?" Incredulity laced his words.

"That's about it, sir."

Jenkins stood toe-to-toe with her. "Chaplain, that's the biggest piece-of-shit story I've ever heard. When you're ready to tell me what really happened, I'll be glad to hear it." He turned abruptly and stalked off the way he had come.

With him went the very last of Jaime's energy. She felt any extra adrenaline seeping out through her toes and wondered that she was able to stand up at all.

She looked around for Rodriguez and found him in deep discussion with the battle captain. They turned to her as one. "What's the good news, Captain?" she asked.

"Yesterday, while you were on the road, the 2nd Brigade of the 3rd ID moved in from the south of Baghdad and took control of the presidential palaces. Third Brigade destroyed the Iraqi troops on the northwest side of the city, isolating Baghdad from outside military help."

Jaime tried to find the energy to look happy at the news.

"Did the Fedayeen really try to kidnap you?" Whittaker asked.

The question made her shiver. The image of her abductor's face, the evil in his eyes, was burned into her memory. But his face had been thin and had seemed tanned rather than Middle Eastern.

"You know," she said, "I don't think he was Fedayeen. He spoke English. But yes, he tried to capture me—before he killed . . ."

Adam Whittaker put his hand on her shoulder. "Jaime, go get some rest. We'll try to figure this whole thing out in a few hours. At least all the soldiers are here safely."

He realized the minefield of his last statement, but Jaime shook off any apology. "Thanks," she said simply, and turned to go. She and Rodriguez exited the tent in step. Outside, dawn was breaking over Southern Iraq. Jaime squinted past the perimeter, to the desolate landscape. "I never thought I'd hear myself say this, but Jenkins is right. None of it makes any sense."

"Why don't you go get some rest?" Rodriguez said. "Let me head over to Mortuary Affairs to see if they can help make arrangements for a burial for your friend. You said you don't know that she has any local family?"

"She told me she was from London," Jaime said. It made no sense at all.

"I'll let you know what arrangements are made," he said. As an afterthought, he fished something out of his pocket and turned back to her. "Here. She threw this at the last minute. I guess she wanted you to have it. Now go."

Jaime took the object he held out to her. It was a golden bracelet, about two inches wide. *Go get some rest.* She still felt as though she were swimming underwater in slow motion. Her mind was as yet refusing to process what had just happened. She knew from years of counseling people in crisis that lack of sleep made difficult things seem insurmountable. And she was running on a severe lack of sleep. The convoy had stopped by the side of the road for three hours last night. Many of the soldiers were able to throw down a cot by their vehicle or even doze off sitting up.

She couldn't. These were her people . . . all of them. Even Jenkins. And if something happened, she needed to be there, to be alert and ready to help. Last night, knowing she needed rest, she had tried sleeping on top of her vehicle, as Rodriguez had done the night before. He'd wedged a piece of plywood between the roll bars and the canvas top of the Humvee to make a sort of platform. But even this added luxury had not done the trick.

Here at the Tallil base, the headquarters company had thrown up a couple of medium tents for sleeping. Jaime got her cot, found a spot inside the officers' tent in which to throw it, and sat down. She pulled out some baby wipes and removed the top layer of grime from her face and hands. She didn't even consider releasing her hair from its French braid. She was certain that "sandy blond" had taken on an entirely new meaning in the current landscape. She threw away the baby wipes and stretched out on her cot.

A mentor of hers had once said that an effective counselor had to have been broken herself to be of help to others in pain. *Just how broken do I have to be?* she screamed inside. *Mom and Dad . . . and Paul . . . wouldn't that do the trick? We had to add Adara, brilliant, gentle Adara—murdered?* Jaime couldn't help but add that most useless of questions: *God, why?*

She knew she was in danger of old scars ripping open. In fact, she was purposely keeping her mind anesthetized while she tried to think of some way, any way, to keep from plunging again into the overwhelming grief of having lost Paul. She found herself unconsciously clutching the wedding ring she wore on the necklace behind her dog tags. That was the final push. She lost her emotional footing and stumbled backward yet again to that sunny September day, the warm scents of summer still in the air. Jaime had been in Maryland, assigned to Aberdeen Proving Ground, where they'd felt a female chaplain could provide some stability to a training unit that had been wracked by a sexual harassment scandal earlier that year. She'd been visiting soldiers in a truck maintenance class, which was held in a large four-bay training garage. One of her favorite parts of her job was keeping up with what the soldiers did as daily routine. Four students—three privates, one specialist—and a noncommissioned officer were there, all in requisite green coveralls. They were pulling an engine out of the chassis of a Humvee with an overhead crane. Jaime had been looking over their shoulders, asking questions, kidding with them, when the battalion commander and the brigade chaplain had appeared at the open bay door.

"Group, atten-hut!" said the NCO. All the soldiers snapped to attention. And every soldier in the garage had exactly the same thought: *Oh, shit.*

The commander and the chaplain together looking for someone was never good. Someone was either in serious trouble or about to get really bad news. The commander was the notifier. The chaplain was there for support.

"As you were," said the battalion commander, Lieutenant Colonel Greg Spenser. He was with Chaplain (Major) Vincent Diaz, a Catholic priest affectionately known as Father Vince.

The group had only a split second to notice and process the discrepancy: battalion commander, brigade chaplain. For a notification, the battalion commander should have found, and brought, his own battalion chaplain. Unless, of course—

"Sergeant, please continue with your class," Spenser said distractedly. "We need to borrow Chaplain Richards."

Unless, of course, it was his chaplain he needed to notify.

That 60-second walk, from the Maryland motor pool to the parking lot in 1997, had ricocheted Jaime back even earlier, to 18 years before, when she had learned of her parents' deaths. That same feeling of unutterable dread overtook her again in the time it took her to walk with Vince and Lieutenant Colonel Spenser out of sight and hearing of the soldiers in the garage.

"OK, tell me," she said, with the mistaken idea that the agony of uncertainty was worse than the news itself.

"Let's go somewhere and sit down," said Spenser, a 38-year-old white male. Six feet tall. West Point grad. Imposing presence. He motioned to a minivan nearby, the door standing open.

But she'd stood, arms crossed, feet not moving.

"Please, Jaime," said Vince.

Jaime, more than anyone, knew how much commanding officers hated this part of their duty. It wasn't high on the chaplains' list, either. But she didn't care about making it easier for them. She just needed to know.

Lieutenant Colonel Spenser gave in, with a sigh, and said, "Very well. Chaplain Richards, I am very sorry to inform you that yesterday at 1550 local time, your husband, Paul, was killed in an explosion in Israel."

At 1550 local time, the world as you knew it ceased to exist.

And now, again, in 2003, Jaime was forced to wonder—how many times could she be expected to rebuild her world, only to have it blown apart?

Was it happening again? What was going on? And she knew that, as tired and drained as she felt, she had to focus.

What was Adara doing in Iraq? Who had shot her? How had she known about the ambush? Who was that man in black robes? How on earth did he know Jaime's name—and why had he tried to kidnap her? Why had he made the killing of Adara so personal?

None of it made any sense.

And the message. Adara had been trying to tell her something. Numbers. Something about a sword. Adara had been so focused on the message. The urgency in her voice was haunting. Perhaps she had even died to deliver the message.

Then something else Adara had said made Jaime sit up and swing her feet to the ground. She put her head in her hands to stop the spinning, then looked at her watch. It was 0630.

Adara had said 0800. If this message was really important enough to die for, if those numbers were indeed a rendezvous time, it seemed Jaime had less than 90 minutes to figure the whole thing out.

April 8, 2003, 6:48 A.M.
Logbase Rock
Tallil Airfield
Southern Iraq

Jaime hated the taste of coffee. If she could have taken her caffeine intravenously that morning, she would have happily done so. As it was, it sat before her, black and vile and only partially effective. The chicken noodle soup, also available in the mess tent adjacent to the mobile kitchen, was more inviting.

She had finished half of it. She sat by herself, staring at her small notebook.

0800. 3057. 4606.

Bring home the lost sword.

Where the Fourth Sister points.

What did it mean? *Adara, why were you here? You didn't tell me anything about your family. Do you even have sisters? Are the "four sisters" some sort of local landmark? A rock formation? A punk rock group? What?*

Jaime reached into her pocket and pulled out the bracelet Rodriguez had given her. The attacker had dropped it, and Adara had used all her strength to pick it up and hurl it to Jaime. It looked like a woman's bracelet—in fact, as Jaime looked at it, the fine gold filigree work, the beautiful inlaid gems, each different, she seemed to remember Adara wearing it back when they were in school together. Jaime resolved when this was all over to find Adara's family and return it to them. It looked like a precious heirloom. She was certain the gems were real. Ruby, carnelian, turquoise, lapis, jade, mother-of-pearl.

"Chaplain." Jaime looked up. Sergeant Moore from the convoy stood behind her.

"I am so sorry," she exhaled. "Is everyone all right?"

"Sorry for what? That transmission sounded totally authentic. What I wanted to say is thanks for driving into the middle of an ambush to get our asses out of there. That took balls." He realized to whom he was speaking and looked momentarily chagrined. "So to speak."

Jaime almost smiled. "Any time."

"And thanks for the loan of the GPS," he said, handing it back to her. "I'm going to ask for one of these for Christmas."

"I've heard there's a RadioShack in Tikrit," she said. He smiled and headed out to the truck for some food.

She absently turned on the GPS, then looked again at the numbers. 3057. 4606.

It would make sense if those were grid coordinates—somewhere to go to drop off the necklace. She toyed with inputting the digits, trying to figure out ways they could add up to somewhere. No luck.

She again took out the necklace Adara had given her before they'd driven into the ambush. It was a simple silver rectangle on a chain, divided into three sections, with the imprint of a flower on each. But no numbers, no clues. Unless there was some sort of numerical value to the spelling of the names of the flowers? Only problem was, she didn't even recognize these flowers. They weren't exactly roses or daisies.

She looked at her watch and shook her head. Adara must have thought she had all the information she needed. Why wasn't she seeing it?

Yes, it was coming back to her. This bracelet was one that Adara had worn every day to class. Once when they'd been doing research together, Jaime had complimented her on it. "I've never seen one like this, with all the different jewels," she said.

"They're common where my family comes from," Adara had said, smiling.

"London?" she asked.

Adara's laugh had been infectious. "Before that," she said. "My favorite is the lapis. The blue is so rich and vibrant. But I like them all, really. When my mother was young, these jewels were worn together all the time. They were called the Six Sisters."

Jaime sat straight so quickly that she spilled her coffee. Fortunately, it had gone cold.

Where the Fourth Sister points.

Were these the Sisters Adara was talking about? Jaime picked up the bracelet and looked at it more closely. There were indeed six gems. She studied the lapis. There didn't seem to be anything carved into it at all. It was oval and burnished, shining brightly. But it didn't point anywhere.

Which would be the Fourth Sister? She found the hinge where the bracelet opened to allow the wearer to slip it on and off. She counted four to the right of it. Unless it was from a society that counted to the left?

The lapis was the fourth to the right. Each gem had a setting, with tiny lips holding it in place. She ran her finger around the perimeter of the jewel. Then, thinking of the hinge, she put her finger on top of the lapis and shifted it to one side.

Much to her astonishment, the jewel sprang open. It was on a tiny hinge as well. And something seemed to be written under it. It was so small that she fumbled quickly in her pocket for her reading glasses. It contained two numbers. On the top, 45. On the bottom, 15.

3057. 4606.

45. 15.

Think simple, she told herself. *Adara thought you could figure it out.*

All right, then. Of course it wasn't grid coordinates for GPS. The bracelet was too old. But what if, going back in time, it was latitude and longitude? Then, she'd need degrees, minutes, and seconds. OK. There were 12 digits. That could be. How did they fit together? She started with the obvious: 30 degrees, 57 minutes, 46 seconds; then, 06 degrees, 45 minutes, 15 seconds.

She turned her GPS on again and instructed it to use latitude and longitude.

Algeria.

OK. Supposing the two digits under the stone were the missing seconds? That would make it 30 degrees, 57 minutes, 45 seconds; 46 degrees, 06 minutes, 15 seconds. She punched the final number into her handheld device, then moved the pointer until the readings matched the numbers.

She needed to look at a field map to be certain. But it seemed the pointer indicated a spot less than two kilometers from where she sat.

April 8, 2003, 7:15 A.M.
Satis's headquarters
16 kilometers west of Baghdad
Central Iraq

One of the great things about Saddam Hussein, thought Coleman Satis, was that the man knew how to build palaces. People like Trump or Helmsley could call their buildings palaces, but in truth, they were boxes made of steel, glass, and chrome. Whereas when Hussein called something a palace, it was a by-god palace.

Even the underground portions of the 18 completed presidential palaces were stunning. In fact, Hussein seemed to revel in the underground.

Satis's office reflected their shared appreciation of opulence. The carpets were plush and thick, the walls painted in gold leaf, the couches brushed velvet, the handles on the john in the attached washroom 16-carat gold. But the practical had not been overlooked. The walls were soundproofed, the door carved cedar over reinforced steel. His personal generator ensured that his needed electronics would always be operational. The space in the palace basement had served him well, although his time there was nearly finished.

To that end, he had retired his closetful of hand-tailored suits. Instead, he now wore mahogany brown combed-cotton trousers and an ecru silk turtleneck shirt. He was planning to leave the shark-infested waters of the business world behind 41 hours from now, when he would use his trained foot soldiers to take over a country that had no army. The foot soldiers would recognize him as the Stark von Uber—the Strong One from Above.

And his compatriots would recognize his rightful place in the New World Order. When he was powerful even beyond his own wildest dreams, he would wear whatever he pleased. To that end, he had left his toupees in his villa in Nice. He thought he looked rather distinguished with a receding hairline. His skin was still firm, though the perpetual tan was beginning to look weathered. He'd let that go, too. "Control in comfort" would be his slogan. One of his slogans.

He looked at the most recent fax in his hand. *Our uncle is in urgent need of a suitable place to stay,* it said. *Time is short.*

He couldn't help but smile. "You have no idea how short, 'Uncle' Saddam," he said. The ruthless dictator had financed the final stage of Satis's search, had supplied him with this suite of offices. Saddam himself had searched in vain for decades, had even drained seventy-five hundred square miles of marshland where the Tigris and Euphrates rivers crossed, looking for the prize that was in his own backyard. True, the decimation of the wetlands and resulting environmental catastrophe were blamed on the uprising of the Marsh Arabs against Hussein's regime and the need for military transport through the region. In a delightful use of doublespeak, Saddam's engineers had called it an irrigation project.

So the Cradle of Civilization had been plundered, the Marsh Arabs hung out to dry, literally, and Saddam still hadn't found what he was looking for. That was when he decided to hedge his bets by financing Coleman Satis's own search for the prize.

Satis had decades of research and unlimited power.

Hussein had given him the final piece: free movement within Iraq.

Saddam Hussein had also double-crossed him. As Satis's organization had gotten within a whisper of the answer, Hussein had captured and tortured one of Satis's operatives. Using the obtained information, Hussein had obstructed Satis's way and sent his own men on the final search.

As irritating as this setback was, it wasn't unexpected. But time had grown impossibly short. If Satis's men could not walk into the National Museum in the light of day, they would do so under cover of war. The launching of a war could be arranged. It had been arranged.

Now Hussein was suddenly in need of a suitable long-term hiding place. He'd come back begging. It was always heartwarming to have someone who'd double-crossed you come crawling back. If Saddam wanted information, it would cost him. Enormously.

"The door to your dwelling closes tomorrow at midnight. If we've not found it by then, the game is over, Uncle Saddam," Satis muttered.

More than the game would be over. Everything Satis had worked for his entire adult life. Every corporation he'd raided, every CEO he'd slammed to the ground, and every broken piece of the companies he'd sold off. The empire he'd built, the governments he controlled. The secret army of foot soldiers he'd commanded. It had all led to this.

Baghdad, Iraq, April 9, 2003. Tomorrow.

He was so close he could taste it. Jean St. Germain had successfully acquired the final items, items that had kept their secrets for over four thousand years. With that step taken, all that kept Satis from claiming his natural inheritance was having the person who could interpret its message.

He was surprised to hear the fax machine click to life once more. He picked up the paper. It read, in English: *The*

*museum in Mosul was raided before we arrived last night.
Taken: Nothing of importance. Cuneiform tablets. Old atlases. What we needed was still waiting.*

Satis read the message and read it again.

Cuneiform tablets and old atlases.

My god, why hadn't I realized?

Cuneiform tablets and old atlases. He absentmindedly
fed the paper into the shredder by the fax.

His gamble had paid off. He had been right to let the
kidnapped old man, Kristof Remen, go free. Remen alone
knew how to find what Satis, and Saddam, so desperately
sought, but he was far from cooperative. However, once
freed, Remen, in his effort to protect the last remaining
keys to the puzzle, had led Satis straight to the museum,
straight to the final puzzle pieces.

They'd entered the final round of the game.

Satis grinned. He did enjoy a good game.

April 8, 2003, 7:23 A.M.
Logbase Rock
Tallil Airfield
Southern Iraq

Rodriguez was going to be royally pissed off.

The air control tower for Tallil Airfield was a two-story cement box with a picture window on top. As Jaime drove the road that ran parallel to it, it seemed only slightly odd that that building and what served as an airstrip in front of it was important enough to have murals of a gloating Saddam Hussein claiming credit for it, let alone making it important enough to be a U.S. military objective called Firebird. But it was a place to land aircraft, and those were in short supply in this neighborhood.

She checked her watch and tried not to ride the gas pedal. She didn't want to look like she was making a run for it. Which she was. Rodriguez would be back any minute now from Mortuary Affairs, looking for her. When he discovered she'd gone off by herself, he would not be happy. To put it mildly. Part of her still thought she should have waited for him. He was, after all, her security. But she wasn't leaving the perimeter. She should be safe.

The larger part of her knew she couldn't explain to herself what she was doing, let alone to anyone else. But she had complete trust in Adara, and time was of the essence. The terrain was flat, with a top layer of loose dirt; the shrubs dotting the landscape were spindly and brittle. She glanced down at the GPS and continued toward the coordinates she'd programmed in, arrows now pointing her way, drawing her to the exact location. Now that she knew where it was, her excitement increased.

The drop point was in Ur.

In her mind, she pictured herself driving away from the military bustle of the airport, back in time. Six thousand years back, give or take a decade. In the landscape before her, the ziggurat loomed on the horizon, like a textbook come to life. She felt her pulse accelerate.

Ur. Perhaps the first city. Anywhere. Ever.

Home of the Sumerians, who invented written language, the concept of a code of laws, and the wheel. The Sumerians, who had an advanced culture, with finely worked jewelry, epic plays, and engineering that allowed them to build a skyscraping ziggurat. Ur had been a humming, advanced city for two thousand years before a man named Terah had a son named Abram, who got married there to a local girl named Sarai.

Then they left. And the world had never been the same.

The ziggurat was drawing her like a beacon. But she was running out of time. Adara's coordinate was in the ruins near the huge structure. There were no other vehicles in sight. She found a place that seemed closest to the ruins, without driving into them and risking damage to some ancient structure. She pulled to a stop and exhaled.

It was all flooding back to her, the hours she had spent looking at maps of Ur, writing a seminary paper on the emergence of monotheism from this very spot. It had always seemed a bit surreal—knowing she was being deployed to the land of the Tigris and Euphrates rivers, where, according to the Book of Genesis, life began. Just the fact that these were actual places you could go to and stand on, and touch: Nineveh, Babylon, Ur. These places had always been mythic to her. Not mythic as in untrue—mythic as in larger than true.

Larger than true. And she was here. She was walking into the pages of Genesis. Not to take anything away from the Liberty Bell, but there was history, and there was . . . Ur.

She picked up the simple silver necklace and felt the outline of Adara's bracelet under the sleeve of her right wrist.

She looked at her watch. Seven thirty-one.

Jaime grabbed her GPS and got out of her Humvee.

The morning was still cool. Before her, bricks rose from the desert floor, undoubtedly part of the ruins. She moved toward them with purpose. She could see walls with arched doorways cut into them, the door frames outlined with sand-colored bricks.

Then a swath of movement caught her eye. Her adrenaline surged, and in that instant she rethought the wisdom of coming to this rendezvous unarmed.

She wasn't alone.

She stopped where she was, mentally calculating the distance back to her vehicle. She thrust her GPS into her pocket. A man emerged from one of the doorways. He wore a simple black robe, with a large right-front pocket. She guessed him to be in his late thirties and just under six feet. His skin was tan, his black hair was long enough to emerge beneath his wound turban of common red-and-white-checkered material, and his face was clean shaven. They studied each other for a long moment.

"So," he finally said: "You here for the tour, eh?" And his face broke into a smile.

Jaime continued to stare at him. "The tour?"

"Abraham's house. The death pits. The temples. You'd like to see it?"

"You give tours?"

He walked forward, extending his hand. "Ahmet Muhsen. I live here with my father and my brothers. We take care of Ur. Give tours. You are Christian, yes?" He motioned at the cross on her helmet.

"Yes," she said. "Chaplain. Army."

"Noticed that," he said. "So you know Abraham. Called out of Ur of the Chaldeans. His house is over here. Come see."

Usually she'd be thrilled to discover the ruins came with a tour guide. But it was now 16 minutes before 0800, and she still didn't know exactly where she was going. How to seem nonchalant?

How to get rid of this guy?

"Abraham's own house?" she asked. "How do you know which one is his? Did he leave an 'Ur Sweet Ur' sign or something?"

"No, a bumper sticker. 'Go, Rams.' Sorry. Little thicket joke."

Jaime smiled in spite of herself.

"My grandfather worked here on the dig with Lord Woolley in 1923. Great excavation. Very important. Come see."

He turned and walked back toward a walkway that flanked a number of arched entryways. She could think of nothing to do but follow.

Ahmet led her down onto a narrow dirt path, which ran along the walls of the houses. The bricks looked very clean. The mortar between them still held.

"These are original?" she asked.

"Ur was a fantastic city," he said. "Very well built. But in this section only the doors and below are original. The walls were reconstructed by Saddam Hussein for a visit by the pope—who never came, by the way. But we can see how they lived. Many rich merchants in this place. I will show you how the houses were. Step up. See, houses are a step up. That keeps them dry. Even back when this was the Fertile Crescent." She followed him up into a beautiful room. Double-arched doors were carved out of the wall beside them.

"OK," he said, "This is how it went, if you had a nice house. You step up, come in. Door to the right leads to the entertain room, where you entertain guests. Door to the left leads to kitchen, where your servants busy. Would be nice, eh? Stairs in center lead to bedrooms upstairs. Those are pretty much gone. Nice arched doors straight back lead to private gardens. Not bad place to live. Especially considering the neighborhood four thousand years ago."

Jaime stood, stunned, in the middle of the floor and looked at the stones beneath her feet. "It's really incredible," she said. "I don't know that I've ever stood on a floor that will be around in four thousand years."

"These extra doors make it easier to walk house to house. These weren't here. Ur people like their privacy. Had their own walled gardens."

He looked over at her, as if to gauge her reaction. "You know what? If this is not Abraham's exact house, it is house of his neighbors."

She nodded.

"Come. I show you the temple. There everything is original, maybe the oldest known arch in the world."

"Mr. Muhsen," she said. "It's fantastic. I would love a tour, maybe tomorrow? Right now, well, I'm really tired, but I just wanted to take a look. Would it be OK if I just wander for a minute? Only a minute."

"If that is what you'd like," he said. But he didn't move.

She had eight minutes. This was not going well. Then it struck her.

"You and your father, you are guides? That is what you do for a living?"

"And my brothers. We care for the ruins."

"That is a great service," she said. She fished out her wallet and pulled out a $10 bill. "Thank you so much."

He took the bill and gave her a small bow. "Thank you. You take the time you need."

And he vanished as abruptly as he had appeared.

Her shoulders slumped with relief. She pulled out her GPS. She was close—perhaps one hundred meters from her target point.

She waited a moment and walked through one of the double arches into the house next door. The floors were completely swept and clean, a miracle in this desert environment. She stepped down out of the front door and back into the walkway that ran along the residential section. Ahmet was nowhere in sight. She looked at the GPS and worked her way around a large dirt mound beside a deep quarrylike pit. Back on the original path, she passed a structure with waist-high ruins and continued toward another brick edifice that seemed more intact.

Jaime tried to recall the maps she had studied at Princeton. She'd bet the first set of rubble was the ruins of the palace. Which would mean the ruins she was now approaching were the temple. Many of the walls were still intact, and the entry included a very ancient-looking arch—undoubtedly the one the guide had mentioned.

And then, according to her GPS, she was there. Or at least within a foot or two of there. The target point was at a place where four stairs went up into another arched doorway.

Now what?

Was she just supposed to drop the necklace on the ground, to be found by any passerby? That didn't seem likely. Was she supposed to stand here till 0800 for the handoff? That seemed equally unlikely.

She climbed the stairs and ran her hand over the smooth silhouette of the archway.

And then she saw it. Plain as day in front of her face.

The instructions on where to leave the necklace.

The instructions were at her fingertips. Under her fingertips, to be more precise.

"KUS masku DILI," Jaime whispered, awed by the thought that a message from four thousand years ago was still completely legible. "Hidden under the first brick."

She crouched by the first brick on the bottom step. She placed the ball of her hand against the front of the brick and lifted. Nothing. But she saw that the step was longer than the adjacent wall, protruding about half an inch. She grasped the brick from the side. It still didn't lift. Then she noticed what looked to be a small track. She urged the brick forward in the track.

This time, it moved easily. Beneath it was a small cylinder, one of those used by Sumerian scribes, with images of birds carved on the sides. The cylinder was affixed somehow to the ground, but the top was a golden sphere that was attached by a simple link chain. She removed the top and dropped the necklace into the cylinder. She replaced the top and slid the brick back into place.

Then she looked for somewhere out of sight that she could hide. She didn't know who was going to pick up the necklace or what the importance of it was. But Adara had been murdered trying to get here, and Jaime felt she at least had to know why. It now seemed clear there was a reason Adara had suggested they take the class in cuneiform together.

Had Adara been planning to involve her in something? But neither of them had any way of knowing Jaime would be coming to Tallil. It was all too baffling.

It was then that she heard footfalls approaching quickly. She darted up the steps into a small roofless courtyard, turned to the left, and flattened herself against the wall. The footfalls stopped but didn't approach. She silently dropped to the ground and peered around the corner. She saw a figure looking through the archway where she had entered the temple. He seemed to be looking for something, and even as she caught a glimpse, the figure turned and hurried away.

Jaime waited a few moments after the newcomer disappeared, then followed him out through the archway, away from where she'd left the necklace. He was walking the opposite direction from which she had come, and Jaime could now see him clearly. He wore a Kevlar helmet and khakis.

Then the figure stopped short, turned around, and looked at Jaime. She saw to her surprise that it wasn't a man; it was a woman. The woman locked eyes with her for one brief second and cocked her head silently as if to say, *Come on.* Then she turned and continued. It didn't take long for Jaime to realize where the woman was headed.

The grand ziggurat.

Jaime was torn. Should she follow this newcomer, this woman, or should she wait where she'd been, hidden, to try to see if anyone came to pick up the necklace? It seemed the woman had beckoned her forward. Maybe she knew something about what was going on. Curiosity got the better of Jaime. She couldn't resist following the woman—

especially since she was heading toward the incredible ziggurat.

As amazing as the ruins of the residential section of Ur had been, there were not words to describe the nature of the huge ziggurat that swelled from the ground before her. As Jaime approached it, she remembered it as it had been illustrated in one of her textbooks, with each terrace covered with trees and other plants, made to look like a bountiful mountain to honor the gods.

She moved slowly toward its massive base. In a way, it now looked like a gigantic sand castle. Each side had four flat indentations, like long panels that ran the vertical length of the ziggurat. So immersed was she in another time that she was shocked to crest the hill in front to find what looked like a large, flat parking lot, complete with flagpole. Today, at least, there was no flag.

Then she turned and found herself squarely in the center of the bottom of the longest flight of stairs she'd ever seen. It was a golden staircase to the sky. She'd gotten there in time to see the woman climb the stairs, becoming smaller and smaller and finally disappearing onto the top. Should she follow?

This day had become so surreal. Had this person actually seen her and beckoned her forward? If so, why? Did she somehow have answers? Or was Jaime being lured into another trap?

The bricks of the ziggurat were burnished and flat, 10 across on each step. There were wide brick walls on either side. It didn't seem like a tall, frightening climb. To the contrary, it called you to put your foot on the first step and keep going.

God help me, she breathed, and she started up.

At first, she noticed that you could still see four-thousand-year-old pieces of straw that had been ground into the mortar between the bricks. Twenty steps higher, she began to notice again that she was wearing long sleeves, long pants, a flak jacket with a high collar, and a helmet. She was glad it was early April. She could imagine the heat in the months to come. This morning it was still comfortable, near 80 degrees Fahrenheit. Thirty steps past that, and she was relieved that the end was in sight.

Then, she was there. She was on top.

And as she expected, she was not alone.

On the dashboard of his 1973 Chrysler Newport, Gerik's radio crackled to life. "Parcival Ten, this is Wotan Four, over."

"Wotan Four, this is your opera. Over."

Coleman Satis's voice continued, "We've heard from Mr. St. Germain, and we have an item for pickup. Over."

Gerik settled back into the fraying seat of the rattletrap that looked like a clone of every other rattletrap in the Iraqi countryside. Some of them were all white. His had the creative touch of bright orange front and rear fenders.

His earlier disappointment at losing the chaplain was still as sharp. But now she was within the confines of the air base where the Commander could easily have her watched. Gerik would know the minute she left Tallil. And this latest news was enough to bring a smile to his face.

Wotan's message could only mean one thing. It was all happening.

"St. Germain knows where to drop it? Over."

"There will be no drop. I'd like you to meet Mr. St. Germain in person to thank him for his help. Over." Satis was nonchalant, as always.

This day was getting better. Gerik gunned the vehicle

down the dirt road through the godforsaken countryside. No one looked twice at the beat-up car driven by the anonymous "local" man in ubiquitous black robes.

Soon the New World Order would begin.

Before the next 24 hours were gone, he'd meet the chaplain again, and she'd help them, whether she wanted to or not.

Richards. The name was familiar.

She'd just have to wait her turn.

He adjusted his Moschino sunglasses and headed into the northern sands.

"I know this was built in honor of the moon god, but the sun is also very strong right here," said the woman in khaki who had preceded Jaime up the massive structure.

As she turned around, Jaime saw that she had a camera around her neck, under which hung a lanyard with credentials. Her nut brown hair was longer than Jaime's, but it was braided and fastened up.

"You don't have to say that twice," agreed Jaime. "Let me guess. Embedded photographer."

"French credentials, but don't worry—I'm not French," she said.

"Chaplain Jaime Richards," said Jaime.

"Photographer Liv Nelsson," said the woman. "Chaplain Richards . . . wait. Are you the one who was in the ambush this morning?"

Jaime looked at her, trying to get a read on what she knew. Was she involved somehow, or did she just happen to be out exploring? "How did you hear about that?"

"Most exciting story of the day so far here at Firebird."

"You're not going to—report it?"

"I'm a photographer. I only report what I have photos

of. So, what happened? Rumor has it you're more than just a chaplain."

Jaime looked at her, aghast. "No such thing as 'just' a chaplain," she finally said. "Being a chaplain is more than enough."

"So, you don't know anything more about what happened?"

"No. How about you?"

"Me?" Liv asked. "I only know what I see."

Jaime turned back to the view. Behind her, she could clearly see the ruins she had just walked through to reach the ziggurat, including the walled section she had skirted while heading to the temple ruins, the royal cemetery, perhaps. Farther in the distance, she could see the airfield at Tallil. This view must be spectacular at night.

"The stars must be brilliant from here," commented Liv.

"I was just thinking the same thing," said Jaime. "Have you been over to the death pits?"

"Death pits?"

"I guess they've been renamed the royal tombs. Much more tourist friendly," she said. "Some of the greatest ancient finds came from there. They were originally called death pits, because when the king died, he apparently took all of his servants with him. It seemed they all brought the items of their service—chalices, swords, whatever—and were positioned very carefully according to rank. Then they must have done a sort of Jim-Jones-Kool-Aid thing, and all followed the king into the hereafter. They found roomfuls of the bones of well-dressed, dead servants."

"My guess is that their job satisfaction would have a lot to do with their belief in an afterlife," commented Liv. "But I don't know. This place feels to me to have a stronger life vibe than death vibe."

"The view is exhilarating, anyway," commented the chaplain.

"Do you believe in fate?" the photographer asked.

"I'm Presbyterian. We just call it by another name."

Jaime grabbed her canteen to take a drink, but it was empty.

"Whatever you want to call it, you and I were supposed to meet," said Liv.

"On top of a ziggurat in an ancient city?"

The woman laughed. "That's one assurance we'll never forget. Are you thirsty? I have some water."

Jaime gratefully accepted Liv's canteen. "So, if we were supposed to meet, Liv Nelsson, is there anything you want to tell me?" She was practiced at the art of giving people the opportunity to talk.

"Just that there's something else important going on here, and you're a part of it. Nothing you don't already know," she said simply.

Jaime used all her remaining emotional strength to appear impassive. Was this photographer being canny, or was she just a space cadet?

"Can I ask where you've been getting your information?" Jaime asked. The water was warm, but she could feel the strength returning to her legs as she drank.

Liv shrugged. "Everywhere and nowhere. I told you, I'm press. I hear things."

Jaime felt creeping fatigue and knew she didn't have the patience to play games. If the woman had nothing coherent to say, she needed to use her remaining strength in other directions. Or was Liv a diversion so her accomplice could pick up the necklace? Either way, she didn't seem to be forthcoming. "OK. I'm going to head back down. I guess I'll catch you later." Jaime handed back the canteen. "Thanks."

As she headed back down, she felt the ball of dread drop into her stomach. *There's something else important going on here, and you're a part of it.* Was the photographer somehow right? The man in Fedayeen robes knew who she was and zeroed right in on her. And Adara— Adara didn't seem at all surprised to find her in the convoy.

She tried to clear her mind. She knew she needed to return to the war, already in progress.

When she reached the ground, she was again overwhelmed by exhaustion. She followed the path back past the temple ruins. Her watch read 8:43. She couldn't help herself. She stopped at the movable step and shifted it, then took the cap off the cylinder. It was empty. The pendant was gone. She closed it, replaced the brick, and headed back toward her vehicle, this time veering to the left so she could get a look at the tombs along the way. They looked like interesting areas for future exploration, but she was too tired to explore anything at the moment. The walk along the dusty ground back to her vehicle used up what seemed to be her last ounce of energy and motivation.

Let Rodriguez say whatever he needed to. She promised herself that she wouldn't ditch him again. Maybe he'd let her get a little sleep before he expressed his indignation.

She reapproached the ruins of the city and cut back down the path alongside Abraham's house. She reached the series of entryways along the residential section but didn't slow her pace.

Until the strong arms reached out from one of the arched doorways and she was jerked backward, falling off-balance, a hand tightly held across her mouth.

She was dragged through a low door and suddenly there was no floor beneath her. With a muffled cry, she fell into the darkness.

In the split second before she landed with a thud, she made a vow.

She would never, ever again ask what else could go wrong that early in the morning.

April 8, 2003, 8:50 A.M.
Residential Ruins
Tall Al Muqayyar
Southern Iraq

She landed on her back on something soft, but it was enough to knock the wind out of her. Her captor jumped down beside her a moment before the rectangle of light from above disappeared. The darkness was complete. The air was cool.

She lay a moment, trying to begin breathing again. Whoever was there with her moved off the mat. She quickly assessed her physical situation. Her ankle throbbed, but she didn't think it was broken. The most noticeable pain jabbed through where she'd sprained her right shoulder during a successful slide into second base while at Camp Stanley. She gritted her teeth and willed the pain to subside.

"Where's Adara?" The voice that spoke from the darkness was male. American. Angry. "The woman who was supposed to bring the chain. Where is she?"

"Who wants to know?" Jaime asked. While the pallet had initially seemed soft, she realized now that it was stuffed with straw—or something like it—and "lumpy" would have been a kind description.

"The person she was supposed to meet."

"She gave the necklace to me. You need to know more,

I'm wearing dog tags. Name, blood type, and Social Security number."

"So, the military is involved? The military has her?"

Now she detected a slight British accent to the words, a non-American cadence to the phrases.

Without warning, Adara's death replayed in her mind. The man holding Adara, calling out to her—"Jaime." Looking her straight in the eye, and killing her friend. Adara slumping to the ground. *Adara!*

"No," she said. "The military doesn't have her. But they will come looking for me. People know I'm here."

"They know you're here? And where might that be?"

Point taken.

"Look. I don't know who you are. I don't know what's going on. A friend asked me to do something she thought was very important, and I did it. As a matter of fact, I would like a little information myself. I'm not usually kidnapped twice this early in the morning. Maybe we could help each other out."

There was silence. Then, "Adara gave you the pendant."

"Yes."

"You know where she is?"

Jaime closed her eyes while the physical ache in her chest subsided. "Yes."

"And you're not going to tell me?"

She sat up and turned toward the voice. "Why should I? I don't know who you are. You say you're the person she was supposed to meet, but how do I know that's true? There seem to be sides here. Stakes are very high. But since I don't know what's going on, I'm pretty much in the dark. As perhaps you've noticed."

There was a single click, and light burst from a small battery-powered lantern.

The room she was in was square. The floor was dirt, but it was smooth from centuries of being packed down. The walls were the same kind of brick that lined the houses above. The cellar was not large, maybe 12 feet by 12 feet. The pallet on which she sat was directly under the rectangular frame of the trapdoor she'd fallen through 5 feet above. Otherwise, the room was bare.

Except for her captor, who sat against the back wall. They stared at each other a long time. He was still wearing the guide's robe, but the turban was gone. His hair was black, tousled, and slightly curly. Without the turban, he'd lost five years. He now looked to be in his mid-thirties.

"So I guess we're in Abraham's neighbor's basement," she said.

"Actually, all the houses have cellars, though they're not all excavated. It's where the Sumerians buried their dead relatives. The family graveyards."

"Lovely. This isn't on the standard tour, I take it?"

"The Muhsens are very understanding about having a phantom brother who pops up now and again."

"So there really is a Muhsen family?"

"Oh yes. Father and three brothers. Dhief, the eldest, is the chief guide just now."

As he was speaking, something he saw caused his spine to stiffen. He sat up straight and pursed his lips "She's dead."

"Sorry?"

"Adara is dead. Isn't she?" He scooted across the floor in a practiced move and grasped her wrist. As he held it up, her sleeve fell back, revealing more of Adara's bracelet. "You wouldn't have this if she was still alive."

Jaime looked at him. His eyes were searching hers, and they were full of pain.

She nodded slightly. It was enough.

He held on to her wrist and ran his finger along each of the gems. Then he looked up again. His eyes were a deep green. She had never been looked at with such intensity. She felt as if he were trying to see inside her.

"Were you there?" he asked quietly.

"Yes."

"Tell me what happened. Please."

"Who are you?"

He released her. "I'm her brother."

"Her brother? I don't remember her mentioning . . ."

"Did she mention any family?"

"Not really. She said she was from London. I knew her when she was studying History of World Religions."

"At Princeton Theological Seminary. I know. You're Jaime Lynn Richards."

Oh, man. "Yeah. And you are . . . ?"

"Adara's brother."

"Do you have a name? I take it you're not really Ahmet." She only hoped her voice sounded calmer than she felt.

"Does it matter?"

"It does to me."

"I have many names, depending on where you meet me."

"What did Adara call you?"

He exhaled, as if making a decision. "Yani. Adara called me Yani. Now. Please."

"She died saving me. She wasn't afraid. She said it was very important that I deliver the necklace."

"When did she die?"

"This morning. Just before it got light. I was traveling with five other vehicles coming here, to Tallil. My Humvee was stopped by a bale of concertina wire that got wrapped around the tire. While we were trying to get free, Adara came stumbling out of the desert. She'd been shot. She gave me the necklace, said something about returning the lost sword. Then she told us the others had driven into an ambush. We took her with us as we went forward to tell the others it was a trap."

She shook her head. "This is the part that doesn't make sense. There was a man—in the robes of the Fedayeen. He tried to kidnap me during the ambush. But Adara hit him with a tent peg. If she hadn't, I don't know if I'd have gotten away. I think this guy must have taken her bracelet, because it fell out of his pocket. Adara grabbed it and threw it to me and told me about the Fourth Sister. She said it was important."

"She died of her injuries?" His voice was measured.

"No. The guy dressed like Fedayeen. He killed her."

"He—?"

"Yani, no. That's enough."

"It's not. Tell me!"

"He broke her neck. He was holding her, and he called me so I'd look. She was so calm, though. She didn't seem to be afraid at all."

He turned and went back to the cellar wall where he'd been sitting before. He sat. His face was expressionless.

"She is a wonderful sister," he said.

Jaime started toward him, but he motioned her away.

"I am so sorry," she whispered.

The silence hung heavy between them.

"I need help," Jaime finally said. "Someone killed Adara. Someone tried to kidnap me. Who are they? What do they want? What was Adara doing in Iraq during a war? It makes no sense. If I'm going to get killed over this stupid necklace, I'd at least like to know what it is. And why is it so important that people would kill for it?"

Yani looked at her. Then in a voice that seemed almost nonchalant, he said, "It's the sword that's worth killing for. But if you want to see why the necklace is so important, I'll show you."

He beckoned her over. As she came to kneel in front of him, he held up the small pendant she'd left under the brick. He took out a device that was about as big as a Post-it note and a quarter of an inch thick. He slipped the ancient-looking pendant into it. The screen in front sprang to life, a full palette of colors radiating from it.

"Here," said Yani. "Let me give you your own viewing screen." He took a pair of sunglasses from the pocket of his robe and offered them to her. She took them, and he nodded that she should put them on.

She saw nothing through them, the basement was so dark. But suddenly a dual pair of screens appeared on the left side of each shade. And she was looking at an old Christmas card photo of herself, her older sister, Susan, and younger brother Joey. She must have been about eleven. Their full names appeared as a caption under the photo.

"Look familiar?" Yani asked.

The photo disappeared, and in its place appeared a photo of her parents. *James and Ingrid Richards*, it said. *Occupations: medical doctor and R.N. Killed 1979, returning to a Pakistani relief camp.*

"Where are you getting this?" was all Jaime could ask. She was afraid of what she might see next.

And then it was in front of her. A photo of Paul, smiling, standing in front of one of the pyramids in the Valley of the Kings. It had been a brochure photo for one of the rare non-school-sponsored trips he'd led. Across the bottom of the photo, in blue electronic letters, it read: *Paul Irvington Atwood. Married to J. Richards, 6 July 1997. Killed 4 September 1997, by suicide bombers, Pedestrian Mall, Jerusalem.*

The next photo was a current one of Jaime—the photo from her military I.D. *Ordained Presbyterian minister. Chaplain and Commissioned Officer (Major) United States Army. Current Status, Chaplain, 57th Corps Support Group. Deployed to Kuwait 16 February.*

"OK," she said hoarsely. "Whatever your point is, I think you've made it. So you've ransacked my personal life. Isn't turnabout fair play? Is there an introduction to your life in there?"

"I have no life," he said simply. "I am my work. There is no one close enough to me that their kidnapping would be a threat."

"Except Adara." Jaime spoke softly.

"Yes," he admitted. "And someone threw her life away without even knowing what he had."

Jaime looked at Yani more closely in the dim light. He had Adara's thick black hair, just long enough to show a propensity for curl. His face was more angular than hers. The set of the jaw was harder. And although he was being civil to Jaime, she could see steel behind his eyes.

"So, you're an assassin?" she asked.

He shook his head. "No. I'm . . . an anti-assassin." He saw her studying him, assessing, trying to decide how much to trust him. "Think of what you knew of Adara. Did she seem to you to be genuine?"

"She was one of the most genuine people I've ever met."

"Do you think she would love a brother who was an assassin?"

Jaime considered the question seriously. "I think she would love him. But I don't think she would be willing to die to help him."

"Adara is my strongest credential with you."

"OK, so who are you with? Even the Army doesn't have stuff like this. Not for general distribution, anyway."

He didn't answer. Instead, he reached out again and touched the bracelet. This time, Jaime hit the spring, and when the bracelet opened she took it off and handed it to Yani.

He accepted it and again ran his fingers over the set jewels. "You wanted to know why the necklace was so important. It holds valuable information I couldn't have gotten any other way. It told me about Adara's backup, the only person qualified to complete the mission if something happened to her. You."

"Do I not get a chance to agree to something here? Is there no fine print to read and sign? The military is pretty sure I'm here with them. They're not big on sharing."

"I'm afraid there's no time for lengthy explanations. Something important has been taken, and I have only a matter of hours to retrieve it. That's what this necklace told me."

"What you're after is the missing sword."

"Yes."

"And it's important enough to die for."

"Obviously, some people think the sword is important enough to start a war over."

"What? You're trying to tell me someone started this war over an artifact?"

"Suffice it to say that the wrong people have it. And it's my job to get it back. Within a matter of hours."

"How do you know where it is?"

Suddenly, inside her glasses, she saw a screen that looked somewhat similar to her GPS. A small dot glowed in the center of it.

"That's it?"

"Yes. Another reason this necklace was so important. If I know what I'm looking for, I know where to find it."

"Where is the missing sword?"

"South of Baghdad. And moving."

"And what do you need from me?" She took off the sunglasses.

"It seems likely that the quickest way to get there, given the current situation, would be in military transport."

Her jaw dropped. "You're joking, of course."

"Even in these circumstances, I would never ask you to do anything that would compromise your oath of allegiance, or endanger United States troops. I know you would never do that, even if your life was threatened. It's precisely because of who you are and what you stand for that I am asking you at all."

"Yani. Adara's brother. I don't care who you are. The two basic flaws in your plan are, first, I'm not going to Baghdad. My TOC is here, in Tallil. And second, the Army doesn't pick up hitchhikers!"

"The Army wouldn't need to know."

"Oh, OK, that works. And which should I choose, Leavenworth for the rest of my life, or blindfold at dawn?"

"Richards. I repeat. If CENTCOM knew what the situation is, there would be no question. They would order you to help."

"Fine. Great. Let's go explain it to them, and I will gas up my vehicle."

"I am unarmed. I will do nothing to hinder Operation Iraqi Freedom. I will hitch a ride north and disappear."

"Having saved the world." Her tone was sarcastic, but she didn't care.

"One corner of it," he said.

"For God's sake, and I choose my words carefully, *tell me what's going on.*"

"You know what you know now because you've been given a high level of clearance." He held up the minicomputer. "But I can only explain things on a need-to-know basis. Not want-to-know, need-to-know. The less you know, the less you can tell."

"That's to your advantage, not mine," she said, an edge of anger in her voice. "Translation: They can torture you because they think you know something, but you don't, so I'm safe. In other words, Jaime's lack of information is all about Yani's safety."

"That's the program," he said simply.

"Well, here's another point of view. Yani's lack of transportation is all about Jaime's lack of information."

He was getting exasperated, as if he were a father with a young child who wasn't listening to reason. "Look. Whether you help me or not, we've got a problem. Your identity has somehow been compromised. Someone besides me knows you're involved. You're in this. You might as well decide to help the good guys. And the clock is ticking fast."

"*I don't know who the good guys are!*" she rasped with fury through gritted teeth.

He sighed. "There's no good way to do this. I didn't want to . . . not yet, anyway."

"Look. All I want is information. You're right that I'm in this. And I'm not leaving until I understand what 'this' is."

"Your parents. How did they die?" His tone was flat.

"What? What does that matter?"

"You've asked for more information. I'm trying to give you what you've asked for."

"They were killed in an accident, back when I was in high school."

"What kind of accident?"

"They were returning to a Pakistani relief camp from India during a monsoon. It was a mud slide, on a mountain road that was bad to start with . . ."

"And only their ashes were returned," he said simply.

"Yes."

"Would you believe me if I told you that was not how they died?"

Wordlessly she shook her head. Why would he even joke around with something like this? Her world had broken in half that day when she was a teenager, as had her heart. Ever since, her life had been defined by the terms "before" and "after."

He picked up his handheld and hit something on the screen. He sat looking at it. "It happened in a hotel room in Mahattat al Jufur, near the Jordanian-Iraqi border. I don't know as much about your mother, but I can tell you that your father had been tortured, and his neck was broken."

"*Dear God!*" she said. "Why should I believe such a thing? No one would have done that! My parents were helping in the camps. My mother was a nurse; my father was a doctor. He was working on a process to quicken the body's return from the brink of starvation. Why would they be in Jordan? And why would they be killed?"

"They knew where the sword was," Yani answered. "They would not tell."

"*My parents* knew about this sword?"

He nodded.

"They were in Jordan? I don't understand. . . . My brother and sister, do they know how they died?"

"No, they don't. They still believe the cover story. There's no reason for them to know."

"Do you think the same people responsible for killing Adara . . . ?" She couldn't speak the rest of the question.

"It's certain. The sword has remained hidden for twenty-two years since then. But now they've found it." Yani navigated his handheld. He looked up at her. "This was recorded just before that time." Suddenly a voice spoke clearly from the small speaker in its side.

"Jaime, it's me; it's Mom, my P.B. Girl. If you're hearing this, all I can ask is that you help the person who has it. And the Lord watch between you and me when we are absent one from the other."

Jaime sat, stunned, her hand over her mouth, her world reeling.

In the thundering silence that followed she heard footfalls from above. And, filtered through a layer of stone, a voice. "Chaplain Richards? Chaplain!"

She and Yani locked eyes.

"It's my chaplain assistant," she said.

"You should go."

"He must have seen my vehicle. He's seen to Adara's burial arrangements. During a war, the military can't do anything special with civilian burials, but now that her brother's here . . ."

"I'm not here," he said simply.

"How can I find you?"

"You can't. I find you." His tone had become hard and businesslike. "As soon as your assistant has moved into the next house, I'll help you out."

"Chaplain Richards!" The call was more urgent.

"This is so much . . . Who are these guys? Why do they want this sword so much?"

"Power," Yani said simply. "These things are always about power."

But all she heard was the inflection of her mother's

voice, replaying in her mind. Her mother, asking her to help this stranger. "What is it you need me to do?"

"Get me a ride north."

He came over to the pallet. Together they put their hands on the trapdoor. As Rodriguez's footsteps moved off in another direction, they lifted it slightly and pushed it aside. Yani made a cup of his hands and hoisted her up. But by the time she'd swung her legs out of the way, the door had closed again. She looked at the floor with awe. The outline on the ground was barely visible; in fact, she wondered if she could find it again.

"Chaplain?"

"Rodriguez?" she answered, moving slowly toward the sound of his voice.

"Chaplain Richards?" he said, his tone a mixture of incredulity and relief. She went through one of the double-arched doors and found him in the next room.

"I was just visiting Abraham's house," she said.

He let out a long sigh. "Actually, he lived over there, in a section that hasn't been excavated yet," said the staff sergeant. "This was his cousin's house. But he slept over."

Jaime shook her head. "Everyone's a tour guide," she muttered. "Let's get out of here."

Rodriguez had found the terse note Jaime had left him and
had hitched a ride to the ruins with a couple of Marines who
were now halfway up the grand ziggurat. He drove Jaime
back to base. He didn't say anything about her excursion.

"They had a doc take a look at Adara, in case questions
come up later," he said. "She'd lost a lot of blood. It's
likely she would have died of her injuries."

"So, she was dying before Mr. Fedayeen murdered her."

"Yeah."

As they jostled together over the dirt road, Jaime looked
back at the ancient city of Ur disappearing behind them.
She was beginning to feel that she had crossed the berm
into Iraq and entered an alternate reality, one that was over
four thousand years old.

"So, what do you think, Rodriguez? It must have been
tough to be Abraham. Living in a society with so many
gods. And then, suddenly, there's this voice talking to him,
making promises. How does that work? How do you know
what to believe? Ever after, God could say, 'I am the God of
Abraham.' But what did God say to Abraham? Would you
have had the faith to follow the Voice? Would I?"

"Isn't that what life's about?" asked the staff sergeant,

as if he was used to chaplains throwing out philosophical questions. "Finding answers to questions like that?"

"What do you do when you start hearing voices?" she asked. "How do you know which voices to trust?"

Rodriguez looked at her but said nothing. He continued to drive. "I asked the guys at Mortuary Affairs to let us know where Adara's grave is. I figured you'd like to bless the site," he finally said.

"Thanks," Jaime said. "It's the least I can do."

"I was able to grab a couple of guys and put up our tent," Rodriguez said, "but I haven't unloaded the Humvee. Where did you leave your stuff?"

"Parked in the officers' tent."

"I'll drop you there, then."

"Thanks."

When she got out, she quickly realized the first thing she needed to do was find water for her canteen. Then she'd find the chaplain's tent Rodriguez had pitched and try to clear her head. She turned toward the mess tent and had only taken a couple of paces when someone called her name.

"Major Richards!"

She stopped and turned around. The man coming toward her was dressed in jeans and a navy blue T-shirt, with a navy blue windbreaker on top. The day was already warming up, and Jaime was certain the windbreaker served the sole purpose of concealing his sidearm.

"*Chaplain* Richards," she said, a mild correction.

"Frank McMillan," he responded. He pulled identification from his pocket. "CIA. I need to talk to you about the ambush this morning."

Jaime tried to keep her expression passive, but some of her reticence must have been apparent.

"I know that some people are wary about speaking to government agents," he said. "I can go through channels, if that will make you more comfortable. But there's a chance we've got someone on the inside with an objective different than that of the rest of us. Someone who has access to radio codes and frequencies. If we work together, we can figure this out sooner rather than later and prevent another incident."

They both stopped walking. "Got a minute?" he asked.

How did CIA guys always get the cool reflective sunglasses? Jaime wondered. And she said, "Yeah. I guess so." But did she? A clock was ticking. She just hadn't figured out her next move.

As it turned out, reflective sunglasses were the least of what Frank McMillan had.

His office tent was huge, and it was full of state-of-the-art equipment. Goodies. Stuff the Army would salivate over. He was obviously not your average field agent.

To start with, he had his own generator outside. Which implied he had lackeys to keep it running, since keeping one fueled was a mess and a pain. But it also meant he had a small refrigerator, from which he offered her a can of Pepsi.

"No Diet Coke?" she asked.

"Lemon or vanilla?"

"Vanilla," she said, certain he was joking. Until he handed her the can. She took it, watching the beads of condensation form immediately and run traces down the silver side. She briefly wondered if this could be considered a bribe.

She opened the can, took a long drink, and resolved to think about that at some point in the near future.

He sat behind his desk and indicated a chair for her across from him. It was a folding canvas chair, but it had one of those armrests with a place for a drink.

His chair was higher than hers, and he rocked it back on two legs, studying her casually. She returned the favor. His hair was short, but not a military cut. It was dark with hints of silver, and clean, and neatly combed. She just bet this was a man who had access to private showers. That alone was enough to make her sarcastic side rise to the surface.

A small poster written in cuneiform was displayed behind him. It made her flash on that restaurant chain, Apple-bee's, which bills itself as "your hometown restaurant." Meaning that in each chain location they put up some sort of local posters on the wall. Like this was Frank McMillan's Ur poster.

She didn't trust him, of course. Oh, she was sure he was a rah-rah flag-waving American, but the distrust between the Armed Forces and the suits ran deep. Maybe it was just that compared to, say, the Army or Navy, the CIA never fielded any sort of decent football team.

But, on the other hand, Frank McMillan was right. Someone had made that radio transmission this morning.

"I'm just trying to figure out what happened on the road this morning," he said. She had the sudden fear that he was questioning her as a suspect or a possible accomplice.

"You and me both, Mr. McMillan," she said.

"That's what I figured. Why don't we see if we can help each other? Do you remember the call sign of the phantom radio transmission you received this morning?"

"Rock Three November," she said.

"Did you recognize the voice?"

"No. It sounded like he had a bit of a Southern drawl, but that could have been put on."

"And it sent you into an ambush."

"Square into it, yes, sir."

"But your vehicle stayed behind?"

"Yes. We had tire trouble."

"And while you were there, a civilian—a woman—approached you and told you the others had been sent into an ambush."

"Yes."

"You knew this woman?"

Jaime looked at him to see if he already knew the answer to this question, as he had known the others. He did. She obviously was not the first person from the convoy he'd interviewed.

"Yes," she said.

"Her name was?" He didn't look up from the notes he was taking.

"Adara. Dunbar."

"And you knew her from?"

"She was in my master's program."

"Princeton, New Jersey. Although you initially attended Union Theological Seminary."

I might as well be wearing school colors, thought Jaime.

"So, how is it the two of you came to rendezvous in Iraq?"

"Here's where my answers run out," she said. "I haven't a clue."

"But obviously, Adara Dunbar knew where to find you."

"It seems so."

"And what did she say to you? Did she give you any information? Or anything at all?" Frank stopped writing and looked up. Jaime took this to mean he'd run out of answers, too. In fact, if he hadn't talked to Rodriguez—and Rodriguez would have mentioned it to her if he had, she was sure—he couldn't have the answers to these questions.

So, how much should she tell him?

If he was really trying to figure this out to save the lives of American troops, she should tell him as much as possible. But her talk with Adara's brother led her to believe that the pendant she had dropped at Ur had nothing to do with the military.

She took another swig of the cold soda.

"She said something about finding a missing sword," Jaime said. "But I don't have the slightest idea what she was talking about."

"Ah. She mentioned a missing sword. But someone killed her before she could tell you what or where it was."

"As it turns out, she'd been shot before she found us. So, she may have died anyway. But yes, this guy dressed like a Fedayeen murdered her when we arrived at the ambush."

Obviously, Frank had gotten enough of the story already that he didn't look surprised when she talked about arriving at the ambush.

Instead, he leaned back in his chair again—not rocking it this time, but playing with the stylus he was using to make notes in his handheld. And he was looking at her.

"Have you heard of the Spear of Destiny, Major Richards?"

"No, sir, I have not."

"How about the Ancestral Heritage Society?"

"No clue."

Frank stood and walked around the folding table that served as his desk. He leaned against the front of it. "I know you're a specialist in the history of world religions," he said. "Let me tell you why I'm here and see if it might clarify your thinking. I'm working on the assumption that you know something important, something you might not even know you know. So, feel free to stop me if anything starts sounding familiar to you."

"I'll try."

"The Spear of Destiny. 'Who holds the Spear rules the world.' It is purported to be the spear that pierced the side of Jesus Christ during the crucifixion. It had a long line of owners who did quite well at trying to rule the world. The most recent was a fellow by the name of Adolf Hitler. The minute the Reich took over Austria, they looted the museum where it was held. They say Hitler used to stare at the spear for hours each day.

"One of the first things the Allies did when they took Berlin was find and capture the spear. That was the day Hitler committed suicide."

Jaime sat, trying to process this information. "Interesting story," she finally said. "Wrong war."

"Well, wrong spear, as it turned out. There are three Spears of Destiny, and the one Hitler used is now safely back in the Austrian museum from which it was taken. There's a different weapon in play at the moment, which seems to have everyone scrambling. The Dagger of Ur,

also known as the Sword of Life. It was found right here, in
the royal tombs of Ur. It's from about 2400 B.C.E."

He reached behind him on the desk and found a color
printout. He handed it to her. She recognized the sword
from her studies but had forgotten how truly breathtaking
it was.

"The blade and the sheath are gold. The handle is lapis
lazuli. The gold beads and the filigree work on the sheath
are the products of master craftsmen. It would be worth
millions, even if it wasn't over four thousand years old."

"It is the most beautiful dagger—or sword, whatever—
I've ever seen," Jaime said, trying to seem cooperative.
"And I do remember that it was discovered right here, dur-
ing the excavations of the 1920s, by Lord Woolley's team.
Dug up from the royal tombs. It's been in the National Mu-
seum for eighty years."

"Until this morning," Frank told her.

"This morning?"

"Yes. Coincidentally, about the time your small convoy
ran into the ambush. The way the museum was looted was
obviously the work of professionals. They not only knew
what they wanted; they also walked right past the exact
replicas to the real things. One doesn't want to be dramatic,
but it's almost as if they were just waiting for a war to start
to get what they wanted."

*Obviously, some people think the sword is important
enough to start a war over,* Yani's words replayed in her
head.

"I wish I was with you here; I really do," Jaime said.
"Are you telling me that these items—spears and swords,
whatever—have some sort of magical powers that make
people start wars so they can rule the earth?"

"No, Major Richards. I'm telling you that these items
are associated with primal stories that capture people's
imaginations and can even incite them to act in specific
ways. Certainly you're familiar with such items. Even
commonplace ones. The sound of the shofar. The feel of a

prayer shawl. The sight of a crucifix. Primal feelings. Religious feelings. We all know those can be strong enough to cause people to put their lives on the line."

"This is not a religious war we're fighting. We're deposing a tyrant, whom the whole world knows to be a butcher. It's not about one religion versus another. Saddam Hussein lives by the laws of no religion anyone's ever heard of."

"That's not completely true. He lives according to the laws of the cult of Hussein."

"OK. Granted."

"What military people sometimes don't understand is that often the army most willing to fight is the one crusading for deeply held spiritual beliefs. Take World War Two. That was a religious war, if there ever was one."

"Over the Spear of Destiny."

"Hell, no. That was a prop, though a very unlikely one. The prediction was very clear. The Strong One from Above would show up just about the turning of this millennium and would purify the Aryan race once again, bringing it back into its full glory, making men the gods they were created to be." Frank was clearly warming to his topic. "A priesthood of pure Aryans would be waiting for this. You haven't heard of this? Nothing is ringing a bell?"

Jaime shook her head.

Frank got up again and strode to her seat. "Stand up, Richards."

She stood, looking askance. He fingered loose wisps of her hair, looked in her eyes, put his hands on either side of her face. "Open your mouth, please."

"Now wait . . ."

"Humor me."

She complied.

He tsk-tsked. "You almost made it," he said. "You have the hair, the eye color, the skull shape. But those fillings would have kept you out of the SS. You see, they were not just a fighting unit. They were the highest priesthood of the New World Order."

"Not the same 'New World Order' that President Bush Senior kept talking about, certainly."

"No, of course not. Although, interestingly, both had their germ in the ideas of the philosopher Georg Hegel. Those Germans do have quite the history of philosophers." He grinned and went back behind his desk. "Don't look so glum. You probably could have gotten a waiver to be an SS bride. But the fillings would have killed any dreams of being a Brood Mother."

"I don't even want to know," she said. "Seriously."

"But it does make you feel kind of special, doesn't it?"

"You're nuts."

"I know. But I'm just trying to show you the seductive power. You know you're one of the Elect, it all suddenly starts to sound pretty good. But, if it will make you feel any better, you yourself are currently an affront to the Teutonic Brotherhood."

"That helps some. In what way?"

"It is quite clear, at least to them, that from the beginning of time, society was supposed to be a paternalistic Aryan dictatorship. But there you stand. A woman, not only in uniform, but in a position of religious authority. Never supposed to happen. Proof positive that civilization is spinning out of control."

"You don't have to be a rabid Aryan to believe that," Jaime replied with a sigh. "So you're telling me that the ruling class of this Aryan stuff is still intact and active. That they stole this Sword of Life from the National Museum this morning, and somehow Adara knew about it."

"That's what I'm trying to figure out," he said. "So many pieces, but such a large puzzle. I do know the Society is still active, and I do have good information that their center of operations has moved here, to Iraq. I know the pursuit of the powerful pure Aryan blood has gone on, unhindered, for the last sixty years.

"When the Nazis were in power, they sent teams out searching for the Remnant, that small group of people whose blood had never been defiled. They searched in Tibet, in South America, Greece, Rome, wherever there had been great civilizations founded by Aryans. They were searching for the Remnant of Eden."

"A remnant of people from *the Garden of Eden*?"

"That's a whole different discussion. But yes. Which brings us to Iraq. The likely site of that famous garden."

"One of the possible sites."

"And the missing Sword of Life, which holds the clues to find the Remnant."

"Which has to do with why someone tried to kidnap me this morning?"

"That knife, or dagger, or sword, whatever you want to call it, that was stolen this morning is mystical enough in its own way. Have you put together how it got the name of the Sword of Life? How old did I tell you that dagger was?" Frank went back and sat behind his desk.

"You said from 2400 B.C.E. That would make it roughly forty-four hundred years old."

"And what was happening in these parts, twenty-four hundred years before the birth of Christ?"

"Abraham, the patriarch of the world's three largest monotheistic religions, was trying to have kids."

"Very good, Richards. But let's take it a step farther. How did these religions—Judaism, Christianity, Islam—start? Abraham, per God's instructions, took his son out to slaughter him as a sacrifice. He got as far as tying the boy, laying him on wood for a burnt offering, and raising the knife. Then God stopped him. Some versions of the story have it that God himself stayed the knife. And which knife would this be, do you suppose? Which dagger would come to be called the Dagger of Life? Abraham's."

"Surely you don't believe this."

"It doesn't matter what I believe. But I have spent the last two decades discovering what my friends of the Ancestral Heritage Society believe. That's why I'm here.

And, whether you know it or not, that's one of the reasons you're here.

"I believe that a member of the Society is embedded here. I believe they arranged a sabotage of our troops on the road this morning. And I believe that, somehow, you know how that happened. You're at the fulcrum of all this. Whether you want to be or not."

"But," she said, looking to answer him in kind, "I have fillings."

"Think about it. And if anything, any theory, no matter how cockeyed, comes to mind, let me know."

She picked up her helmet. She wondered briefly if she could ask for another Diet Coke. She handed him back the printout of the stolen dagger. Then she looked again at the cuneiform poster behind him.

"The answer is '*edubba*—a school,' " she said.

"Beg pardon?"

"The cuneiform poster behind you. It's the oldest riddle in the world. The house that one enters blind and leaves seeing. The answer is 'a school.' "

And on that note, she turned and left.

April 8, 2003, 10:15 A.M.
Satis's headquarters
16 kilometers west of Baghdad
Central Iraq

Andy Blenheim's footfalls were silent on the smooth marble floors beneath his slippered feet. His arms ached from
carrying yet another 10-gallon can of fuel for Mr. Satis's
generator, and Andy himself reeked of the gas needed to
keep the office up and running.

But all their efforts would soon pay off.

He was proud to have been chosen to personally serve
Coleman Satis but would not mind being back in a world
with its own supply of uninterrupted electricity. Yet he
served in whatever way he was asked.

It wouldn't be long now. He wished he could see the
looks on the faces of his parents, and his turncoat sister,
back in West Virginia when they discovered that his "crazy
ranting" had been right all along. If they could even know
he was in Iraq this very minute, guarding a palace! That
soon now, once they'd joined the Remnant, he'd likely be
awarded a wife and become a father.

He groaned as he hoisted the can forward and turned his
concentration back onto the task at hand.

Sleep in peace, Mom and Dad, he thought. *The end is
coming sooner than you think.*

"What on earth was going on in there for so long?" Rodriguez asked her as she exited Frank McMillan's tent. Rodriguez had taken the opportunity to clean himself up.

The camp around them was bustling with activity. Richards could see Marines, Army, and Air Force all working purposefully in different quadrants of the perimeter. The airstrip was already partially operational.

"You wouldn't believe what's going on in there," she said. "*Diet Vanilla Coke* is going on in there."

"You want to get a cup of joe?" he asked.

"Today, I do. If they had something stronger, I'd be mighty tempted."

As they turned, she nearly stepped into the path of three American contractors who were deep in conversation. It was always slightly jarring to see civilians in jeans and T-shirts and baseball caps, but these were the guys who knew how to get things up and running quickly. Two wore Halliburton identification; the other was from DynCorp. All three nodded to her as they passed. The third paused a yard farther on and lit a cigarette. He was wearing tight jeans and a golf shirt with a sports logo above the pocket. He had a nice rear end.

He turned back to Jaime and asked in a Texas drawl, "Care for a smoke?"

"No, thanks," she said. "I don't smoke."

"Nah, me neither," he said. "Take one for a friend." And he shook the pack toward her. She tried not to let her mouth drop open. She took the protruding cigarette. A piece of paper was wrapped around it.

She looked at his face again, then stared at his DynCorp credential. "Y'all keep up the good work now," he said.

Yani turned and left, putting the pack of cigarettes into his breast pocket, under the embroidered NFL mascot for the Rams.

As he did, Jaime surreptitiously unrolled the note. *You're in extreme danger,* it said. *Come back to Ur at once. It's the safest place to talk.*

Staff Sergeant Rodriguez was waiting for her. She didn't want to lie to him, so she didn't say anything, and he didn't ask. She followed him to the mess tent, grabbed a steaming Styrofoam cup of coffee, dumped all the milk in it she could, and collapsed across from Rodriguez at a table in a corner.

What should she do? If it was Abraham's sword that Yani needed to save, why didn't he just say so?

"So, what's happening today?" she asked.

"War, ma'am." He put a plastic bag on the table between them. "Adara's personal effects."

"Dear God," Jaime said. She put her hand over her mouth and pursed her lips, trying to contain the emotion.

"I know, Chaplain."

There wasn't much. An inexpensive Timex watch with a gold band and a face that lit at a touch of a button. A pair of blue lapis earrings. A beaded scarf.

"I wonder if she had more, but it was taken from her by whoever shot her," Jaime said. "I mean, her murderer had her bracelet already. He might have taken anything of value."

"We may never know." He paused a moment to change

the subject. "Also, about an hour ago Specialist Cindy Bar-net stopped by the TOC looking for you. She seemed pretty upset. You might want to go talk with her."

His words hit her like an ice-cold shower. She'd gotten so caught up in her own saga that she hadn't been focusing on the fact that she was here to do a job. Jaime tried to clear her head. On the most obvious level, she was really tired. She doubted her ability to muster the appropriate concentration for any sort of counseling session. Then there was Yani's note. She figured it would take something serious to make Adara's arrogant, focused brother give her such an urgent warning. And if Frank McMillan was right . . .

She didn't want to be shot in the back on the way to meet Specialist Barnet.

On the other hand, she was here to help the Barnets deal with the tragedies that came their way. And it was best not to wait too long if a soldier was dealing with a serious issue.

Rodriguez was quiet, sitting there like her own personal Jiminy Cricket, waiting for her to make the correct decision.

"Do you know where I can find her?" Jaime asked. She knew the clock was ticking, but since she hadn't decided what she was supposed to do, she might as well do her job.

He tried not to smile, studying the grounds at the bottom of his own Styrofoam cup. "She was on a detail stacking sandbags around the headquarters tents," he said.

Yani would have to wait. And if she got shot in the back, well, one of her chaplain basic course instructors had once proclaimed, "A chaplain must be prepared to preach, pray, or die at a moment's notice." She grinned at her own sense of melodrama. Truth be told, she had no interest in becoming a casualty. She knew that, at the moment, she was using the fantasy of getting shot as the easiest way out of whatever the hell was going on.

"I'll head on over," she told Rodriguez.

It wasn't hard to find Barnet over by the headquarters tents. She was working with two other soldiers. All three had taken off their desert camouflage uniform tops and were wearing flak vests directly over their brown T-shirts. They wore their Kevlar helmets, but their M-16s were stacked to the side as they worked.

Jaime walked up to the young woman who was digging a trench around the outside of a tent with her entrenching tool. Her short dark brown hair was covered with a layer of dust. A pile of sandbags stood waiting to be placed around the outer edges of the tent once the ditch was dug. The other two soldiers were out of earshot, filling more sandbags about 50 meters away.

"Can I help?" Jaime asked.

Specialist Barnet looked up, startled. "What? Oh, Chaplain—oh no, you don't need to . . ."

"Sure I do. I can use the exercise." She picked up a sandbag and slung it over to the corner of the tent. "Whoa, what are they filling these sandbags with, concrete?"

This coaxed a smile from the young woman, a switch from the stoic expression she wore upon Jaime's arrival. "It's Grayson. He prides himself on filling them until they burst!"

The two soldiers worked in silence for a few minutes, Barnet digging and Richards dropping the sandbags into strategic places along the tent line. When they'd gotten a ways ahead, Jaime said, "I need some water. You ready for a break?"

"Suppose so," said Barnet.

They sat down, leaning against the sandbags. Jaime pulled out her newly filled canteen and Specialist Barnet grabbed her Camelbak, sucking water from the tube. She rubbed vigorously at her pants below the knee. "Ugh," she said. "These sand fleas are the worst!"

"The worst. You bitten bad?"

"Just since we got here, to Tallil."

"Sergeant Rodriguez said you were looking for me. What's up?"

"Well . . ." Cindy Barnet was having a hard time getting

the words out. Jaime guessed that she was in her early twenties. "You know 5th CSB is forward with the division, and some of our ammo trucks were supporting 1st Brigade in the battle for the airport the last few days. I just got word . . . my best friend's truck was hit by an RPG. The medics couldn't save her. . . ."

"That's really horrible! I'm very sorry."

"I just . . . I can't believe Becka's gone."

"Becka—was that short for Rebecca? How long have you known her?"

"We were best friends in high school. Stillwater, Oklahoma."

"So, you must have joined the Army together, on the—"

"Buddy system, yeah. Basic, AIT, and first assignment together." Cindy was still looking straight ahead, but she wiped at quiet tears that tracked her cheeks. Her voice was still fairly strong.

"I bet the drill sergeants had a hard time smoking you two, huh?"

Barnet gave a small laugh. "Oh, they tried . . . but we leaned on each other a lot. If I got tired, she pushed me on. If she was pissed at a drill, she complained to me instead of mouthing off and getting an Article 15."

Jaime smiled as well. "Sounds like a great team."

"We were a great team . . . but now . . ." And the floodgates burst. Her body convulsed with sobs.

Jaime just sat next to her quietly, giving her permission to cry. "This really sucks, doesn't it?" she finally said.

"Yeah, big-time. This whole stupid war sucks! Life will never be the same without Becka."

"You're right, Cindy. Life won't be the same. You will miss her, horribly, some times more than others." They continued to sit side by side. Finally Jaime asked, "Are there others who will miss her as much as you?"

"Oh God, yes, her mother will be devastated. She must just be finding out!"

"Is there any way you can help her mother?"

Cindy wiped her eyes with the backs of her hands, leaving a smear of wet dirt across her cheeks. Jaime took out a wet wipe from her pack and handed it over. Cindy took it gratefully and cleaned off her face. She sniffed. "I could e-mail her . . . tell her how sorry I am . . . what a brave soldier Becka was. . . ."

"Anything else? What do you believe about death? Is that it, or is there something more?"

"Oh, Chaplain, I believe there's a heaven. I'm a Christian, and Becka was, too. We used to go to youth group together. She even told me once, she was looking forward to heaven, to see her dad again. . . ."

"So, what else might you say to her mom?" Jaime asked.

Cindy teared up again as she said, "That I know God's watching over us, and Becka, and will take care of us until we meet again."

Jaime knew tears were streaking her own cheeks, but she let them. "You could be a chaplain one day, Cindy. I couldn't have said it better myself."

They looked at each other with tentative smiles. Jaime fished around in her cargo pocket and pulled out a small card. "Here, I want to give you this for your wallet. Pull it out whenever you feel like you miss Becka so much you can't stand it."

She watched as Specialist Barnet took the small piece of cardboard and read the words imprinted there: *May the Lord watch between YOU & ME when we are absent one from the other. Genesis 31:49.*

What Jaime's parents always said to their children before leaving on a trip. What her mother had said just this morning.

"Thanks. I'm gonna stick this in my helmet band."

"Well, I'd better let you get back to work before your cronies over there think you're shamming. But before I go, would you like to have a prayer with me?"

"Yes," she said. "Please."

Chaplain Richards reached over and took the grieving girl's hands. They were still trembling. "Lord, we thank you for the gift of friendship you brought to Cindy and Becka, for the good times they shared, and the strength they gave to each other. We thank you also for the certain knowledge that Becka is not dead, but is alive with you forevermore. But we are still here, in grief, missing her. Bring strength and peace to Cindy, and help her to share that peace with Becka's family, as they face the difficult days to come. This we pray in your name, Jesus, the Christ. Amen."

She looked up to see Cindy's eyes misted over again. Jaime took one finger and brushed away the single tear and gave a smile to the girl that she hoped conveyed understanding and strength. Even though Cindy had no way of knowing Jaime's own situation, the parallels had not been lost on the chaplain.

"Thank you so much," said Specialist Barnet.

Jaime stood and slapped the new dust from her pants. "Catch me any time you want to talk some more." She headed out.

What do you believe about death? Is that it, or is there something more? Jaime knew what her faith taught her, what she wanted to believe. But so many emotions were churning inside her. She wanted to think that Paul, and Adara, and her parents were not just gone forever. She wanted to believe that someday you'd hear a voice and it wouldn't just be a recorder; they would really be together again.

She wanted to remember what it felt like to trust that the people you loved would be there for you, not ripped away without a moment's notice. To believe that those you should be able to trust—the government, the military, the church, God—were telling you the truth. That when her new husband said, "I'll see you Thursday," he would be home on Thursday, not in a coffin in the belly of an El Al airplane. That someone had not put a cosmic KICK ME sign on her back.

She wanted to sink down on the dirt road and weep.

But she had given herself a cardinal rule, many years ago. She would never weaken the faith of someone else, even when she was questioning her own. She wasn't even questioning her faith, really. She just wasn't feeling it. She missed feeling the Presence of God as she had so many times in her life. When she'd felt called to seminary. When he had given her Paul. Now, and for so long, nothing. When she most needed a faith of the heart, not the head—nothing.

It had been hard for her to let Paul in, to her inner self, after losing both of her parents. She had just been starting to take small steps back to intimate trust when she'd been open with Adara.

And now this. She didn't know if she'd ever heal enough to trust someone, intimately, again. Especially when God the healer seemed so very far away.

But she had no time to indulge in whining. She'd have to muddle on the best she could. She used the backs of her hands to wipe the tears from her own cheeks and took the baby wipe she still clutched to clean off the mud.

She took a breath, shook her head, and said a prayer for Cindy Barnet. She looked up, and the young woman gave her a small wave. That communication was all it took to bring her back to herself. She was here for the Barnets. That was one fact she could hold in her hands, one fact she knew was true.

As Jaime left the headquarters tents, she stood straight in the late-morning sun. Early April was still not bad, even in Southern Iraq. The temperature had reached the mid-eighties. The barren terrain was what she had gotten used to during their weeks in Kuwait. Talking with Barnet had cleared her head.

As she walked, she felt she'd returned to Planet Earth, to sure footing. She also knew how she could get Yani up north to Baghdad.

If she could only keep from getting killed before she got back to Ur.

She made sure no one was in the immediate vicinity as she moved with purpose to her vehicle and climbed inside.

Which meant there was no one to see her struggle as someone covered her mouth and pulled her into the back of the Humvee.

The Americans had blasted the Palestine Hotel that morning. Just the thought terrified Jean St. Germain. He hadn't been staying there this trip, but he had stayed there before. His driver had told him that initial CNN reports said several journalists had been killed in the attack on the hotel. Aljazeera television had also been hit in an air raid. There was heavy fighting southwest of the city. And a residential compound was destroyed in Baghdad when intelligence indicated that Saddam Hussein and his sons were meeting there. Hussein was probably dead.

St. Germain hated this. He had never wanted to be James Bond. Had never even played cops and robbers as a kid. He liked things neat and safe and predictable. He understood the importance of what was happening, and his role in making it happen. But he'd never been one of the flashier, more high-profile members of the organization. In fact, he had been shocked when he'd originally been tapped for membership, and his feeling of inferiority had never completely dissipated. Yet he'd done his bit, and now he wanted to go and stay somewhere safely on the sidelines until this whole mess was cleaned up. He wanted a shower and a glass of Burgundy.

Instead, he was in the passenger seat of an old car with a torn white sheet flapping from the hood driving down Highway 1, heading with his prize out of Baghdad.

"We're almost south of the Army brigade at the crossroads of Highways 1 and 8," said his driver, a local man, who seemed to take everything with a grain of salt and a dash of humor. "Once we're safely south of them, we'll cut back west. Don't worry. We'll make your appointment."

His appointment.

Jean tried to be thrilled that he would be meeting Grosskomtur Gerik Schroeder, one of the Triumvirate, along with Wotan and the Commander, and giving him the great treasures. When history was rewritten, Jean's name— his true name—would have a prominent place.

But now he was miserable. They could be stopped or shot at any moment, by anyone. This country was in chaos.

He closed his eyes. Soon he would get rid of the burlap sack at his feet. Soon his part would be over.

It would all be over.

April 8, 2003, 11:21 A.M.
Logbase Rock
Tallil Airfield
Southern Iraq

Jaime banged her left shoulder as she was dragged over the seat into the back of her vehicle. She was held in a fierce grip on top of her captor, his right hand so tightly over her mouth that no sound could escape. The note on a torn piece of paper that was held in front of her said: *Don't make any noise. You are bugged. Do you understand?* She nodded her head with difficulty.

Yani did not release her for a moment. Slowly he took his hand from her mouth. She was lying on top of him, her head against a box of Bibles, Jewish prayer books, and copies of the Qur'an, their feet scrunched against another brown box, this one filled with communion supplies. A couple of rolled prayer rugs were under the small of his back. The supplies of a chaplain to all faiths, as all military chaplains are. He couldn't have been comfortable.

She willed herself to remain silent as his fingers explored beneath the collar of her Kevlar vest. She couldn't help but notice a slight tingle as his hand brushed along the bare skin on her neck. Under the left shoulder, he found what he was looking for. He held the small oval microphone for her to see. He let her sit up and sat up beside her, still in silence. He motioned to the window at the front of the Humvee and she nodded. She climbed forward, he handed her the bug, and she tossed it out the window. She mimed starting the vehicle, and he nodded.

She drove a couple of kilometers, until she was far enough out of sight of any tents that she felt safe pulling over to the side of the road. She sighed. "I want to show you something," she said. She put a finger up to her lips. Then she motioned him forward with her hand. He moved up to the rear seat.

"What?" he said.

"That was it," she said. "The first one meant 'shhh.' The second meant 'come here.' They're signals I respond to. *So please stop grabbing and dragging me!* Sheesh!"

"I had to make sure you didn't talk," he said with no remorse. "You were bugged."

"How did you know?"

"Static," he said.

"Excuse me?"

"That transmitter was causing very annoying static over my own airwaves."

"What? You're saying you have me bugged, too? Could you be so kind as to remove it?"

"Here's your lesson for the day. You get to find this one. Think: Where did I touch you?"

Jaime thought back to the basement room, to him sitting against the far wall. "You never did."

He waited.

She replayed the meeting yet again. She remembered the sadness in his demeanor as he had run his fingers over the stones on Adara's bracelet. She took her left hand off the steering wheel and ran her fingers under the fold of her cuff. Sure enough, there was a flat silver circle, about the size of a watch battery. *You weren't mourning your sister. You were bugging me!* She breathed deeply, looking straight ahead through the windshield. *Remember with whom you're dealing. Remember the steel behind the eyes.*

She pulled her hand back to toss this bug as well, but

just as quickly he caught her hand. "Not this one," he said. He took it from her.

"Things have gone farther than I thought," Yani said simply. "It's obviously no longer safe for you here, even inside the perimeter of the base—especially now that you've announced to anyone listening that you can read cuneiform."

She had to agree: Obviously, she wasn't safe, even here. But there was something even more urgent in her mind that had to be dealt with first.

"Look," she said. "We need a plan of action and we need to be on the same side. But first we need to be clear about something. I will respect your need to withhold certain information from me. But I ask that you tell me as much as you can. And also, I want you to tell me anything you know about my family. They were my parents. As far as they're concerned, it's 'need-to-know.' "

"OK. I agree to those terms. I will tell you all I can. As for your parents, you basically know what I know. Everything I told you and your mother's words were on the chip you brought me this morning. I had no idea who you were, or that you were backup, until then. What makes these less than ideal circumstances is that you had no idea you were Adara's backup, either. So we're both starting at a disadvantage. But we're going to have to trust each other."

"Why were my parents in Jordan? And why were they killed? And who decided to make up a story and tell us they were killed in a mud slide?"

"I wish I knew more. It had to do with the sword. They were there of their own free will. I hope you could tell from your mother's message that she felt they were doing something important. There is someone who could probably tell you more. In fact, he's the one with whom I'm supposed to rendezvous south of Baghdad."

Try as she might, she couldn't get her mother's voice out of her head. She hadn't heard it for so many years. But there were other issues to deal with—like the fact she had been bugged, twice. "So, with all the static, did you hear the incredible things Frank McMillan was telling me? That all of this is basically a glorified case of art theft? Granted, the sword is over four thousand years old, but it's preposterous to think it's the knife that Abraham used. Why all the fuss? And who basically cares that I can speak Hebrew and Greek and read Aramaic and cuneiform? It's not something that usually gets me very far at parties."

She was keeping an eye out for other passing vehicles, but so far, so good. It wouldn't really cause problems if she was seen talking to a DynCorp contractor, but she didn't want to have to explain anything she didn't have to.

"OK," he finally answered. "This stolen Sword of Life, or Dagger of Ur, whatever you want to call it, it is worth millions as an art object. You're also right that it holds no mystical or magical powers—none that I know of, anyway. Its true worth is that it holds the key to the location of the original Garden of Eden. That's why it's so important. That's why everybody wants it."

She didn't say anything. But she was staring at him with a look that said, to put it politely, *Uh*-huh.

He almost smiled. "So, perhaps you see why I didn't just go blurting this out at our first meeting."

"*The* Garden. Of Eden."

"You have a problem with that?"

"I have so many problems with that it's hard to even let a dozen rise to the top."

"Give it a try," he said.

"Assuming the Garden was a true, literal place, and given the time frame in which it would have existed—well, suffice it to say, even though the Tigris and Euphrates rivers still flow, the topography around here has changed. A lot. There have been floods and aridity. The other two rivers mentioned in the Hebrew Scriptures have totally disappeared. How could the site still exist somewhere? And if it does, how come no one has found it in the last six or seven millennia?"

Yani considered briefly. "I wish we had time for a nice archeological chat," he responded. "However, I will point out that Ur, which is behind you, is over four thousand years old. It was the bustling capital of the Fertile Crescent—despite today's lovely arid look, it was fertile here once. Ur was finally excavated by Lord Woolley in 1923. In the context of history, that's yesterday."

"I suppose, if such a site does exist, it would be the archeological find of all time." She had to grant him that.

"There seem to be a number of people who agree with you. And that is the stolen sword's greatest value. To decipher the location, you must have the sword, a certain ancient atlas, and ancient cuneiform tablets—the very ones that have been stolen from the museum in Mosul. Obviously, someone knows what he's doing. The final thing he will need is someone who reads cuneiform."

"And that's me."

"Yes. Although someone obviously had you bugged before you affirmed that piece of information. It's not your sole use, but it's a nice bonus."

"It was Adara's idea that we take the cuneiform class together."

"And you've already used it once today, to deliver the necklace."

"Everything is happening so fast," Jaime said.

"Actually, it's taken years for this all to happen. But it's only just barged into your life."

"If what you say about my parents is true, it barged in decades ago. I just didn't know it."

"So this whole conversation brings us back around to my original point: You're not safe, even here. You could be killed at any moment."

"Yani. You don't have to scare me. I'll help you. I'll get us up north. Exactly where is it you need to go?"

"The Third Sister. I need to be there by sundown, which happens today at 18:25. The Third Sister is in what used to be Babylon. And it's a four-hour drive from here, without war. So we haven't much time."

"That will be cutting it tight, no matter how we manage it. I'd better go get us a ride."

"How?"

She couldn't help the slightly smug tone. "I'm not the only one who gives information on a need-to-know basis. Where should I meet you?"

"I'll turn up," he said. "As long as you understand that we have to be the first ones to the rendezvous. If anyone beats us there . . ."

"Someone else knows your rendezvous?"

"Someone knew where to find Adara. Someone knew where to find you."

"Give me half an hour."

"Just hurry. I'll be around."

"OK. You want a ride to Ur?"

"No," he said, one foot already out the door. "This is fine."

"Yani," she called, using her authoritative, commissioned-officer voice. He turned back to her expectantly.

"You're lucky you're cute," she said.

She'd hoped to throw him off-balance for once, and from the look on his face, it seemed she'd succeeded. Jaime smiled to herself and gunned the Humvee back toward base.

April 8, 2003, 11:31 A.M.
Near the Biwage Water Treatment Plant
south of Baghdad
Central Iraq

"More good news," came the voice of Coleman Satis over the radio in the dash. "The old man we freed did indeed head straight to secure the final items from the museum in Mosul. He's even been kind enough to bring them practically to your doorstep. Once your appointment with Mr. St. Germain is finished, he should be easy to intercept. He seems to be heading in your direction, even now."

"He doesn't know he's being tracked?"

"It shall come as a delightful surprise to him, I'm certain."

"Excellent. What is it he's carrying?"

"An old book of maps and some tablets with Sumerian writing."

"I'll call you when my appointment with Mr. St. Germain is complete."

"Until then."

The differences in Iraqi terrain never ceased to be a source of wonderment for Gerik. As he approached Baghdad from the south, the terrain had gone from arid to lush. Farm fields dotted the landscape; palm trees grew in profusion. Cattle and sheep grazed. You could tell the pecking order in the country by who got the green.

The passing from lifeless to verdant matched Gerik's own mood. After decades of work, years of planning, by this evening he'd have the objects of his quest. These were the final days of the old order. Within the hour, he'd have the sword. The sword. A heady feeling of transcendence was washing over him. It was so apparent that humans were meant for something higher, something more.

Gerik's own grandfather had been a high-ranking member of both the SS and the Ancestral Heritage Society. Those connected with these organizations knew that within the root races that populated the earth some were founders of civilization and culture, some were maintainers, and others were destroyers. Of the races, only the Aryans were founders. That had been proven time and time again by their expeditions: to Tibet, to South America, to Greece, to Rome. The Aryans, in their undefiled state, were god-men. They understood all things, built all things, understood the future as well as the past, and could connect with one another easily through telepathy. Transcendence was the normal state; euphoria was common. And then they intermarried with other races; they muddied the blood. They had lost their natural abilities; they could no longer consort with the Astra, who were pure spirit. Only a return to purity of the blood would make men the gods they were meant to be.

Didn't people, even of the other Root Races—didn't they feel it? These longings, this knowledge that life is about more? Didn't they sometimes cross the void and touch the spirit world? Didn't they know in their bones that telepathy and transcendence were possible? Didn't they wonder? Didn't they have Wonder? If not, how did they live?

Gerik's grandfather had been hung for "war crimes." Proudly. Apparently it was a crime against humanity to try to save the earth.

Gerik's father was also a high-ranking member of the Ancestral Heritage Society. He had married a beautiful, pure-blooded girl, and they had produced Gerik.

Gerik, as predicted, had even outshone his father. He

had been indoctrinated into the Society at 18 and had a bride chosen for him at 21. She was of the purest blood, the daughter of the former *Grosskomtur*. But Gerik knew he was called for a higher purpose. He declined to marry her, choosing to wait, believing that they would find the Remnant of the original Garden in his lifetime—the pure Aryans—and that his bride was awaiting him there. Sometimes he had visions of the perfect, ascended children he would have with her, visions of her blond hair and white robes blowing. Sometimes he heard her calling to him.

Oh, he had impregnated the *Grosskomtur*'s daughter, as she had asked, as he had many of the girls in the Society. It was his duty as they ascended toward the purity of the blood. But as enjoyable as it had been, it was not his final purpose.

Gerik had finally become *Grosskomtur* himself. The Society had no leader as committed, as ascended, as focused, as willing to be ruthless. And that was what had brought them to this crossroad of history.

Gerik had serious doubts about the enlightenment of Coleman Satis. He was a necessary piece of this final battle, however, as was the Commander. It was exciting in itself that the three leaders whose foot soldiers had pulled this all together had each come to Iraq. Gerik was well aware that the other two belonged to another organization that demanded their top loyalty. Yet thus far their goals had coalesced and they'd been able to work in tandem with him and the Ancestral Heritage Society. He had long suspected they each had separate ultimate aims. His hope was that these aims would serve them well in the Order to come, not splinter them. Best they each had a different but equal role to play.

Now the time was upon them. None of them was represented by his lieutenants now. They were each here, in person, for the triumph.

He smiled to himself and turned right onto the small local road that led to Baghdad's water treatment plant.

Jaime found Lieutenant Colonel Ray Jenkins with the hood open on his Humvee. As she approached, she could see that he was checking fluid levels and testing the belts for wear and tear. He turned to her and leaned with his back against the front fender. He seemed relaxed but hadn't lost that expression of superiority that pervaded his features on those rare occasions when he wasn't actually angry.

And his greeting was typical Jenkins: "Chaplain, I hope you had a good excuse for blowing off the BUB today."

Officers' attendance was required at the daily Battle Update Briefing, and usually, given the circumstances, she was plenty interested in attending. But not today. It irked her that she always had to get past his petty accusations to have a conversation.

"As a matter of fact, I did, sir. I was counseling with a soldier."

"About what?"

She didn't even dignify that with an answer. He knew better than to ask.

"Yeah, yeah, I know," he said, "confidentiality and all that crap. So you can't tell me what you talked about; is there anything you can tell me?"

"Well, yes, sir, there is. I'm concerned about 5th CSB. I understand they just lost some soldiers in a firefight taking the airport," she said, referring to the unit of Specialist Cindy Barnet's friend. "Their chaplain is young, straight out of basic. I doubt he's ever done a memorial service before. I need to go forward, check in on him, and offer support. There's a convoy of fuelers leaving for Objective Lions. I'd like to fall in with them."

Jenkins turned back to his vehicle. "Not a chance. I'm not putting anyone on the road right now for anything less than mission-essential business."

"But this is mission-essential!"

He swung around, in his best eye-flashing mode. He took a step closer, coming nearly toe-to-toe. "Bullshit. Everyone tries to find an excuse to get close to the front. To get a piece of the action."

Jaime was close to sputtering. "*A piece of the action?* Did you forget what happened this morning? I've had enough 'action' for one day. This isn't about glory; it's about doing my job."

The executive officer was beginning to gloat. He loved this part. "Yeah, well, you can do your job from right here. Call him on the phone. You're not going forward."

"But . . ."

"And that's final." He turned back to his Humvee. She was dismissed.

April 8, 2003, 11:53 A.M.
Satis's headquarters
16 kilometers west of Baghdad
Central Iraq

The thing that most people didn't understand, Coleman Satis knew, was that governments didn't run the world. Corporations did. Or if people did understand, they didn't care—as long as it didn't keep them from having a comfortable home, three televisions, and two game systems, and letting their kids play soccer.

What did they care that 50-odd independent book publishers were now imprints of four conglomerates? Or that their choices for television viewing, magazine purchase, and film-going were dictated by three media moguls? If Coleman Satis couldn't dictate to the citizens of the world what to think, he could at least tell them where to focus their attention. And as any magician will tell you, if you've got people watching your right hand, you can do as you please with your left.

Satis's one regret was that his mother, Federica, was not alive to see this. He had often heard the story of how she had been forced from her home, penniless and pregnant, to find the only job she could get, at a garment sweatshop. How she'd been paid pennies for each piece, but how she had worked long hours, and through lunch, to earn what she could. How when her situation—single and expecting—

became evident she had been taunted by the other girls in the shop. How she had come to the attention of the manager and had gained his confidence. And how she'd used the information he'd given her to get him fired and her hired in his place. How she'd then fired the girls who had taunted her and replaced them with workers she could control; she had taken the one girl she liked off the sewing machines and hired her as nanny. How she had diverted some of the payroll and had bought the company 18 months after she started working there. She had gone on to turn it into one of the largest, most productive factories in West Virginia. By the time Satis was in Yale, she owned a textile empire.

He had learned his lessons well. She had delighted in the fact that her son walked the corridors of power, that families who'd presided over privilege and position for generations had tapped him and accepted him as one of their own. She had enjoyed his knack for acting as a fierce corporate raider. The more ruthless he was with companies he'd acquired in hostile takeovers, the more she patted his hand at dinner in their eighteen-thousand-square-foot Manhattan triplex. She stayed out of his personal life—for which he had little time, anyway. She had her own floor of the triplex. She also had half a dozen homes around the world.

She had given him the purpose and drive he needed to succeed. He was about to succeed in reaching the one goal that had been beyond her grasp. If only . . . if only.

It was in reach now. And it was for her.

"Tomorrow night, Federica," he said, touching the gilt frame on his desk in the palace basement Saddam had outfitted for him. "Your son will go home in triumph."

Jaime purposefully regulated her breathing as she stood on the new path. Everything here was dusty with the top layers of whitish gray soil that permeated the air even without a wind.

She had to get to the Third Sister by sunset at 1825 so that Yani could intercept the sword.

She had to find out what really happened to her parents.

She had to not stay here and get killed.

She had to not sock Jenkins.

She turned down the row of officers' tents, looking for the tent of Colonel Abraham Derry, the 57th CSG commander. Colonel Derry was a veteran of Desert Storm and had the respect of all under his command. Abe, as he was known to his peers, led with quiet confidence. He was a tall, muscular African-American, whose every feature—and every personality trait—spoke of a man who was the exact opposite of his XO.

Jaime found Colonel Derry outside his tent, hanging up laundry he was pulling from a wash bucket. He had stopped, soggy T-shirt in hand, and was staring into space. She waited a moment before finally saying, "Sir?"

He snapped back to reality, shaking his head a bit, then

smiled at her. "I was about to report you AWOL," Jaime said, and as he laughed, she asked, "Where were your thoughts taking you?"

"Oh, I was wondering what my kids are doing right now. And wondering what they would think if they could see their dear ole dad doing his laundry."

"Well, the first answer is easy," Jaime replied, looking at her watch and doing the math. "Knowing your teenagers, they are sacked out right now and will remain so for the next few hours until your wife drags them out of bed to rush for school. The second answer isn't very hard, either. Unless I grab a picture of you with my digital camera, they won't believe you do your own laundry."

"I believe you've called it. So, what's on your mind? You're wearing your intense Jaime-in-mission-mode look."

She was embarrassed that he could read her that easily and touched that he devoted the attention necessary to truly know his officers. "The 5th CSB, sir."

He nodded solemnly.

She continued. "Their first combat losses. Suddenly the fantasy of combat becomes the harsh reality of blood and death. I want to help the battalion commander and her soldiers get through this and continue on."

"Karen was pretty shaken up by the incident. One of the soldiers used to be her driver. What do you recommend?"

"Chaplain Henderson is a good kid, but brand-new at all this. I have resources he can use and experience in these kinds of situations. I need to link up with him and help provide critical incident debriefs for the affected soldiers, to include the command group. And, most important, the unit needs closure. We honor those fallen soldiers with a proper memorial ceremony and this serves as tacit permission for their battle buddies to return to the mission." She meant every word she was saying and hoped that she would have had the wherewithal to make the same plea without the current circumstances.

Colonel Derry finally wrung out the T-shirt in his hand

and threw it over the line. "Makes sense, Chaplain. I want nothing but the best for these soldiers. The roads are still dangerous, though. How do you propose to get there?"

"There's a convoy of fuelers leaving within the hour for Baghdad. My assistant and I were going to fall in with them."

"As of 1100 hours, that convoy now has a secondary mission. They are going to stop in Al Hillah to test some fuel. The 101st has been fighting there all morning, and they just captured fifty Iraqi tankers. There are still many pockets of resistance. It could be risky." He stood straight, gazing over the camp, putting his thoughts in order.

"I'm willing to take the chance," she said. "Besides, God has brought me safe this far. I'm sure I won't be abandoned at this point."

The colonel looked straight at her. "Like that card you gave me with Psalm 91 on it: 'No evil shall befall you. Nor shall any plague come near your dwelling. . . .' "

" 'For he shall give his angels charge over you. To keep you in all your ways.' Did you memorize the whole thing?"

"I read it every morning." He fished another shirt out of the bucket. The water was brown with mud. "Do what you need to do, Chaplain."

"One more thing, sir?" For the first time, she was nervous. "The XO . . . he . . ."

"Probably told you no, right?" The colonel chuckled, and she felt sheepish.

"I'll take care of it. You just worry about my soldiers."

"Yes, sir." She held the triumphant part of her grin in check until she turned around to head back to find the convoy commander.

"Hello, Cousin!" said his driver as they passed through the chain-link fence surrounding the Biwage Water Treatment Plant. Jean didn't know if he was more shocked to be waved through the gate or that there was anyone there at all that day.

"Why is your cousin here today?" he ventured to ask.

"It is a very brave thing, I think," said the driver. "There is a good chance that dirty water will kill more Iraqis than bombs during this war. Already in Basra, the water treatment plant is down. Cholera is spreading. These plants are in bad shape—embargo on industrial parts since the last U.S. war, you know. But it's all we have. Anyone vandalizes these plants, many, many people die. Brave of him to stay.

"Already in Baghdad, bombing has hit water mains. Pressure is bad. Then locals shoot at the water pipes to get at the water, and—hah—worse pressure. Poor people, at the end of the pipes, they have no clean water at all."

How was it that his driver was in such a talkative mood and such good spirits? It was like he was a cabbie pointing out the points of interest in Manhattan, not chatting about people dying of cholera in a war zone.

Large rectangular holding tanks of water appeared before them, with white concrete walkways and metal railings, with chipping white paint. The concrete administration buildings, which seemed deserted, were low one-story affairs, also painted white. His driver passed them, though, and continued past the large round enclosed water storage tanks. Low buildings and sheds dotted the landscape.

The car came to a stop. "This is the conference room," said the driver. "We get out here."

The driver stepped out, came around, and opened Jean's door. He reached down for the burlap sacks at his feet, but Jean pushed his hands away. "I have it," he said.

"As you please," said the driver. He walked ahead of Jean into a small rectangular building that only charitably could be called a shed. The door was unlocked. Inside, an old door on two sawhorses served as a table. Canvas tarps were stored under a window that had been nearly completely taped over.

"This is where we're meeting Grosskomtur Schroeder?"

"Yes, this is the place," said the driver, still chipper. "Makes for privacy, don't you think?"

"I don't think we'll be disturbed."

"That is my point. I am wishing you all the best." His driver, a thin local man with a large smile, extended his hand.

"You're leaving?" Jean was stunned.

"It is not for me to meet such important men. I drive only."

Before Jean could object, the driver had taken his hand, pumped it twice, and left the hut, pulling the door closed behind him.

Outside, the car roared to life, the old muffler making that peculiar *baa-daa-daah* sound. The sound became fainter as the driver pulled away.

And Jean looked for a place to sit with his burlap bag. Was the *Grosskomtur* here already?

Jean was tempted to remove the items from the bag but didn't want to be caught looking at them. It would seem disrespectful. So he sat on the dirt floor and waited to meet the great man.

"Hello. I'm Bill Burton, the contractor who'll be hitching a ride with you," Yani said, extending his hand. He still wore his black Rams polo shirt and jeans, but thank God he'd dropped the Texas drawl. She wasn't sure she could take five hours of it. His curly hair was brushed straight. He wore shades.

"Hello, Mr. Burton."

"Bill."

"Bill. I'm Chaplain Richards, and this is Sergeant Rodriguez."

"Pleasure."

"I guess you've checked in with the convoy commander? It sounds like we've got a convoy briefing at 1240, and are leaving at 1255. I see you came prepared for the ride."

"I'm ready, yes, ma'am," he said. He was carrying a black nylon case the size of a laptop slung over his shoulder, with a flak vest and a plain Kevlar helmet in his hands. He dropped the protective gear in the backseat of the Humvee.

Rodriguez was reshuffling supplies in the back of the

vehicle. Yani lowered his voice. "I need to speak to you in private before we go."

"Rodriguez, I'll be back," she said.

"I'll finish up here," he answered.

Jaime and Yani walked back over to the line of tents, to the SICPS—Standard Integrated Command Post Shelter—that served as the chaplain's office. A small desert camouflage flag with a chocolate brown elongated cross in the center hung over the small entryway in front of the door. The vinyl tent was 12 feet by 12 feet and provided somewhere to counsel in private. Rodriguez had left most of their supplies there, as they'd only be gone for two days. He'd already set up a cot, a table, and two folding chairs. All three window covers were mostly down, leaving only about an inch at the bottom to let some light filter in.

Yani turned and Velcroed the door panel shut. "We don't have much time," he said.

"You're welcome," she answered.

"OK, good job furnishing the ride, Chaplain. But this is only the beginning."

She rolled her eyes. "I can see you're not easy to please. I take it you've been cleared to hitch with us by the SPO?"

The Support Operations Officer, or SPO, was the commander's key staff officer for planning what material went where, to whom, and in which convoy. "And by the way, where did you get that helmet and vest? How do you come up with this stuff?"

He paid no attention. He took a seat on one of the gray folding chairs and zipped open his case. "Here."

"What?"

He had something in the open palm of his right hand. It was fluorescent green. "Take it."

"It looks like Flubber." She offered her hand and he dropped the small blob into it. It wasn't as dense as Flubber, more like green gelatin. Not even that dense. "What is it?" More like goo. But it didn't leave residue.

"It's a tracking device."

"You do have all the latest toys."

"I need to inject you with a small ball of it, which will allow me to track you for the next forty-eight hours, should we get separated. It's not toxic, and it will disintegrate within a few days."

She stared at him, aghast.

He remained unfazed. Businesslike.

"You expect me just to trust you on this?" She knew her voice was rising.

"You have no choice. I'll do it with or without your permission."

All of the emotions inside her suddenly folded together into one roaring boil. "*Who are you?*" she spat. "You say you're Adara's brother, but you take news of her death without missing a beat. In fact, you use it to plant a bug on me. You've already asked me to put my career on the line for you. And my safety. Now, what, you want me to bet my health as well? This does not look like something I want inside my body. As a matter of fact, it looks like the *definition* of toxic."

This guy was driving her nuts, and he'd just found her tipping point. She continued, "Every time I trust you with something, you take that as an invitation to bounce it up to something even more impossible. Well, there are limits. And this is one."

It happened so fast that she had no time to defend herself. He had stood, turned her around, brought her left arm up behind her, and with the other grabbed her in a headlock. Within that moment, she careened back to the morning, to the man in Fedayeen robes holding Adara just this way. Yani's grip was absolute. She knew she could be dead in one second. Instead of breaking her neck, he forced her arm up farther behind her, high enough to make her gasp. She felt his breath as he spoke, barely audibly, into her left ear. "This is to answer any future questions before they come up. And to remind you that you are not *my* superior, Major."

Tears burned her eyes as adrenaline burned her veins. What had she gotten herself into? Had she guessed wrong? Was Rodriguez going to find her body here on the ground, her neck snapped? It seemed the method of death du jour.

She let her body go limp. He continued to hold her, her arm socket burning.

After a minute, he released a breath, let her go, and stepped backward.

His mistake was to take her exhalation as acquiescence. Before he had a moment to think, she turned and slapped him—really walloped him—across his face with an open hand.

Then she stood, six inches from him, staring him down. "That was a reminder that although my faith teaches me to turn the other cheek, it doesn't require me to be a punching bag," she said.

They continued facing each other, jaws clenched, fists clenched, until he finally said, "Understood.

"Jaime." He changed his tone as he changed his tack. "Someone went to a lot of trouble to try to kidnap you this morning. And he, or someone else altogether, also went to the trouble of bugging you. We're about to undertake a hazardous journey, to make a dangerous rendezvous. This is procedure," he said, nodding toward the gel that had fallen onto the ground. "It's necessary procedure."

She put her palm to her forehead and rubbed it as if an answer would appear.

"We don't have much time. Please. Cooperate. Please."

She tried to think of some appropriate training or even an appropriate verse of Scripture, but all that came was the old adage "In for a dime, in for a dollar." The frightening truth was, if she couldn't trust Yani, she was probably as good as dead, anyway.

"All right," she said. "All right."

"OK," he said, his shoulders relaxing slightly. "It'll be easiest if you just lie on the cot."

"Oh. Don't tell me."

"It's not how I get my jollies, Richards; don't worry."

"I know. You are your job."

"Yeah," he said. "But how about you?"

"What do you mean?"

He sat down on the folding chair again and was prepping the syringe where she couldn't see it.

She mouthed a very unchaplain-like word to herself, took off her vest, and shrugged off the suspenders of her chemical pants. She hadn't had time to change since they'd rolled in that morning. Which would actually be handy, as they were heading out again.

"I mean, why are you here?"

"In what way?" She sat down on the cot. She was suddenly drenched with fatigue. She undid her pants and loosened them around the top. Then she lay down on her stomach on the cot. And she realized she could sleep for two weeks. Perversely, her body wouldn't cycle down when she was supposed to sleep. But now, with the convoy leaving in minutes, she could barely remain conscious.

"I mean, if you asked a typical soldier out there why he or she is here, he'd probably say something along the lines of 'to kick Saddam's butt.' But I'm guessing that's not your main purpose. So why are you here?"

She put her chin on a fist in an effort to stay awake. "I'm here because war is hell," she said. "Every soldier out there is going to face some sort of spiritual crisis, and they shouldn't have to do it alone."

He came and pulled the second chair up beside the cot. "Interesting answer," he said.

"So, who's the guy?"

"The guy?" With a practiced move, he tugged the clothes several inches down off the left side of her hip.

"If we were to get separated. Who is the person who can tell me about my parents' death?" The swab was warm, and she exhaled as the needle slid in and, momentarily, was withdrawn. She was, unfortunately, as practiced at receiving injections as he was in doling them out.

"That wasn't bad," she said.

"I know. Wait just a minute for it to kick in. And sorry," he said. "You can't know his name, in case we *do* get separated."

He went back to his bag on the first chair. She couldn't help herself. She closed her eyes. Just for a second . . .

She pulled herself back to wakefulness as she felt another swab on her hip, an inch higher than the first.

"What?" she said.

"Last one," he said. "You're good at this. Relax one more time."

This time she felt more of a pressure than a puncture, but it was constant and uncomfortable.

"So, you want to know why I'm here?" he asked.

She knew it was a diversionary tactic, but she had nothing against diversion under the circumstances. "Sure. But I assumed you wouldn't tell me."

"It's a calling," he said. "And it's not an easy one."

"That's really revealing," she said. "I could have said the same thing."

"I know," he said. "And it would have been truer than you knew. So, does it ever bother you, being a noncombatant? I mean, suppose you saw someone in your convoy about to be killed. Wouldn't you want to grab a gun and start shooting?"

"Honestly? I don't know. I pray I would have the strength not to. If I did, it would put every other chaplain—on both sides—in danger. Kind of like if a Red Cross convoy opened fire on a town."

He sat up straight. "OK. We've got it. Here, hold this. Put pressure on it."

She held the gauze bandage against her lower back as he set the syringe down on the chair and knelt beside her with more gauze, a bandage, and some white tape. He replaced the gauze several times before he finally taped the bandage into place.

"Stay there for a minute while I clean up. Then we're ready to roll," he said.

As he moved away, she saw the syringe for the first time. "Good Lord," she said. The needle was huge. "How did that not hurt like hell?"

"First shot was like Novocain," he said. "Better to have your hip asleep for a couple of hours during the drive than to have you in pain."

"Why didn't you ask?" she demanded.

"Look, I wasn't shooting you with some meds. The gel had to nest. The insertion can hurt."

"Nest?"

"By the iliac crest."

"Yani—"

"Bill."

"Bill." She sat up. Her left side tingled like crazy. "There's only one problem with your plan. As you so clearly pointed out, I don't carry a weapon."

"So?" He was making a clean sweep of his supplies. And he knelt to pick up the original sample where it had fallen into the dirt.

"So, Rodriguez is riding shotgun. And I'm driving you to Babylon." She tried to stand up. It was hard to get her balance. More than hard. "Shit," she said.

For the first time since they'd met, he looked sheepish. "'Shit' is right," he said. "Please tell me the Humvee doesn't have a clutch."

"Everything in order, Sergeant?" Jaime asked as she and the contractor returned to the Humvee just in time to head over for the convoy briefing.

She was met by a look of mild astonishment on Rodriguez's face. She quickly realized that unlike when they'd left 15 minutes earlier, she now had a limp. And Yani, who had an arm around her to help her toward the vehicle, had a swath of red across his left cheek and the bridge of his nose from where she'd slapped him that was particularly impressive in the daylight.

She couldn't help herself. She grinned. And her chaplain assistant sent a silent communication that she read as: *Just when I thought you could no longer surprise me . . .*

As they rounded the back of the Humvee, Jaime became acutely aware of the strength of Yani's arm and the care with which he was guiding her in the guise of nonchalance. She also became aware of the prickle of heat where his flesh touched hers and found the sensation a little unnerving.

"Let's go," she said to Rodriguez.

"Um, ma'am," Rodriguez said.

"Yes?" she asked.

"We've got another rider."

She and Yani turned, in concert, to where another person stepped out from in front of the Humvee.

"Liv Nelsson," Rodriguez said. "Embedded photographer."

"Hi," said Liv, shielding her eyes with her hand and addressing Jaime. "We've met." She turned then to the contractor. "Liv Nelsson," she said. "I'm heading north for Baghdad Airport. The SPO told me there might be room in this vehicle."

He gave her hand a curt shake. "Bill Burton," he said. For some reason, she kept her grip a moment longer and studied his face more carefully. "It's good to meet you," she said. Then, "Wow. What a group."

Yani casually continued around to the other side of the vehicle. Jaime stood by the driver's side door, trying to figure out how to board the vehicle without either calling attention to herself or falling on her face. Her left leg remained fairly useless.

"All aboard," said Rodriguez. He didn't know exactly what was going on with Jaime, but he came over, opened her door, and unobtrusively helped her into the seat.

"You all right?" he asked.

She nodded and kept her voice low. "We're definitely down the rabbit hole now," was all she said. Jaime turned the lever on the dash and cupped her hand around the glow plug light so she could tell when it went out. Then she pushed the lever the rest of the way to start the engine.

"Yes, ma'am, I'm right there with you," Rodriguez responded, and closed the driver's side door.

—PART TWO—

Al Hillah/Babylon

"Oh, my God. Grosskomtur Schroeder!" Jean said, leaping to his feet. He was slightly shocked to find the man entering the "conference room" dressed in the black robes of the Fedayeen. But there was no question of who it was. Jean had known this man's face from the photos for nearly 16 years. Gerik Schroeder carefully closed the door.

"You have the items?" the *Grosskomtur* asked Jean.

Jean had spent the last hour running different versions of this very moment through his mind. Now it was upon him.

He stood, picked up the burlap sack, and said, "It is with great humility that I, Adrian Montreat, give this gift to the glorious cause." He gave a small bow and extended the sack to the man before him.

The *Grosskomtur* accepted the sack. He put it down gently on the door/table before them and lifted out the two brown velvet sacks inside. He then carefully laid out the burlap. It was clear to both men what was in each package from its shape.

The *Grosskomtur* chose the flatter package and from it withdrew the sheath. Both men inhaled. It was beyond belief. The craftsmanship was unparalleled. There were four golden squares at the top of the sheath, each with a differ-

ent star pattern design. A rectangular divider also displayed
fine filigree work, and beneath it were three more squares
of descending width as the sheath came to its point.

All Adrian's fears were forgotten. This moment, of being here with Grosskomtur Schroeder as he received the
sacred objects, transported Adrian far from this dark shed
south of Baghdad. He no longer heard the constant helicopters overhead or smelled the must in the air. No one
else on the planet was here to share this moment with
them. No one.

Adrian barely noticed that Grosskomtur Schroeder had
moved to stand behind him. "Thank you, Mr. Montreat,"
he said, and those were the last words Adrian ever heard.
His neck broke easily. His body slumped to the ground
with a thud.

Gerik stepped past him to pick up the last item. He reached
into the museum storage bag and grasped the handle. Just
the feel of the small, pea-sized golden balls in the palm of
his hand caused a tear to course down his cheek. And then,
with a smooth pull, the Sword of Life glanced fully before
him. Even in the dim light, he could see the brilliant blue
of the lapis handle. He could feel the power of the long
golden blade. He drew his thumb along the straight line
that ran down the center. And through it he could hear the
scream of everyone who had ever had his life extinguished
by that sword; through his hand vibrated the victory of
everyone who had ever slain an enemy with its might.

The might now belonged to him.

"We are back!" he hissed through gritted teeth. "We are
coming home!"

April 8, 2003, 1:34 P.M.
Satis's headquarters
16 kilometers west of Baghdad
Central Iraq

For Andy Blenheim, the biggest mystery in the palace was the identity of the person at the end of the lowest hall. Was he a prisoner? Or an honored guest? Why did no one ever speak of him by anything but his first name?

As much as Andy wracked his brain, he couldn't figure out what importance the person would have—unless he was somehow the One. Perhaps by his birth.

That was how Andy chose to think of him. So he talked to him with great deference and kindness. It could be that he was in the presence of greatness.

Even now he knocked before he put the key in the lock and turned it. The light was on when he opened the door. The opulent furnishings—the crimson divan, the gilt chairs—seemed somehow sterile and uncomforting.

"You must be hungry," Andy said.

The little boy turned around from where he sat on the floor, on the other side of the divan. Andy put the tray down on the wooden Louis XIV dining table. He had been having trouble finding food the boy liked. Andy had tried macaroni and cheese, hamburgers, and even the universal language of french fries. They didn't exactly have a kitchen going at the moment. All they had was a freezer and a microwave. Though Andy had finally come up with some bread and half a jar of peanut butter.

The boy stood. His hair was dark, his bangs long, which made him look very young. Andy guessed him to be seven or eight. The boy spoke so seldom, Andy hadn't even figured out his first language. He did seem to at least understand English.

Andy offered the sandwich with a sweep of his hand. He had also brought a small carton of milk.

The boy came forward.

"It's peanut butter, Master Stefan. I hope you will like it. I am doing my best, and I know you must be hungry."

"It's not—been poisoned?" he asked. He seemed near tears.

"Heavens, no! I made it myself." Andy broke off a piece and popped it into his mouth.

Stefan came and sat down at the table. He picked up the sandwich, took one bite, and then wolfed down the whole thing, followed by the carton of milk.

"Are you still hungry, then?" asked Andy.

The boy nodded. He was crying now.

"No need for that," said the older man. "Let me see if I can find you a treat. And then you'd best get some rest. I think we have an adventure ahead of us, we do."

He winked at the boy and went back out into the hall, locking the door again behind him.

April 8, 2003, 2:24 P.M.
MSR (Main Supply Route) Tampa
64 kilometers northwest of Tallil
217 kilometers southeast of Al Hillah
Iraq

The countryside through which the convoy was driving was flat and desolate. The greatest point of interest so far had been a small flock of sheep in the distance. But that had been miles ago. Now there was really nothing to look at but the fuelers up ahead. And no matter how you looked at them, they looked like nice fat, round targets for any old rocket-powered grenade.

The 5th Corps Support Battalion, whose chaplain Jaime was going forward to support, was with the 3rd Infantry Division at the Baghdad Airport. That was where the convoy had been headed originally. Now they had a secondary mission—to test the fuel in the 50 Iraqi tankers that had been captured in the city of Al Hillah. That was especially fortuitous for Yani, as Al Hillah was the modern city next to the ruins of Babylon.

Jaime's Humvee was near the back of the convoy, with three vehicles behind. There had been no chitchat since they started. Driving in convoy was noisy enough that you had to raise your voice and nearly shout to be heard above the engine. Jaime knew; she'd been hoarse more than once after a conversation on the road. If she'd had either Rodriguez or Yani in private, there would have been a lot to talk about. But as it was, there wasn't much that could be discussed in the midst of all the riders.

Also, she didn't know what to think about Liv Nelsson. It wasn't Jaime's nature to be suspicious of people, and yet . . . Liv had been in Ur. Coincidence, most likely, but there wasn't much room for coincidence that day. Worst-case scenario was that Liv was working for whoever had been tailing Jaime and that here she was, merrily riding with them to the rendezvous.

Jaime thought back to their meeting atop the ziggurat. Could Liv have been the one who planted the bug? Jaime didn't remember Liv touching her, although she had given her a drink.

Dear God, was this what she'd come to? Being suspicious of a photographer who'd shared her water?

Jaime hoped Chaplain Henderson was doing all right up ahead with the CSB. He was a good kid, just out of the chaplain basic course, and she knew he was in the midst of his baptism of fire. The last time Jaime had been involved with deaths on active duty had been with a chopper crash while stationed with 2nd Infantry Division in Oijongbu, Korea. As sad as it had been, the other soldiers had been able to move at their own pace through the stages of grief and to concentrate on saying farewell to two of their peers. War was, sadly, a whole different animal. You said good-bye to two today and five tomorrow, one the next day. It was good and bad that there was so little time to process individual deaths. But they had to do their best, in part so that the others would know that should tomorrow be their day to die, they, too, would have a fitting send-off.

By the time Chaplain Henderson got home, he would be a rookie no more. But the first battlefield memorial ceremony was always the hardest. She was glad she was heading up.

And then suddenly, without warning, Jaime missed Paul with an intensity that seized her physically, making her chest ache and her eyes brim with tears. This used to happen fairly often, but she hadn't felt the longing so viscerally in several months.

Paul would love this. Chasing through Iraq in search of Abraham's dagger—it was right up Paul's alley. He loved history and he loved the Middle East. He could be in the direst of circumstances, and it never occurred to him to be afraid. Just didn't come up.

Jaime had always figured it was because Paul was always so interested in the people around him, what they believed, and what made them tick. He had broken bread at home with families in so many cultures, and he loved it. He loved them. As much as he'd dedicated his life to defusing extremism, he could also look at a terrorist and see the person there, driven by limited education, injury, and fear. Paul was probably one of the only people on earth who could have a normal, down-to-earth conversation with a terrorist wearing a suicide vest loaded with dynamite. Which was why it was so ironic that he was killed—as just a nameless, faceless person in the crowd—that September day five years ago, on Jerusalem's Pedestrian Mall.

You killed the guy who could have helped! she'd wanted to yell, so many times. *You killed my husband. My Paul.*

But he'd prepared her even for this: *Whatever happens, Jaime, if anything bad ever happens to separate us, don't give in to the hate. Don't let hate win. That's all I ask, my love. Promise. Promise me.*

It was like he had known.

She had promised.

The worst thing about Paul's death coming so soon after their marriage was that they hadn't had time to get tired of each other yet, or even to truly irritate each other. The only way in which she could drum up any anger at him at all was to wish he had contacted her earlier after she'd graduated from seminary. It wasn't kosher for professors to date students, but they'd lost five good years between the time she'd graduated and the day they'd met in the airport in Rome.

"Didn't you notice me when I was in your Bible history class?" she'd asked. "Did you not remember sitting on that hillside with me overlooking the Sea of Galilee on your Israel trip that year? I had a pretty profound moment there, and I thought you did, too."

"Did I notice you?" he'd rolled over to ask. "It's a damn good thing Bible professors can't get fired for their fantasies, put it that way."

"You fantasized about me? And who else?"

"See? With you women, that's always what it comes to: Who else?" He laughed and tousled her hair. "Fact is, you were definitely the standout, girl. And I remember those sweaters you wore. It wasn't hard to imagine the size and shape of your breasts pretty darn close to reality."

"Yeah? So which is better, fantasy or reality?"

He'd kissed her then—her mouth and her breasts—and said simply, "Back then, I didn't have the details, Richards. God is in the details."

She loved that he'd wanted her to keep her name after they were married. She got a kick out of him calling her Richards, as he had ever since she'd been in his class.

Another time, she'd asked, if she was the standout, why he hadn't kept in touch. Why he'd let her go.

"I've felt this sense of purpose to my life, this sense of calling, very strongly, since my early teens, I think. It's not something I could give up to be tied to the responsibilities of a wife and family. The thought of giving up my work, especially in Israel and Palestine, and staying home in a cute little house near campus, spending my whole life grading papers and watching TV—I couldn't stand it. And I knew a woman would have a right to ask it of me. When you have dependents, you don't go running off to war zones.

"That's before I knew there were women like you who were running around to the world's hot spots on your own. I had no idea that, with you, for a year I'd have to fly all the way to Korea just to get laid!"

The fact was, if he had kept in touch right after she'd graduated, she probably wouldn't have joined the military. She would have wanted to make herself free to be a minister near the town where he had his "cute little house near campus." She would have become the woman he'd fled.

Yet the way things had worked out, between their two careers, spending time together was a great challenge. The days of their married life that they'd spent at either his house or the house she'd bought near her post in Maryland felt wonderful and exotic. They hadn't come to any conclusions on who would embrace a career change first. It had seemed to Jaime that they both loved their careers—he had been tenured; she had been promoted to major that spring—but both could see themselves going together to live in the Middle East, either founding or working together for some sort of hands-on problem-solving organization or institute.

Until they had a home together, they couldn't think of having children. So they hadn't. And now they never would.

But Paul would think this was a wonderful adventure. She could almost feel him smiling down on her now. It gave her courage. She sat up straighter. She was beginning to get feeling back in her left leg.

"So," said Liv, unbuckling her belt and sitting forward in her seat to be heard. "Did you two know each other before today?"

She was pointing between Jaime and Yani.

"Nope," said Jaime. "Never had the pleasure."

She was guessing the silent part of the trip was over.

She was right.

April 8, 2003, 3:00 P.M.
Ruins at Babylon
Six kilometers northwest of Al Hillah
Central Iraq

The old man had not been to the ruins of Babylon in over 20 years. He had kept up whenever he saw that there were photos in *National Geographic* or on the Internet. But nothing had prepared him for the reality of the changes. Rumor had it that at one time Saddam Hussein had considered making it the capital of his new empire, following in the footsteps of King Nebuchadnezzar II, who had made this city on the banks of the Euphrates River's fabulous Hanging Gardens into one of the Seven Wonders of the Ancient World.

The site used to be fantastic ruins, much of which was excavated in the first two decades of the twentieth century by German teams. Now Hussein's workers had "rebuilt" Babylon on top of the ruins. For archeologists and historians, this was a disaster. Important sites were to be left as discovered so they could speak of history—not built over. Kristof had to smile at that. As if despots followed the rules. As if despots even let people tell them what the rules are! Nebuchadnezzar himself had rebuilt Babylon atop the ruins of the city of Hammurabi, the king who had ruled one thousand years before him and found his most enduring fame by instituting the first written code of laws. Hammurabi then had the laws carved onto diorite columns—all thirty-six hundred lines in cuneiform—and distributed to all the major cities he ruled. One of these columns, found in Susa in 1902, was now at the Louvre in Paris.

It was also quite possible Hammurabi was the same king mentioned in the Book of Genesis who built a temple that became known as the Tower of Babel.

This was a site shimmering with history. Kristof used to know it like the back of his hand. Never before had he wondered if he could stay safe here in the few hours until sundown.

It wasn't that the place was crawling with mercenaries. There were no other humans that he could see from his concealed vantage point in the ruins of Hammurabi's palace. But fighting was continuing in Al Hillah, the modern city built across the Euphrates from the ruins at Babylon. His driver, an old friend, had told Kristof that the Fedayeen had warehoused supplies of food, water, fuel, and munitions in Al Hillah and would not give them up without a fight. The driver had also told him that while there were certainly pockets of support for the Fedayeen in Al Hillah, most of the citizens were appalled by the mass graves dug in their city, into which thousands upon thousands of Saddam's enemies had disappeared. They had no wish for their city to become a fighting ground. It was also rumored that Syrian mercenaries had joined the Fedayeen for the fight.

From the mortar bursts still coming from the city, and the gunfire answering back, it seemed the fight was continuing. There also appeared to be a frenzy of looting taking place up at the palace. Certainly the chandeliers and gold-plated bathroom fixtures were long gone by now. Kristof wasn't sure what was left to loot, but by any standards, Saddam's new Southern Palace, adjacent to the ruins of Nebuchadnezzar's former palace, defined ostentation. It covered the area of four American football fields and was shaped like a four-storied ziggurat. And if it was anything like his other palaces, it would be floor-to-ceiling marble, gold plating, and mosaic.

What was the man thinking?

Did he not see the irony in building his own palace so near the unearthed throne room of Nebuchadnezzar, who had led his armies to conquer Jerusalem and brought the Jews back as slaves? If Hussein believed the story in the biblical book of Daniel, it was in the king of Babylon's throne room that the finger of God etched the original "writing on the wall," spelling the end of Belshazzar's reign. Why not build your own throne room next door and see if history might repeat itself? Hussein had even gone so far as to finish Nebuchadnezzar's walls; the bricks laid by the ancient king's masons all had praise to Nebuchadnezzar inscribed on them. The new ones said: *In the era of Saddam Hussein, protector of Iraq, who rebuilt civilization and rebuilt Babylon.* Although these new bricks were barely a decade old, they were already cracking, whereas the originals were still intact. Probably not the legacy Hussein meant to leave.

Kristof decided to start making his way toward the rendezvous point near the ruins of the Hanging Gardens of Babylon. He wanted to look into the rebuilt amphitheater but felt it would be too risky. The structure was massive, with modern signs and ticket-taking booths flanking the entrances. But it was very open, and he was unsure there would be protected places to hide. No, best take his items and head for the Third Sister. Three hours and 15 minutes until rendezvous. He hoped the secret entrance to the underground chamber was still there, still available, still hidden. There was one way to find out.

The old man began deliberately making his way across the ruins.

April 8, 2003, 3:44 P.M.
MSR (Main Supply Route) Tampa
28 kilometers northwest of As Samawah
151 kilometers southeast of Al Hillah
Iraq

"So," said Liv Nelsson again, leaning farther forward from where she sat behind Jaime, speaking loudly to be heard above the rumble of the Humvee. "Alejandro tells me you're an expert in world religions."

The chaplain shot Rodriguez a look that conveyed interest at both Liv's use of his first name and the subject matter. Rodriguez didn't take his gaze from the landscape outside, but his smile somehow contained a shrug that said, *What could I do? Neither piece of information is exactly classified.*

"Yeah, that's my area of specialization," Jaime replied.

"It must be exciting, being over here where so much religious history happened," the photographer continued.

"You mean, like Ur?" Jaime asked, remembering their meeting atop the ziggurat.

"Yes. Not to mention Nineveh, Babylon, even the Tigris and Euphrates rivers."

"They don't call it the Cradle of Civilization for nothing," Jaime agreed.

"Yeah? So you think this really was the Cradle of Civilization? Like Eden was here somewhere?" Liv asked.

OK, so this conversation seemed a little too on-the-nose for comfort.

"You mean the Garden of Eden?"

"Yeah. Genesis gives its location by referencing four rivers, right? The Tigris, the Euphrates, the Pison, and the Gihon. And we've got two of them right here."

Jaime took a second to frame her response. "If you're asking if I have any idea where the site of the Garden of Eden actually was, in today's topography, I haven't a clue."

"Didn't think you did. But what I'm really wondering is why you think people, like ordinary Americans, care about an old Jewish creation story. It was written, like, what, three thousand years ago?—about an event long before that. So why does anyone still care? Or do they?"

It was an intriguing question. A fascinating question, actually, although you didn't need to be a religions expert to have studied it. First-year seminary would do. How could Jaime begin to explain the fact that interpretations of the second Eden story were still loaded enough to cause major rifts between groups well into the twentieth—and now the twenty-first—century. The famous Scopes "monkey trial" and whether to teach children both creationism and evolution . . . Jaime smiled to herself. Throw one of those terms into a modern-day school board meeting and see what happens.

Liv was still sitting forward and leaning in to hear her answer. Richards shot a glance back at Yani, but he was looking out the plastic window, his thoughts seemingly miles away. He and Liv were both wearing flak jackets and helmets as required of everyone in convoy, which gave the conversation a slightly surreal feeling.

The chaplain sighed and steeled herself for the eventual raspiness with which she would pay for another shouted conversation. "You're referring to the second creation story, I take it?" she asked.

"The second one?"

"Genesis has two. Likely written by different authors,

two or three hundred years apart. The first one, the one that opens Genesis, is shorter, more poetic, sort of told from the heavens looking down. It also happens to be egalitarian. 'So God created man in his own image, in the image of God created he him; male and female created he them. . . . And God saw every thing that he had made, and, behold, it was very good.'

"Then, in Genesis 2, the story starts all over again, this time culminating in the creation of Adam and the discovery of the need for Eve, made secondarily from Adam's body."

"Wait a minute," said Liv. "I thought the first five books of the Bible were supposed to have been written by Moses. Either dictated to him or handed to him on the tablets by God on Mount Sinai. Isn't that what Jews and Christians believe?"

"Well, some people do think that, and when I'm talking to someone whose faith depends on thinking that, I'd let the conversation be over. But most seminaries—Christian and Jewish—accept the idea that the text in the Pentateuch was woven together from multiple strands of stories and tradition. Not only are several stories—such as the creation—told in dual versions, but the vocabulary and voices of the two main authors and two main editors are very distinctive. It's sort of like one version was written by Shakespeare and another by Arthur Miller. Both excellent writers, but separated by centuries, so it's fairly easy to tell who wrote what."

"OK, so then who wrote the long version—you know, about Adam and the rib and Satan and the apple?"

"That one was written, probably about 922 B.C.E., by the writer referred to as 'J.' He was originally called J because he refers to God as Yaweh. In the German spelling, that's 'Jahwe'—hence J. German theologians were responsible for working a lot of this out. The other earliest source was known as E, because he uses the name Elohim to refer to God. Studying the text, it's likely that E was a priest, while

J was a layman. And it's also likely that these two were writing down oral traditions that preceded them, at the time that Israel was divided into a Southern and Northern Kingdom. E was likely from the Northern Kingdom. J was likely from the South."

"So, E wrote the first creation story, and J the second?"

"Well, no. The stories of J and E were joined fairly early, when the kingdoms were reunited, about 722 B.C.E. It was almost two hundred years after that when a writer named D added Deuteronomy—and likely some other books—and a redactor called P, another priest, pulled them all together into coherent documents. P did a lot of merging and explaining and probably added the first creation story. He wrote very poetically and, in many cases, liturgically. Much of what he wrote down was most likely used in worship for centuries. For example, his account of creation was probably meant to be chanted back and forth, with repeated phrases, such as: 'morning and evening, the seventh day.'"

"But that would mean that P wrote long after the event," Liv said. "And added stuff to explain with his own agenda?"

Jaime couldn't keep a straight face. "Well, unless God wrote it down personally, there were no eyewitnesses to the creation of the world, or of Adam and Eve. Whoever wrote it down did so long after the fact, and yes, with an agenda.

"And you just retold it to me with another layer of interpretation. There is no mention of an apple in the story, or of Satan. We do have a fruit and a serpent, but those things would have been interpreted much differently by folks three thousand years ago.

"Another example is the line 'For this reason a man will leave his father and mother and be united to his wife, and they will become one flesh,' which appears after the creation of Eve. That was added as an explanatory aside. And whatever reason that person had for the addition, well, it's now being used as proof that gay marriage is wrong, by people with a different agenda altogether."

"So you're telling me that this story, which has been used to prove everything from the inferiority of women, to the evils of birth control, to the sinful nature of mankind, comes from a story that has been interpreted completely differently over time?"

"Yeah. And don't forget that the creation story has also been used to give humans the right to abuse animals. Also, once you get into Cain and Abel and their wives, who mysteriously pop up from somewhere, you've got the basis for people to explain the 'tribes' of the earth and who is blessed and who is not."

"Why would God do that? Why would he tell a story that allows its readers to justify the subjugation of other sexes, or other races, or even of animals?"

Jaime looked at Rodriguez. He was scanning the terrain outside their vehicle, but he flashed her a look that said, *I'm interested in your answer to this one.* It was times like this, she imagined, that he was glad he wasn't actually clergy.

She turned to Liv long enough to see that she was asking seriously. "I like the way you put it: God tells the stories. But it's us humans that use them as a power play. It's the thing we do best, isn't it? Use anything and everything to gain power for ourselves. Even the stories of God. One interesting aspect is that most Jews regard the creation account as a wisdom story that has important lessons but isn't necessarily thought of as literally true. The Jewish writers of the Hebrew Scriptures never mention Eve again outside of that one Genesis account, whereas other women, such as Sarah, are much more important and are discussed again and again."

"Is that true?" The photographer did seem genuinely interested in the conversation.

"Eve doesn't come up again in Scripture until the early Christian theologians brought her up. Jesus never mentioned her that we know of. She finally appears with a serious agenda behind her in First Timothy. In fact, that's the first time this new interpretation appears: Women can't teach men because Eve was the second created and the first to sin."

"But isn't that the whole point of the Christian faith? I mean, excuse me if I'm wrong, but doesn't it go that Adam and Eve brought sin into the world, and Jesus paid for Christians' sins to reconcile people to God?"

"OK, now we're getting into the finer points of theology. Have you ever considered going to seminary?"

"Sorry, Chaplain, I'm not exactly a Jew or a Christian. But I am trying to understand."

"Well, I'm impressed. You've done your homework. Yes, Jews, Christians, and Muslims all believe that Adam, the first human, was also the first sinner. In Genesis, the word 'adam,' by the way, just means 'human.' So it's understood that the first human was also the first sinner. With the exception of the writer of Timothy, both the Qur'an and the Christian Scriptures tend to come down harder on Adam than Eve.

"But—and this is a big but—the idea of 'original sin,' that the world was a wonderful place before Adam and Eve sinned, but since they did, all humans are conceived in sin and born already with a sinful nature, that is not in either Jewish or Christian Scriptures. To Jews and early Christians, the idea was that Adam and Eve sinned, we all do, and everyone slips up now and then and needs to be forgiven. The whole idea that humankind is inherently fallen and sinful from birth was put forth later by a theologian named Augustine, who was nearly killed for proposing such a heretical idea."

Nelsson sat back heavily into her seat and reached up to unzip the window beside her so she could scan the countryside. "So, wait a minute. If the Jews, who wrote the Eden thing, consider it a 'wisdom story,' how come some Christians, who showed up a couple thousand years later, are telling them they're wrong, it's word-for-word literal truth?"

CHASING EDEN 145

Chaplain Richards focused her attention ahead on the road. "I've run out of answers," she said.

"OK, then a personal question. Doesn't all this arguing over sources and meanings make you lose confidence in the Bible as a book of faith?"

"To the contrary. Just because I don't believe God dictated the Bible word for word to only one ancient holy man doesn't mean I can't hold it in reverence as a work inspired by God. In fact, my tradition believes that God not only inspired the various writers, editors, and translators, but that God inspires each of us even today in the reading and hearing of the Word."

"I have one more question for you," said Liv Nelsson. "When you were studying Eden, did you study the theories of Dr. Leo Zaruf?"

A ball of dread dropped into Jaime's stomach. Had all of this just been bait to bring her around to landsat images and to discuss Garden sites? If people had stolen artifacts and were running around ready to kill to find the site of the original Eden, it didn't seem much of a leap to assume Liv had been placed in the vehicle purposefully to discover what Jaime knew. Come to think of it, if someone had been able to track her movements even inside the military perimeter of Tallil, they would certainly have known when she was leaving. And it didn't make sense that they would just let her go without having some way to follow her movements. The easiest way to do it would be to stick someone in the vehicle with her.

Wouldn't it?

"Yeah, I've heard of him," she said. "Why do you ask?"

"He says he knows where Eden was," Liv answered.

OK, Jaime thought. *Here we go.*

April 8, 2003, 4:10 P.M.
Below the Amphitheater at Babylon
Six kilometers northwest of Al Hillah
Central Iraq

Gerik loved the fact that the fluorescent lights were still on in the underground parking garage. It certainly made his job easier. There were perks to working with officers on the highest levels of the regime of Saddam Hussein. Knowledge of Hussein's private parking garage, accessed through a tunnel that ran from a hidden, unmarked entrance across the Euphrates and led to a bulletproof elevator that ascended to the amphitheater was certainly one of them. Sooner or later all of Hussein's secret tunnels and passageways would be found. But the invaders didn't even know yet to start looking.

More important, Gerik still had the euphoric feeling that there were times the universe conspired in your favor. There was no doubt in his mind that the Astral spirits were working with him and on his behalf, communicating with him even now, through soundless whispers and heightened instinct. The time for the rebirth of history was here. He was in the flow of the New World Order.

The garage wasn't large. There was room for perhaps 15 vehicles—Saddam Hussein, his guests, and bodyguards. The space was square, and it was easy to scope out the fact that he was alone.

He got out of the car and went back to the trunk. If anyone had occasion to inspect his rattletrap car, they would be surprised to find the trunk was reinforced steel and locked with a heavy-duty high-tech series of bolts and codes.

He opened it easily.

First he took off his black robes. Underneath he was wearing a nondescript black knit shirt and dark pants. Perfect for moving around after nightfall. He checked on his supply of chloroform and found it more than sufficient, although it was too early to taint the cloth.

He briefly considered his firearm options. If things went as planned, he would not need a firearm; he would have the old man and the booty in the car without engaging anyone else. However, given the current situation of fighting in Al Hillah, if there was engagement of some kind, it could be significant. He'd best be prepared. He chose the Mark23, the heavier of his two firearms, but left the sound suppressor and the laser aiming module in the case. He looked again at the bag containing his trophies, and he smiled.

April 8, 2003, 4:43 P.M.
MSR Tampa
31 kilometers southeast of Al Hillah
Iraq

"Lots of people think they've figured out where Eden was," Jaime said warily.

"Yes, I know," said Liv. "But don't you think this guy Zaruf makes sense? The way he's put modern technology together with the clues in Genesis, what we now know of the cycles of weather in the Middle East between 30,000 and 5,000 B.C.E., and the appearance of the story, along with the words 'Adam' and 'Eden' in writings more ancient than cuneiform?"

"You've got me interested," said Rodriguez. "I haven't heard of Zaruf. What's his theory?"

Liv turned her focus to Rodriguez. Jaime realized she had tensed her shoulders. She exhaled and purposefully tried to relax her muscles. This set off another shower of tingles through her left leg, but they were much less pronounced. Thankfully, it seemed Yani's drug would wear off by the time they reached their destination. As it did, however, an ache was starting in her lower back where he had injected the gel.

She wondered if Rodriguez had joined the conversation because he was truly interested in the work of Leo Zaruf or if it was partly just to remind her—and Liv—that he was present.

Whichever, she was grateful.

Liv's eyes sparkled, as she seemed glad to now be the person with the information. "Zaruf's theory goes something like this: About 30,000 B.C.E., the Great Ice Age still held sway in most of Eurasia. It caused sea levels here in Mesopotamia to fall substantially. What we now know as the Persian Gulf was dry land all the way south to the Strait of Hormuz. Yet the valley where today's Iraq, Iran, Kuwait, and Saudi Arabia meet was still watered by four rivers: the Tigris, the Euphrates, the Gihon, and the Pison. It was a popular seasonal stop for humans, who were still hunter-gatherers.

"Around 15,000 B.C.E., this area entered several millennia of diminished rainfall, so food became more scarce and the range of the hunt became much wider, of necessity.

"Then, between 5,000 and 6,000 B.C.E., a happy event occurred: a wet phase. The whole area of Northeast Saudi Arabia and Southwest Iran was green and fertile again. The four rivers ran full. Digs within the last decade have found remains of abundant game, intensive habitation, and distinctive pottery in what is now those dry riverbeds. It was truly paradise.

"But this time, there was trouble. The hunter-gatherers returned from the northern lands as the seasons warranted to discover that their southern paradise had been settled by—horror of horrors—"

Liv looked at Jaime, who rolled her eyes but added, "Agriculturalists."

"No!" said Rodriguez, entering the spirit of the tale.

"Yes," Liv said. "It was a cataclysmic transformation, from a society that followed food to one that stayed put and, in effect, made food come to them. These were people who had solid housing, understood planting and harvesting, and knew how to domesticate animals. They claimed

turf. They no longer moved from place to place. They took
things into their own hands, instead of 'relying on God's
bounty.' "

"Bad news for the old-style folks," said Rodriguez.

"Bad news, indeed. They could adapt, or they could
leave. Be cast out of paradise, in a manner of speaking."

"Aha."

"To make matters worse, there's evidence that some of
these local agrarian societies were matriarchal. So those
hunter-gatherers who were 'cast out' were particularly angry at the women."

"OK," said Rodriguez more slowly. "That's an interesting theory about where the idea of a lost paradise came
from, and even why Eve got the brunt of the blame, but
how does this guy Zaruf justify locating an actual place?"

Her chaplain assistant seemed to be fully able to concentrate on both the landscape around them and the conversation at hand. As if in keeping with their conversation,
the countryside was becoming more verdant, grasses
greener, palm trees dotting the horizon. Houses also were
becoming more frequent and more like the walled and
roofed structures of modern buildings and less like the
stick huts of the southern camel herders.

Jaime shot a look back at Yani, who was still removed
from the conversation, looking out the scratched plastic
window, ever the laconic Texan. Not surprisingly, her
adrenaline surged merely at the sight of him and the reminder of the true reason they were on this trip. She would
give anything to know who he truly was and what he
thought of their conversation.

Liv was continuing. "Apparently, he started with clues
from Genesis. Genesis was written, of course, from a Hebrew point of view—so when it says the Garden was 'east-
ward,' he assumes that means east of Israel.

"The story mentions four rivers, as we said. The Tigris
and Euphrates still flow, so that part is easy. The other two
might have been dry even at the time of the writing, since

the writer feels the need to give location clues. The Pison, for example, is said to be near the land of Havilah, which is talked about further, later in Genesis. There it's understood to be located in a Mesopotamian-Arabian area. Supporting this is that landsat images from space clearly show a fossil river there, which the modern Saudis and Kuwaitis know as the Wadi Riniah and the Wadi Baton, respectively. Additionally, the Genesis account says that 'Havilah' was rich in bdellium, a gum resin still found there—and gold, which was still mined in northern Saudi Arabia until the 1950s.

"The last piece of the puzzle was the Gihon, which the King James Bible translated as having 'compasseth the whole land of Ethiopia.' Well, what those scholars translated as 'Ethiopia' is referred to in the original text as 'Kush.' As we know now, 'Kush' is an entirely different entity than Ethiopia. In fact, Dr. Zaruf believes what was the Gihon is what's now called the Karun River, which rises in Iran and runs south. Until it was dammed, it ran all the way to the Persian Gulf. If you look at landsat images, you can clearly see where once these four rivers came to one head."

"So, have people sent crews to dig and prove this theory or find this site?" Rodriguez queried.

Liv was still straining forward, apparently losing none of her enthusiasm in the telling. "Archeological digs have found astounding things along the eastern shore of the Persian Gulf, as recently as the 1990s. Pottery that is very distinctly Ubaidian, animal bones, utensils, and many other clues that the area was 'intensely populated' at the time we're talking about. When the Ubaidians went back up north, they wrote about it all."

"Arguably the first travel writers," said Jaime dryly. "I wonder if they had a Sunday pullout magazine? 'Come visit Eden for the waters. Bring home great pottery!'"

But Liv didn't miss a beat. "Do you see?" she enthused. "It all leads back to where we are now. Isn't this exciting? It only makes sense that once people became agricultural and started staying put, they would begin to build cities.

Hence Ur, and Eridu, Uruk, Sumer, and Babylon. The
world's first cities. Right here.

"Like you said, the beginning of Genesis deals with
Mesopotamia. After Eden, we go straight to Abraham living in Ur of the Chaldeans. So even your Bible places
earth's original civilizations in this area!"

Jaime had to smile at Liv's phrasing—"your Bible"—as
if Liv might be accused of having read it.

Liv was excitedly plowing on. "This is my favorite
part—that written language began about three thousand
years B.C.E. with the Sumerians, right here in Iraq. Place
names like Urak and Ur were codified and written about, as
were 'Eden' and 'Adam.' It was clear from the context that
all those words, and places, existed for millennia before
written language was invented. However, the first time the
word 'eden' appears, in cuneiform, it means 'fertile plain.'
The word 'adam' meant 'settlement on the plain.'"

"OK," said Rodriguez. "How about the pay dirt? Where
is this fertile plain, this Eden?"

"In the southern portion of Iraq, where those four rivers
actually intersected," Jaime broke in. She didn't mean to
steal Liv's thunder, but it was too hard to keep quiet. "But
there's the small problem Liv hasn't mentioned yet."

"That would be?" asked Rodriguez.

Jaime looked at Liv but continued. "A little thing called
the Flandrian Transgression, which occurred sometime between 5,000 and 4,000 B.C. It caused a sudden rise in sea
level. So, unfortunately, according to Leo Zaruf, the Gulf
swallowed Eden. And paradise became solely the stuff of
legend."

"So—we can't go there." Rodriguez sounded truly disappointed.

"Not without scuba gear," said the chaplain. "Even according to Dr. Zaruf."

Richards expected that to be the end of the conversation, but she was mistaken.

"So, don't you see?" Liv continued, more enthused than

ever. "Saddam Hussein spent years and millions of dollars draining the flooded southern swamplands. The official reason given was that he was punishing the swamp dwellers for fighting against him in the first Gulf War."

"Actually, the official reason was that he needed access roads," said Jaime.

"Whatever. But what everybody knows is that, in reality, he's spent the last decade looking for Eden."

"Everybody knows that?" said Jaime. Although, truth to tell, it was a common rumor.

"And rumor is that someone has found it," said Liv. "Rumor has it that that's why this war really started."

"There are a lot of rumors about why this war actually started." Even Rodriguez felt he had to weigh in on that one. "I'm not sure that's one of the most credible."

What is going on here? Jaime wondered. *Who is Liv really? Who is she with? Is someone feeding her this information?*

Jaime sighed a deep sigh. For that matter, who was Yani, really? And what on earth had he shot into her? Why were they heading for the ruins at Babylon when there was obviously still fighting in Al Hillah? Liv's theories sounded completely far-fetched. But Jaime had no doubt that something unexplained was going on here. She just didn't know where to find the missing puzzle pieces.

She never thought she'd consider Tallil, Iraq, as a safe haven. One she'd been cast out of. She wanted to start the day over. To drive into her own TOC in Tallil, where she was stationed, and expected, and stay there and do her job.

But it was too late. Even now they were approaching Al Hillah.

April 8, 2003, 5:15 P.M.
Satis's headquarters
16 kilometers west of Baghdad
Central Iraq

Coleman Satis watched the small flashing dot on the 40-inch GPS screen in his office. The old man had indeed gone to Babylon. And Gerik Schroeder was there to meet him. A euphoric Gerik Schroeder, who had in his possession the sword, and who would soon have the key to decoding the sword.

Satis was relieved that he was not ruled by emotion the way Gerik was. There was, frankly, nothing yet to be euphoric about. They would have the sword, they would have the key to the location, but as of yet they had no one to interpret the key. They had a guide who knew the way, but he wasn't talking. And time was very short.

If they did not have the correct information by moonset tomorrow night, another opportunity would have passed them by. He had waited 20 years for this second chance. Who knew how long he would have to wait for another?

The simple fact was he was not willing to wait. His work, his life, had all pointed to tomorrow. It was now or never.

He pressed the intercom button on his office phone and ordered a martini. He needed something to keep him steady while waiting for Gerik's next call, which would tell him all was in order.

Less than an hour until sunset.

That was all that Jaime could think as the convoy finally reached the outskirts of Al Hillah from the southeast via Highway 8.

They pulled up to a major intersection and were met by military police as the convoy pulled to a stop. The drone of Apache helicopters overhead and the flares from the missiles exploding intermittently from inside the city, along with the answer of bursts of automatic weapons fire and explosions, made it clear they were on the outskirts of a war zone.

A makeshift Operations Center was off to one side of the road, and an officer was shouting orders into a radio hand mike as he consulted the map. A soldier was positioned nearby, alert and with weapon ready, in case they should come under attack while his commander was concentrating on the tactical situation.

Having had an initial conversation with the military police to declare their identity, the convoy commander motioned they should pull off on the south side of the highway. Gratefully, everyone got out to stretch. One of the MPs came back to their vehicle specifically to check the credentials of their civilian riders.

"You're Nelsson?" he asked Liv.

When she affirmed that she was, he told her she was expected at Baghdad Airport and that the journalist she was to accompany was awaiting her arrival. She said good-bye to the other three in the chaplain's vehicle and headed off, following the MP.

The other MP studied Yani's papers with intensity. Finally he took them and headed back for the command post. Jaime tried not to let her nerves show. Was something wrong? If something was out of order with Yani's papers, there was really nothing she could do to help. Not to mention that the situation here in Al Hillah seemed less stable than she'd anticipated.

Even if his papers were in order, there was no way they would just let him wander off in search of a business contact. How on earth was he planning to get to Babylon? And how on earth would she go with him? If the military turned him away, was he planning to make a break for it? Truth was, she had no idea what he was planning.

It occurred to her that the fact he was standing here, in southern Al Hillah, fulfilled her part of the deal.

She understood how people could bite their fingernails and briefly entertained the idea of taking up the habit.

Their convoy commander, Captain Brian Sapp, also headed for the command center.

Jaime circled the vehicle a couple of times, just to get the blood flowing again and to control her nerves. She came to lean against the right fender where Rodriguez was studying the skyline of the city before them. She wondered if he'd noticed she no longer had a limp. Instead, her lower back now throbbed with a dull ache.

She decided to take some ibuprofen, which led her backward into a decision to scavenge the best parts of several Meals Ready to Eat, or MREs, since she didn't want to take the tablets on an empty stomach. She went to the back of the Humvee, where Rodriguez had stashed the MREs, and pulled cheese and crackers out of one, as well as a slice of chocolate mint pound cake. Once she took the first bite, she realized how hungry she actually was and stood munching and drinking water while she waited.

Her adrenaline was pumping. She wasn't sure what would happen if they didn't make it to the rendezvous on time. Would the man who knew about her parents disappear forever? It was imperative to keep the code-breaking items from falling into the wrong hands. And, in the midst of everything, her mother's voice kept replaying in her head. Her mother had asked her to help, and she had decided to do so. She wanted to succeed.

Yani stood against the opposite side of the Humvee. Jaime had handed him a package of pretzels, which he'd accepted and eaten, but the transaction had happened in silence and Jaime left him alone there.

It couldn't have been longer than five minutes after the MPs had departed that a master sergeant came from the Operations Center. His head was shaved, his face and neck covered with dirt—he looked like he hadn't had a bath in weeks. He wore chemical suit pants, with a brown T-shirt, a flak vest, and a 9-millimeter in a shoulder holster over the vest. As he approached, she guessed his height at five foot eight. He was wiry and no-nonsense. He came to stand before Yani, the only civilian in the group.

"Mr. Burton?" he asked. Jaime found she had stopped breathing.

"That's me," Yani answered.

"I'm Sergeant Greg Adkins. Captain Sapp and the rest of the convoy will be occupied with the captured fuelers for a while, so I'm going to provide you escort to Babylon. Get your gear and hop in the back of that truck while I round up some firepower."

Well. Bill Burton was nothing if not full of surprises.

Without missing a beat, Jaime stepped forward. "Excuse me, Sergeant Adkins, but there's no need for Mr. Burton to move his gear. My vehicle will be joining you on the mission."

The master sergeant looked at her with surprise. He immediately sized her up, noting two things, both of which brought doubt to his face. She knew exactly what they were: She was a woman and she was a chaplain. Not that he held either in disdain, but he didn't see the purpose of having her on this mission.

"With all due respect, ma'am, I see no reason for you to come along. We haven't cleared all the areas of the city yet—"

A masterful understatement, thought Jaime.

"And we may have to fight our way into the ruins. We could take casualties."

"All the more reason to have a chaplain with you. Besides, I'm not going to get this close to one of the ancient wonders of the Bible and miss the chance to see it because of a little danger." She kept her voice steady and factual, although it sounded like fairly ridiculous reasoning, even to her.

"But—" Adkins objected.

"My chaplain assistant is an excellent shot. You won't need to worry about wasting assets to protect me. He'll take care of that."

Adkins took only a moment to weigh the pros and cons of continuing the argument if this crazy chaplain was insisting. He had more important issues to consider. "Suit yourself," he said. "We leave in ten." He headed out to make final arrangements.

Jaime turned back to Yani. They were now alone on the left side of the Humvee. "I don't get it," she said. "These guys are bending over backward to get you to Babylon. What kind of contractor do they think you are?"

"Actually, they believe the contractor bit is just a cover story."

"A cover story?"

"I'm actually a WMD expert from the UN who needs to meet an informant in Babylon."

She realized something and felt foolish for not calling

him on it before. "OK, Bill. So it's clear you've got contacts on the inside. Someone higher up—and more creative—than I am. You going to give me any clues, here? Or at least a hint why you need me, when you're obviously quite well connected?"

"You're my backup, Richards. Do you see anyone else standing here with us?"

"No, you're right about that. It's only us with our necks on the line."

"And Rodriguez," Yani said simply. "But there's nothing I can do about that. I will have my hands full being responsible for you."

She had no idea how to respond to the idea that he felt he was responsible for her. She had never asked for that, and she didn't need it. "Let me mention that my lower back is killing me, thanks so much."

"I told you it would," he said. "You won't notice it in a couple of days."

"Assuming I'm still alive."

"Well, either way." He gave one of his rare smiles.

"And would you tell me honestly what you shot me up with?"

He took a step closer to her and lowered his voice. But it was firm and slightly angry. "I've never lied to you," he said.

"Right," she said. "Ahmet . . . I mean, Bill."

"About any factual information, I have told you nothing but the truth. It is gel that will help me locate you. That's it."

"In case I try to get away?" That had just occurred to her, too.

"You're here of your own free will," he said. "I thought we were clear on that. I can't be worried about your loyalty when we're at Babylon. You're with me one hundred percent, or you stay here. Make up your mind now. One way or the other. And then it never comes up again."

He walked away.

He was right. It had been her choice to come. And he was right about the rest of it, too. If she had any doubts, she should bail. But so far, he had meant everything he'd said, and he'd been both willing and able to act on it.

Whatever information he had given the Army here, well, that had worked, too. That much was clear from the arrival of two trucks filled with infantry soldiers and two Humvees with side and top canvas stripped off, chairs welded down facing the rear, and a .50-caliber machine gun mounted behind them.

Sergeant Adkins pulled up in a third Humvee and hopped out, yelling.

"Sanchez, you fall in behind me, followed by Headquarters 25! Carter, you have rear coverage. The other troop carrier is ahead of you. Chaplain, I want you in the center. Keep the pace through town—don't stop for anything! Rakkasans!"

Jaime, Yani, and Rodriguez scrambled into the vehicle. The vehicles in the convoy worked their way into the required positions. It was accomplished quickly. And then they took off.

Into the war.

April 8, 2003, 5:18 P.M.
16 kilometers west of Baghdad
Central Iraq

The Commander considered himself the pragmatist of the Triumvirate. Gerik provided the foot soldiers, Satis provided the media support—and millions of dollars—but he knew Gerik and Satis each had personal agendas. So far, these agendas had been useful. Soon they would get in the way.

The New World Order had morphed for the better. Yes, it was still the same elite group of men—and OK now, reluctantly, a couple of women—who were calling the shots. His fellow Knights were in all the right places, the key positions of power. As they had for the last 150 years, they controlled banking, oil, politics, the drug trade, and the intelligence community. All the strands necessary, finally, for world domination.

Their use of this current "controlled conflict" to change the landscape of the Middle East was heartwarming, as was the way Hegel's "New World Order" had morphed into an American agenda that called for beefing up the military, "challenging regimes hostile to our interests and values," and "accepting responsibility for America's unique role in preserving and extending an international order."

In other words, empire expansion. They now had people

in power who were not afraid to promulgate these values—
in fact, many of them had signed those very principles for
public viewing!

He was thrilled to be present when the United States
had finally reached the point where the few, the educated
elite—the Knights of Eugenia and their friends—were
changing the world map.

A few soldiers would have to die, but that was Hegel's
point. The state is "the march of God in the world" and has
supreme rights against the individual. The state was calling
on men and women to make that ultimate sacrifice. It was
for their own good that they were not consulted.

God, he loved a good controlled conflict. And this was
one hell of a great one.

He was proud to be the point man on the ground. He put
his pedal to the metal and drove down the dusty highway
in Iraq.

For the first time in his career, Kristof Remen wondered what would happen if his contact didn't make it to the rendezvous.

There was nothing Kristof could do about that, should it happen, so he tried to enjoy the fact that the secret entrance to the ruins of the Hanging Gardens and the simple set of dirt steps had not been found during the excavations. They gave him a safe, if dark, place to wait. He was hungry, so he took out the granola bar from his pocket and leaned back against the cool earth wall, savoring the flavors.

He wished he could have seen the Hanging Gardens of Babylon in their heyday. They had been made of mud, with beautiful brick and stone terraces, one on top of the next, reaching over 350 feet above the rushing water of the Euphrates below. Nebuchadnezzar II had built the gardens for his wife, Queen Amytis, because she felt the Babylonian landscape was too desertlike. She was used to Persia, she complained, where there were many plants and fountains.

Her husband's answer was to build her this "Wonder of the Ancient World," ever after giving husbands an impossible standard for pleasing their wives. The many terraces of the Hanging Gardens had been covered with lawns, plants, trees, fountains, flowers, and even miniature waterfalls. The king's engineers had outdone themselves, working out a pumping system to bring water from the Euphrates up to the top of the gardens to run down through channels to water all those "hanging plants."

Amazing what those engineers had been able to figure out twenty-five hundred years ago.

Kristof himself had never had a wife. Never any need for building an incredible homage to a woman. When his niece had accepted a position teaching microbiology and molecular cell sciences at the University of Switzerland in Geneva, he had been happy to retire to his small house in an out-of-the-way Swiss village with his own tiny gardens and his fireplace. He had a green thumb, which he was certain was really nothing more than a heart for plants and a willingness to find out what made them grow. He got to see his niece and her husband and son often, had many friends in his town, and would have been pleased to spend the rest of his days there, looking at the sky and raising roses.

Ah, well.

Life so seldom went as planned.

He checked his watch, which had a dial that lit up in the dark when a button was pressed. It was almost time to start making his way toward the Sister.

Truth was, even if his contact didn't make it, "plan B" would not be hard. Kristof would simply need to hide the items in his sack somewhere that they would not be found for the next 24 hours. Then he could try to find his old friend and driver. It might or might not be possible in these circumstances. But it really didn't matter what happened to him, as long as the items were safe. He'd had a good life, and every day during it he had been ready to die should it be required.

He opened the small wooden trapdoor built in a nondescript place in the great hunk of earth that was now the ruins of the Hanging Gardens of Babylon.

The sun was setting. The air was beginning to cool.

And then, from behind him, he suddenly heard the firing of assault weapons. It came from the direction of the canal bridge from Al Hillah into Babylon. Gunfire answered the opening rounds.

"Dear God!" he whispered, and he turned it into a prayer. "Dear God," he repeated. "Dear God."

It was hard to believe that anyone in Al Hillah was having a normal supper that night. What did you do when war invaded your hometown? For it was clear that the Republican Guard and the Fedayeen were making a stand here. But it was equally clear that Coalition forces finally outnumbered them. Meanwhile, people's homes, and lives, were in the way.

Jaime found it hard to believe what one of the sergeants had told them back at the crossroads: that along with the fuelers and the warehouses of munitions and explosives, they'd found a huge warehouse full of the humanitarian supplies sent to the Iraqi people through the UN. What kind of regime keeps food, clothing, diapers, and baby food from its own people? It was hard to fathom. She wondered again if it was true that Saddam Hussein and his sons had been in the apartment building that had been blown up that morning.

If so, the war should be shorter. But apparently no one had told the Republican Guard's Nebuchadnezzar Division.

Their convoy had picked up speed immediately after leaving the crossroads and was rolling through town at a good 50 miles per hour. There was isolated weapons fire, the ever-present *wokka-wokka-wokka* of helicopters over-head, and even the occasional A-10 "Warthogs" sent by the Air Force to assist with the close fight. Abrams tanks were still on some of the city's main arteries, and infantry troops were moving through the city, searching buildings, talking with locals, surrounding locations from which gunfire had erupted, taking groups of prisoners.

The convoy slowed for nothing. Rodriguez had a task; he never took his eyes from the road around them, his hands grasping his weapon tightly. Even Yani, though out-wardly composed and unperturbed, was sitting straight, muscles taut, paying close attention to the surroundings.

Part of what was so nerve-racking was that they never knew when the Fedayeen or the Republican Guard would hit them with chemical weapons. They'd all seen the pho-tos of Iraqi citizens, women and children included, who had been killed in chemical attacks by the leader of their own country, their bodies left lying out in the streets as a grisly warning. Whole towns wiped out. If Hussein could do that to his own people, would he hesitate to lose some of the population of one of his own cities—Al Hillah, for example—if it meant killing coalition troops with chemi-cal weapons? The chemical suit she wore and the mask that still hung from her belt were of little comfort.

But then they emerged successfully from the city be-hind them. They turned onto a side road that ran along the southwest bank of the Shatt Al Hillah waterway, the canal that separated Hillah from Babylon. The road had nar-rowed to two lanes. But they were here. She looked up and saw the walls of Babylon—the Babylon—rising along the opposite side of the canal.

Was Yani happy? Excited? Relieved?

Was she about to meet a man who could tell her about a whole part of her parents' lives she never knew existed? Were they about to save the Sword of Life, the Dagger of Ur?

As they rounded a corner, Jaime was so focused on the

canal bridge that led to the ruins that she barely noticed the stand of trees across the road to her left. Until a rocket-propelled grenade was launched from the midst of it and sailed cleanly between the first and second vehicles in the convoy. It exploded off the road to the right in a burst of light and an explosive roar.

In the next terrifying seconds, the deadly sound of automatic weapons fire blazed through the night. It was aimed at them.

"Ambush," said Rodriguez calmly.

The convoy came to a halt.

Reflex took over, and the vehicles pulled off to the right side of the road, opposite the attackers. Everyone dove for safety. The soldiers took positions, using the vehicles for cover. Jaime and Yani found a ditch running alongside the road behind them and jumped into it.

Automatic weapons fire continued coming at them from the stand of trees, and it was now returned by the infantry troops of the convoy. Time was suspended and Jaime's senses heightened. She could feel the grainy texture of the sandy dirt at her fingertips as she leaned against the wall of the ditch. She tasted the salt lingering in her mouth from the cheese and crackers. She was astonished at the pink/blue of the sky as the sun began to set, and she was aware of her own breathing.

And then the small puff of dirt as a stray bullet ricocheted from somewhere and plowed into the ground at her feet. Dear God.

The deadly exchange of bullets continued. There's no feeling in the world quite like knowing that you—or the person next to you—could be killed at any moment.

Jaime kept her head down. She knew Rodriguez was

just above her, prone, behind their vehicle, returning fire. He seemed unhurt thus far.

The fight continued for long minutes with no one gaining the upper hand.

Finally, Master Sergeant Adkins deliberately stood up from his position behind a truck and walked back along the line of vehicles. Jaime couldn't hear everything he was saying, but he was gesturing and directing activity, seemingly unconcerned by the rounds whizzing past.

"Sanchez!" she heard him yell. "You and your team lay down cover fire. Hansen, Wright, Carter. You're with me."

The three soldiers led by Adkins moved purposely all the way to the front of the column of vehicles, well beyond the sight line of the enemy bunker. By the time they reached position, weapons fire from the Americans had increased significantly. Jaime heard Adkins yell, *"Go, go, go!"*

There was a pause in weapons fire as Adkins purposefully walked across the road and lobbed a grenade. A moment's silence followed by the *whump* of the grenade hitting, then exploding in the enemy bunker.

Rounds from an AK-47 burst from the trees.

An M-16 returned fire.

Silence.

They held position for a few moments. It seemed they held their breath also.

Finally the call came: "All clear!"

Jaime expelled a long breath, as did Yani beside her.

Above them, the troops swept the area, making certain there were no other enemy soldiers hiding, and looking for weapons caches or other items of interest.

By the time Jaime climbed the embankment, they had cleared the bunker behind the trees. She saw bodies across the road and couldn't help crossing to look. Two of the men were very bloody, killed directly by the grenade and peppered with shrapnel. The third had somehow had the time to dive out of the bunker when the grenade landed, had then taken two M-16 rounds to the chest, and had died immediately.

Jaime turned away, and the prayer that she uttered came from the anguished pain in her gut: "Oh, God, this war— all this death—it's tough. It's hard to see these bloody bodies and know that moments ago they were living, breathing beings. I'm ashamed that I wished them dead because they were trying to kill us. I'm sad that their goals and ours are so different that we must resort to bloodshed. I need your help, Lord, to get through this night, to get through this war . . . to get through this life."

Jaime collapsed against the side of her Humvee. She hadn't realized she had been speaking aloud until she heard Yani's voice softly add, "Amen."

She looked up at him.

Across the road, Adkins was ordering his troops to quickly bury the men in their bunker, to show them that respect.

Jaime looked at her watch. They would be late.

She looked at Yani. He gave an acknowledging nod.

She looked away, purposefully, into the night. For the first time in a long time, she thought she could feel the heart of God. And it, like hers, was broken.

"Mount up!" called Master Sergeant Adkins.

Within moments, the troops were reloaded, and they all headed together across the canal bridge.

They were 20 minutes late.

That seemed pretty good for wartime, but Jaime didn't know what was and wasn't taken into account at a Sisters rendezvous. Rodriguez had parked as the soldiers from the convoy streamed up Procession Street and through the Ishtar Gate to clear the ruins. She knew this was a quick check to make certain there were no enemy ambush positions inside, not an inch-by-inch check. If someone knew the area and knew where to hide, it wouldn't be too hard to avoid detection. Jaime was a little surprised to find a large parking lot surrounding the ruins and an abandoned museum ticket-taking booth at the Ishtar Gate.

The Ishtar Gate.

Oh, it wasn't the real one—that was in a German museum. But it was an incredible reconstruction of the brightly tiled entrance to Nebuchadnezzar's ancient city of wonders. Jaime had known all these places were real. She'd studied them. But there was something stunning about standing on such ancient ground. It was her version of meeting a revered celebrity fans knew to be human but didn't expect to be real. Jaime hadn't been expecting the tourist trap aspect, or the huge signs pointing the way to

"Southern Palace and Amphitheatre Parking." There was also an abandoned open-air bazaar just outside the walls, with a cockeyed sign that read: "All Artifacts Are Fak" in English. Well, in pretty good English.

Rodriguez had parked their Humvee in a spot close by, which was handily marked "Babylon Museum Parking," and the three of them followed the troops to the entrance gate. They'd only been there a minute when Adkins nodded to Yani, who took off like a shot into Babylon. Purposely avoiding eye contact with Adkins or anyone else, Jaime headed in after him, Rodriguez close on her heels.

It was that half hour after sunset when light becomes gray and is slowly vanquished. It was still easy to see the enormity of the ruins around them, although the shadows were long. Near the gate brightly colored maps were posted on the walls of the "Babylon Museum Ruins," but it was all she could do to keep up with Yani without stopping to investigate.

He was heading away from the rebuilt ruins of Nebuchadnezzar's dynasty and moving quickly back in time toward Hammurabi's ruins. Yani didn't look back toward her, and she didn't look back toward Rodriguez. Each simply knew the other was there.

The ruins from the time of Hammurabi had been excavated but not rebuilt. They were streets and foundations of original stone and brick, the foundations of an ancient city. They were also an incredible maze.

She lost sight of Yani several times as he strode ahead of her around sharp corners. He was moving silently and staying low, so his head was not visible above the wall of the ruins. She kept quiet and low as well.

Yani came to a corner turn. But instead of moving ahead, he dropped to one knee. He was looking intently at something among the bricks on the long wall that ended this portion of the maze. Jaime came to a stop beside him and searched for what he was looking at. It took her a moment to find it.

It was a small mirror, completely unnoticeable unless you were looking for it, embedded in one of the rocks of the excavation. It showed a tiny reflection of what was in the passageway around the turn.

There was an old man, leaning low against the wall, also preoccupied.

Jaime pointed. Yani nodded but held a finger to his lips and held up his hand to signal "halt."

Something was wrong.

The old man started moving away from them, quickly. He came to a three-way corner and hesitated only briefly before taking the hard right-hand turn and disappearing up the far passageway.

Jaime half-stood, ready to follow, but Yani gave a small shake of the head. They stayed put. It was a minute or less after the old man had departed that, in the mirror, they saw a second figure appear along the far passageway and take the same path their contact had chosen.

It was the first time Jaime had seen emotion on Yani's face since they'd gotten to Babylon. But the set of his jaw quickly became sheer determination.

He waited only a moment more before moving around the corner and up the ancient street.

He knelt at the place where the old man had been. And, as Jaime had at Ur, he triggered an ancient spring mechanism in one of the bricks. It slid open. As he reached in and pulled out a rucksack, he motioned her to come. She did.

As she knelt beside him in the gathering dark, he said, "Stay with this backpack. I've got to go and make sure the old man's all right. If I can, I'll make time for you two to talk. There's somewhere we can disappear to, briefly, if I can get rid of our intruder."

Without waiting for a response from her, he stole off into the night, taking the same passage as had the two men before him.

It didn't take Richards long to piece together what had happened. When their contact realized he was being followed, he'd stashed the items and lured the interloper away from the pickup point. It had worked.

She crouched down beside the backpack as Rodriguez came past her and looked cautiously around the corner where the other three men had disappeared. He was there, at the corner, when they heard three gunshots, fired from a gun muzzled by a silencer. Jaime's heartbeat accelerated wildly.

She remembered what Yani had told her when they first met back in Ur.

He wasn't carrying a weapon.

April 8, 2003, 7:02 P.M.
The Ruins of Hammurabi
Babylon

Gerik had never been more surprised in his life than he was when the first bullet whizzed past his head. It was closely followed by a second. The shooter was either tremendously good or singularly unlucky.

"Put him down," said Frank McMillan, CIA station chief of Kuwait City.

The newcomer stood tall and confident against the darkening night. Gerik hesitated, the unconscious old man still slung over his shoulder.

A third bullet grazed his shirt. He dropped the old man and backed away.

During the brief seconds Frank was focused on the form of Kristof Remen, Gerik took three steps back to the end of the lane and disappeared around the corner. As Gerik slipped through a doorway into a neighboring passageway, he heard the newcomer say, "Old man. Are you all right?"

Kristof wouldn't answer for a few hours.

Meanwhile, Gerik sidestepped into the dark shadows of an alcove. What on earth was Frank doing here? It made no sense, none at all.

Gerik had only moments to regroup and get out of there. He listened again. No one was following him. He contemplated the fact that Kristof hadn't been carrying anything. That meant the old man must have hidden his valuables to be picked up later.

Gerik stealthily retraced his steps. As he came to the corner from which the old man had emerged, he held up his own mirror to look down the long lane.

And there was that irritating chaplain assistant. Which meant that, somehow, Jaime Richards, his original target, was somewhere nearby!

A plan was morphing in his mind, and he grinned.

He watched the chaplain assistant for a few minutes. It was easy to figure where the chaplain must be, because that was where he was watching with the most focus and frequency. But he'd positioned himself at a difficult intersection, with the paths going off at drastic angles, so that he could not possibly watch all of them at once. For the most part, he had his back against a brick outcropping, from which he could cover the chaplain and two paths.

Gerik had prepared five cloths with hydrochloride and had so far only used one, on Kristof. He felt a certain smug satisfaction that his propensity for overpreparation would once again save the day.

The chaplain assistant turned again to scan the two other walkways. Gerik was silent and quick, and he had the cloth firmly over the sergeant's nose and mouth before he dragged him two steps backward, out of sight of where he assumed Richards was waiting.

The shorter man slumped within seconds, and Gerik laid him silently on the ground. He contemplated the sergeant's M-16 with interest for just a second before reminding himself he needed to travel light.

It was the right choice.

For as he used his mirror to scan the passageway that went off to his right, he couldn't believe his good fortune. There crouched Chaplain Jaime Richards with a knapsack that he just bet contained Kristof Remen's valuables.

Bingo.

This was too good. Gerik admitted to himself that he had wondered for a moment if things were starting to go wrong, if cosmically, somehow, he was losing his footing. But he wasn't supposed to have the consolation prize of Kristof Remen. He was meant to have the Grand Prize— the rest of the items taken from the Mosul Museum—and the person who had been fingered by the Dunbar woman was holding the rest of the information they needed.

He paused only for a moment to listen intently for anyone else. He heard nothing.

He went back along the passageway and climbed up out of the ruins. He stayed low against the darkening sky and walked quickly around the crumbling walls until he came to a spot above the one against which Richards was crouched.

He could see the top of her helmet. She had probably realized Rodriguez was missing and had stood, wondering what to do.

He'd relieve her of all that burdensome thinking.

In one smooth movement he dropped straight down behind her, drugged cloth in hand. He grabbed her shoulder but let her turn slightly, just enough to see who he was.

He knew he would long delight in the memory of that moment, of the horror in her eyes. But before she could scream or fight back, he had the thick cloth firmly over her nose and mouth. She struggled, but there was no point. He held it firm for seconds after she went limp in his arms. He needed her safely unconscious for a lengthy transport.

There was still no sound of anyone else following him. He flung her over his shoulder with ease, for although she was slightly heavier—and more heavily outfitted—than the old man, she was not brittle as he had been.

Gerik used his other hand to scoop up the brown backpack. It was heavy. He took a precious second to unzip an inch of canvas fabric and look inside. Gorgeous bubble-wrapped items crowded the sack. Thankfully, the cuneiform tablets were only about a foot long. Manageable.

He headed back for Saddam's private garage, where his steel-reinforced trunk with airholes awaited his new treasures.

CHASING EDEN

April 8, 2003, 7:15 P.M.
Procession Street
Babylon

Frank McMillan was shocking people that evening.

As he strode out through the Ishtar Gate carrying the unconscious form of the old man in his arms, Master Sergeant Greg Adkins stared at him with apprehension. Frank had arrived at the ruins only minutes after the UN expert, the chaplain, and her assistant had entered. He'd shown his CIA credentials, given the name of the person Adkins could call to verify the importance of his mission, and then disappeared into the ruins of Babylon.

Now here he was, hurrying out, carrying an unidentified adult male who was unconscious.

Adkins expected answers.

Instead, Frank paused only briefly in front of him. "For months, I've been tracking a man who's a known terrorist," Frank said. "He was here tonight. Obviously, I was too late to head him off, but I believe I know the direction he's headed, and I've got to go now. I'm going to get this man to help and have him debriefed. If you have people in there, I don't know what's happened to them. You'd better send your soldiers in to find out."

Adkins opened his mouth to bark orders, but Frank took a step closer to him and said quietly but with the weight of authority, "There's a chance this terrorist may have taken one or more prisoners. If that's the case, it's all the more imperative that I—and the agency—track and capture him as quickly as possible. He won't hesitate to kill. But he is somehow privy to Army communications. Certainly you must report whatever you find in there. But the longer the Army can keep the details quiet, the greater the chance we can bring this to a swift and successful resolution."

Adkins looked at him warily, eager to take control of whatever the situation was inside Babylon.

"Did I express myself clearly, Sergeant?" asked Frank.

"Yes, sir," Adkins replied.

And Frank was off toward his vehicle as Adkins ordered his troops back into the ruins.

—PART THREE—

Baghdad Airport

April 2003, 8:40 P.M.
The Grosskomtur's *home base*
Five kilometers west of Baghdad
Iraq

He wanted to hurt her.

Gerik knew he was breaking every rule he'd ever taught or been taught by not taking his priceless cargo to safety at headquarters immediately.

But Richards made him angry. He was angry, of course, that she had played him for the fool this morning and eluded capture. But it was beyond personal. Everything she stood for: the fact that she was a woman, with an officer's rank, commanding a male lackey who did her bidding was repulsive. The fact that she belonged to an army that was fighting for the cause of democracy was also repellent. Democracy was a losing proposition, mostly because people, en masse, were hopelessly stupid. They needed a strong leader. But beyond that, democracy was evil because it assigned equal value to every individual, no matter what their Root Race. Absurd!

Worse was that she fancied herself to be in a position of spiritual leadership, which was completely against the natural order of the patriarchal world. Not to mention, she was propagating a religion that distracted the Aryans from their true identity.

He told himself it made sense to stop on his way to

headquarters to get her out of her American military uniform. The last thing he needed was to be caught having kidnapped an officer.

Her identity was about to change.

But the truth was, he was currently in total control of her, and he wanted to enjoy the power he held for another 15 minutes. Certainly, although time was racing—indeed, they were nearly into the final 24 hours of possibility—he had earned his 15 minutes.

He also wanted to take his leave of the local farmhouse that had been his home base for the last two months. His Chrysler bounced along the rutted road of red-brown dirt, through the fields of long grass, until he reached the building. It was one level, long and flat, and much larger than he'd needed. It had housed four generations of the same family, including probably three dozen assorted grandparents, aunts, uncles, cousins, and grandchildren. But they had known hard times and had gratefully received the monies Gerik had paid them—more than they would have seen in five years. He assumed they had dispersed happily to other relatives or had used the money to buy a smaller place with a few more amenities. Like running water.

The back part of the building was one long, narrow room. In front were two taller, square rooms, with an overhang running between them, flanked by palm trees. The overhang had a makeshift roof and worked well as a carport. It provided privacy. The whole building was the reddish brown color of the local dirt.

He pulled into the darkness of the carport. He took a minute to look inside the square room to the left to make certain there were no surprises. He never locked the door, as there was nothing there to identify him and nothing worth stealing—unless you counted the small ham radio hidden in the corner.

Gerik returned to the car and entered the code to open the trunk. He'd leave the valuables there, which was akin to leaving them in a locked safe. His violet eyes sparkled as he found Richards's inert form. She was breathing. He took her wrist and counted her pulse. Strong but slow. She was still out.

He scanned the surroundings once again, then picked her up and carried her inside. Against one wall was a hot plate and a sink; across from it on the opposite wall was a cot. He dropped Richards onto the cot.

The floor was dirt, but several woven mats were scattered about, used as rugs. They looked haphazard, but one of them covered a small trapdoor over a two-foot-wide hole in the ground. Gerik opened it and removed its only contents: a box of black plastic storage bags. He glanced up at the short wooden rod that had served as a closet. Hung there were still two tunic-shaped robes, one a woman's, one a man's. There were also two pairs of nondescript black pants and a *hijab* to complete the local woman's outfit.

Perfect.

The remains of the Army officer would rest here, under the floor, while the new, improved Jaime Richards would continue her journey as a modest local woman.

It was a pain to remove the entirety of her Army uniform, but he began with the desert boots and worked carefully and quickly. Each article of removed clothing was folded and stacked in the black plastic garbage bag. The anticipation provided the most exquisite agony.

Finally all that was left were her underpants, bra, and dog tags.

He turned his attention to her dog tags. It felt sexual, invading her privacy this way. He paid little attention to her actual tags; he already knew her name and cared little about her Social Security number or blood type. Last listed was her faith affiliation: Presbyterian. Why wasn't he surprised? Of course she'd belong to a religious group misguided enough to allow its followers to participate in electing their leadership.

But he wanted to see what else she had. What personal items had she chosen to wear that identified her to herself?

On the chain with her dog tags hung a small silver cross—no surprise. She also had a small square silver medal with some saint on it. He squinted and read: *St. Michael, Patron of Aviators, Protect Us*. This confused him only slightly, as he considered saints to be Catholic, but hey, maybe it comforted her to share their superstitions. On the back was etched: *Aviation Brigade, 2nd Infantry, War Eagles*. OK, so it was some group superstition thing. Obviously, St. Michael was out to lunch today as far as Richards was concerned.

What interested him more was that she wore a second chain. This one had only a simple gold band. Most likely a wedding ring. Odd to wear a wedding ring around your neck, not on your finger. Either it belonged to some family member, or she was somehow not really married. Married but not married. Made no sense. But again, if it meant something to her, provided some identity, off it came.

As he raised her head to remove the two silver chains, she moaned slightly and raised the back of her right hand to rub her eye. He didn't know what dreams she was having, but he knew she wouldn't be able to fight her way back to consciousness for several more hours.

He had to tug at the chains to bring them over her plaited blond hair, but once he had, they easily came free and he let her fall back onto the cot.

He nested the chains on top of the uniform, which nearly filled the garbage bag. Then he tugged the red plastic strips together to close it, tied the handles securely, and dropped it with a thud into the hole. He looked at it with a smile, knowing that by the time anyone found it, she would be long gone.

And the world would be much different.

He closed the two short pieces of wood that constituted the trapdoor and replaced the dyed mat. Then he returned to the foot of the cot and stood studying her, a grin of triumph playing with the edges of his mouth. He enjoyed the way that her arms and face had been colored nut-brown by sun and sand—as had his own—while her torso remained delicately pale. He was going to rape her, of course. Because he could. Because she desperately needed to be shown who was boss.

Because he wanted to.

But he was actually doing her a service. If, by any chance, she became pregnant, the child would at least have a high percentage of pure blood.

He reached behind her head and pulled free the rubber band from the bottom of her French braid. He used his fingers as combs to pull the strands free. The hair was coated with dust but seemed to be naturally blond. She looked like a possible pureblood herself. Tainted somehow, certainly— but not enough to excuse her brazenly bad choices.

Fuck you, he thought, and then smiled, because he was about to do just that. His anger returned, and he began by striking her, hard, across the face with the back of his hand.

The blow roused her, slightly. She coughed and then moaned again, moving restlessly against the gray canvas cot.

He sat her up to remove her white cotton bra. As he did, two things happened simultaneously.

The radio in the corner crackled to life.

And Jaime Richards threw up.

Worse than the fact that most of the vomit landed on Gerik's black shirt was the fact that she continued gagging and retching.

It wasn't surprising that a victim would become nauseous after being drugged and driven over bad roads in the trunk of a car. But it was an inopportune time. Especially inopportune because he couldn't answer the radio call until he had cleared her airway so she wouldn't choke to death. While part of him wished he could just let her asphyxiate, he knew they needed her alive.

So he dutifully leaned her face-forward over the side of the cot and ran his fingers through her mouth and as far down her throat as he could, clearing out the remains of the contents of her stomach. Any sense of joyful anticipation he'd had was gone. The smell was repulsive.

Once he was sure her breathing was unobstructed, he stalked to the corner of the room to answer Satis's call, no doubt demanding to know just where Gerik and their shared booty had ended up. And he swore to himself, once Satis was done with the bitch, she'd be dead.

April 9, 2003, 12:18 A.M.
Satis's headquarters
16 kilometers west of Baghdad
Central Iraq

Something very, very cold splashed on her face.

Jaime struggled to open her eyes. Muted colors swirled around her, and it took her a moment even to figure out that she was in a prone position, lying on a floor. With this information, she closed her eyes again.

She tried to center herself and take inventory. It was not a happy process. There wasn't an inch of her that didn't feel wretched. She couldn't yet isolate the worst pain, but she knew her head was pounding, she felt nauseous, and her thoughts were jumbled. She waited another moment until she could identify the side of her body that had contact with the ground. There was the soft nap of a rug under the palm of her hand. She opened her eyes again. The rug was brightly colored with red, gold, and green. Hand-hooked of soft wool.

She looked up to discover she was on the floor of an opulent office. The furniture was dark, carved wood, with matching bookcases. The walls were covered with hand-painted frescoes, filled with fine brushstrokes and gilded with gold leaf.

There was a person, a man, seated behind the tall desk. As she stretched and rolled onto her back, she had a start

when she realized there was another man, a thin, wiry gentleman, on one knee beside her. He had a beak nose and
light blond hair, beginning to go white. In his hand was a
half-full glass of ice water. From the patches of wet carpet
around her head it wasn't hard to figure out where the other
half had recently landed.

As Jaime looked at him, he nodded at the man behind
the desk. "Well done, Blenheim," said the desk man.
"Please help our guest onto the divan."

The thin man reached over to help her sit up. She held
up a palm to stop him and tried to raise herself to a sitting
position. Her head swam. She stayed sitting up and closed
her eyes. In a moment she felt well enough to nod at
Blenheim. He put an arm under her arms and helped her
stand just enough to move her backward to a sofa behind
them. It was covered with a wine-colored brushed velvet.

Where on earth was she?

She pushed herself back, wedging herself into a corner
of the divan, using its arm to help her stay upright. In doing
so, she saw her own clothing, and her mouth dropped open.

She was wearing a tunic of muted seaweed green,
stitched with a design that looked like interlocking *S*'s
around the small *V* cut out at the neck. The tunic reached
below her knees—and underneath it she had on black
pants, with some sort of elastic waist. She couldn't help but
reach up to her head—where her helmet was missing, an
ivory head scarf in its place.

The man behind the desk was watching her make these
discoveries. She sat back against the sofa and waited for
him to speak.

"Thank you, Blenheim. You've been most helpful. I'll
take it from here," he said. His voice was full of easy authority. The thin man gave a small bow and exited through
a carved wooden door.

The first gentleman stood and came around the desk. He
wore dark brown trousers and a pullover shirt about the
same color as the scarf on her head. They both fit him well.

He pulled another chair around to face the divan and extended his hand.

"Coleman Satis," he said.

She offered her hand and he shook it.

Coleman Satis? The media mogul? Why on earth would she be sitting in the office of Coleman Satis? And which office of his offices were they in? London? Prague? Zurich? She looked around for a window to give her clues, but there were none.

"I do apologize for the rough way you were brought here. But you're an important part of the puzzle. In fact, you should feel very special to be in on the real reason for the war—and the real reason it will shortly end."

The war. Iraq. Babylon. The man behind her, grinning. The strong, acrid smell of the chloroform. Its odor still clung to her, and it still seasoned the terrible taste in her mouth.

"Would it be possible for me to get some tea?" she asked.

"Certainly. Is there anything else you'd like? A sandwich? Some cheese or fruit?"

"I'll start with the tea."

He returned to his desk and used the intercom on his phone to make the request. Then he returned to his chair and turned his attention to her once again.

"I hear you're a friend of Adara Dunbar's."

She nodded. It seemed as if his statement had layers of implications.

"And you read cuneiform."

Again she nodded.

"So I don't need to tell you that the war is not really about weapons of mass destruction."

She stared at him. It was all she could do. She wasn't thinking clearly enough to answer six plus three, let alone discuss foreign policy. But he didn't expect an answer. "Nor is it about the 'evil' of Saddam Hussein, or the corporate need for oil. All of those were convenient premises for launching the invasion. A good war—excuse me, a controlled conflict—in the right hands brings us closer to a New, and much preferred, World Order."

Blenheim returned with a tray containing a steaming mug of hot tea and a plate of apple sections and cheese. She disregarded the food but went for the mug gingerly and took a small sip.

It was a black tea, flavored with a hint of orange and spice. It was heaven.

Blenheim left the room, and Satis smiled at her reaction. He gave her a moment to savor the drink. Even though she knew the effects of the caffeine were not that immediate, it felt as if each sip brought her back a bit closer to being able to interact with the world.

After a long moment's silence while she sipped and then set the mug down again, Coleman Satis said, "Would you like to see it?"

"See it?"

"What all this fuss is about. Would you like to see it?"

"Sure," she said.

He went back to a bookcase, picked up a dark blue sack, and loosened the drawstring at its mouth. Then he withdrew a sword in a sheath.

She gasped as he stood before her and gave her the Sword of Life.

It was heavy in her hands, but it was truly magnificent. None of the descriptions had done it justice. The handle was blue lapis—but it was blue beyond blue; it was the color of the deepest sky and the purest sea. The color shimmered with a natural electricity.

The sheath was golden, exquisitely carved. She couldn't help but run her fingers over the filigree work—the six different settings of stars, which had been crafted more than four thousand years before. The intricacy of each strand was stunning.

She was drawn back up to where the dagger rose from the sheath. At the hilt was a golden triangle, which joined the handle to the blade. On the triangle, tiny golden balls were attached, like a miniature pile of golden cannon-balls. Two rows of four golden beads were topped by a row of three, then two, then a single bead at the top, which rose over the lapis. The very top of the handle, also, was covered with golden beads. The juxtaposition of the vibrant gold and blue gave the sword a feeling of being more than a sword, of being the instrument of legend.

Subconsciously she turned the handle and grasped the lapis with her right hand. She glanced up at Satis, who nodded permission. And with one long backward stroke, she withdrew the blade from the sheath.

And then she sat, mesmerized by the Sword of Life.

A long line ran the length of the blade, from tip to hilt. It seemed to flash and sing in her hands.

"Do you feel its power?" Satis asked simply.

There was no way to deny that she did.

"And do you know its true value?"

"I've been told that it somehow reveals the location of the site of the actual Garden of Eden," she said. She carefully returned the blade to the sheath and presented it back to Satis. She continued, "But I've got to ask, even if it does, why does everybody want it so badly? What's there that's so important? Jewels?"

"Ah," said Coleman Satis, receiving the sword reverently. "The riches mentioned in Genesis are indeed there. Gold, bdellium, onyx, lapis . . ."

"Ruby, carnelian, jade, turquoise, mother-of-pearl," Jaime finished.

"It's true," Mr. Satis said. "But whoever told you of the gems knew only half of the story." He sat forward in his chair and leaned in to her. "The true secret is that Eden isn't an archeological site at all. The true secret is that the Garden of Eden still exists."

April 9, 2003, 12:55 A.M.
Satis's headquarters
16 kilometers west of Baghdad
Central Iraq

Was she hallucinating?

That explanation seemed every bit as credible as the idea that she was sitting in the office of Coleman Satis, who owned a fourth of the world's television and newspaper outlets. And that Mr. Satis was telling her, with a straight face, that the Garden of Eden still existed. She could still smell and taste the chloroform that had knocked her out earlier. The neurons in her brain were not yet firing with enough precision to let her figure out which islands of memory were true and which were fantastical creations of a drug-induced state.

And yet . . . she had just held the Sword of Life in her own hands.

The treasure everyone was struggling to possess. The sword her parents had died to protect.

Mr. Satis had paused, waiting for her to respond to his statement.

She decided she didn't have to be brilliant, just attentive. "No," she said. "No one mentioned that the Garden might still exist."

That was the only invitation he needed.

"Then let me tell you a story, Ms. Richards. I'm a man

who has dedicated his career to disseminating stories, both real and created. But I've never heard one to match that of my own heritage."

Jaime sat with both hands cradling the brown mug of tea, which had retreated from boiling to comfortingly warm.

"My own true home is Eden. I was conceived there. Yes, it is a place on this earth. Hidden, but right here in Iraq, as a matter of fact. Before I was born, my mother left on a mission—it was supposed to be a brief one—to the outside world. However, the way to Eden, what they call 'the door,' opens only twice a year, and you must meet a guide to find it. Just when she was supposed to return, there was a crisis with her pregnancy and she was rushed to a hospital. She nearly died. As did I, her unborn child. By the time she was out of danger, she had missed the rendezvous. And apparently, when you leave, you are only given information for meeting one guide for one door opening.

"She made the best of things, of course. Settled in the United States, and raised me. I've tried to make the best of things, too, and feel that in some small way I have succeeded." Satis paused and gave her what she thought was supposed to look like a self-deprecating smile. It wasn't very successful.

"However, my mother never lost her desire to return home to her family before she died. She knew that there was an ancient map, and items that, put together, showed the location of the 'door.' Even with my somewhat considerable clout, it has taken me decades to come into possession of the sword, the cuneiform tablets, and the correct ancient atlases. I also know that the 'door' opens again, this very evening, and then, at moonset, it closes. Given the current military and political circumstances, it will likely close for a very long time. Possibly forever. Which is why it is so very urgent for us to be there."

"Us?" Jaime asked.

"Yes." His smile this time was eager, almost boyish. "I am inviting you to come, as my guest."

"And all I need to do to claim this one-time offer?" Jaime hoped she didn't look as panicked as she actually was. If there was one thing more dangerous than a madman, it was an incredibly wealthy madman with an insatiable feeling of entitlement.

"All you need do is translate these cuneiform tablets." He again stood and stalked behind his desk. The tablets he picked up were fairly small in size. They were also in very good shape. The strokes carved into them had survived the intervening millennia very well.

"I do read cuneiform myself," he said matter-of-factly. "But in a situation like this, there is no time for one incorrectly interpreted figure.

"You'll help me," he said, a declaration rather than a query. "And in return, you will receive the greatest chance of a lifetime."

"And if I'm not able to translate it?"

Coleman Satis waved a hand dismissively. "Oh, but you will. I know you. I can read your intellectual curiosity from here. You would love to know where Eden is, and what really exists there. You were a friend of Ms. Dunbar's, which means you likely have a connection to Eden yourself. I have no interest in forcing you to discuss it with me. Suffice it to say, I will get you there."

She looked at him, hoping she had enough of a poker face not to reveal her true thoughts. "But I've had only first-year Akkadian. If I can't read it?"

A dark wrath suddenly appeared on his face. "You're asking . . . if you *won't*?"

She sat, still.

"You won't survive the night," he said. "So. Easy choice. And," he said, stalking again to his desk and buzzing the intercom on his telephone, "you have an hour."

"An *hour*?" she asked.

"They're small tablets," he answered. "And time is short."

The door opened, and Blenheim shuffled in once more.

"It's time to take Ms. Richards to her room," he said.

The thin man approached her. "Can you stand up, Miss?" he asked.

Jaime looked at Satis. He nodded. "Let me get what you will need."

Blenheim took the mug of tea from Jaime. Then he took both of her arms and helped her stand up. He gently turned her sideways.

"Hands behind your back, please."

She swayed slightly but was nowhere near as woozy as she'd been when she came in.

From his pocket he removed a white plastic set of zip-tie handcuffs. They were plastic, lightweight, very easy to use, and nearly impossible to get out of. He guided her hands through the waiting circles and tightened them quickly. Then he sat her back down on the couch.

He went over to Satis and collected a sheaf of papers and other elements she couldn't quite see. He took them and exited, leaving her sitting forward on the divan, feet on the floor to keep her balance. Satis didn't seem the least bit perturbed by having his honored guest suddenly sitting before him in handcuffs.

"How will I know when my hour is up?" she asked. "Someone has taken my watch."

Blenheim had returned at that juncture, and Satis, who was once again behind his grand desk, said to him, "Would you see to it that there is a clock or a timer of some kind in Ms. Richards's workroom?"

Blenheim left once again.

"Where am I?" she asked.

"In my headquarters," Satis answered. "You don't need to know where we are, because you will only be leaving with me. All you do need to know is that it's labyrinthine and well covered by surveillance cameras and guards. There's no point in using any of your precious moments contemplating escape. I mean, really," he couldn't help but smile, "think of the power I must command to have been able to remove you from the midst of an active military operation and bring you here without being followed."

He gave himself another moment to enjoy his own power.

Then the door opened, and the henchman returned. Blenheim grasped her left arm and brought her to her feet. "This way, Miss," he said.

"An hour," Satis said.

And the henchman pushed her ahead of him out through the carved door.

April 9, 2003, 1:39 A.M.
Satis's headquarters
Central Iraq

Blenheim had done as requested and had locked her in a
tiny square storeroom with nothing but rubbings of the
tablets, paper, a pencil, and a timer. It was quite different
from the palatial quarters occupied by the little boy down
the hall. Blenheim couldn't help but read into it a difference in their purposes.

Satis had been very pleased when Gerik had brought
Jaime Richards in. Mr. Satis had even treated her deferen-
tially in their discussions. But now Andy assumed it was
simply because she could be of use.

Andy Blenheim had a secret of his own. It made perfect
sense that a man such as Coleman Satis would record
everything that went on in each of his offices around the
world. Even here, there was a hidden camera in his office
and in the outer tunnels. Unfortunately, not in Room 322,
whose top-secret goings-on were never recorded.

Satis was canny, though. The recorded sessions in his
office never went onto videotapes or disks that could be
stolen or viewed by the wrong people. They went, encoded, straight onto chips that only Satis had the hardware
to read. So no one else could view the story of Coleman
Satis's life without his permission.

However, there was a tiny, bunkerlike square room where the feed from the camera was downloaded in real time. And someone had, helpfully, installed a tiny viewing screen and sound control panel.

Andy had discovered it by mistake one night when searching for something on command from Satis. He didn't think that even Mr. Satis knew it existed. It was a small, upside-down fish-eye view of what was being recorded.

Andy had said nothing. He was the only one with the keys required to get into that room. For weeks, it had never occurred to him to spy on his master.

But tonight, so much was happening. It was impossible for him not to listen in.

He tried not to be envious that Satis had handed this newcomer the great treasure—the fabled Sword of Life—just given it over to her for her to examine and feel, whereas he had never let Andy Blenheim, with all his loyalty, come near it.

Andy tried to tell himself he didn't need to touch the sword just now. Soon he would have an honored place in the New World Order, and there would be time for rewards such as that.

It had puzzled him at first that Mr. Satis had not talked to their guest about the true nature of Eden, or about the new order. That was what had clued Andy in to the fact that Satis was not really planning to admit her to the inner circles.

In fact, translation or not, she would not live out this night. In a way Andy felt bad for her. It was not her fault she'd never been taught the realities of the world to come.

And yet she had an important part to play.

Andy had deposited her in the small, empty room with the bare bulb burning overhead. He had brought along her mug, and he set it on the floor while he cut off her handcuffs.

"Would you like your tea, Miss?" he asked. It wasn't much of a last meal, but it was all he was allowed to offer.

"Thanks," she said.

"If you finish before the hour, just knock," he said. And he went back to see what was happening next, on this night of nights.

Alejandro Rodriguez lay on his cot, wide awake, staring into the large dome of sky over Baghdad International Airport.

He had come to fairly quickly after the soldiers from the 101st had found him in the ruins. Adkins was livid after discovering the chaplain was missing and had made it a priority to get back to the brigade Operations Center in Al Hillah so he could report the incident and hand Rodriguez off to his own unit.

There Captain Sapp, commander of the convoy from Tallil, and his crew had finished the fuel testing and were ready to move on to Baghdad. Sapp was at a loss as to how he should handle the missing-chaplain issue. This was way above his pay grade. Conferring with more senior officers at Al Hillah, he decided it was best for the convoy to continue on its mission. Baghdad Airport was an hour down the road, and he needed to link up with someone who could put him in contact with his command back in Tallil.

It had been after dark when they'd reached the airport. The trip would have felt interminable if Sergeant Rodriguez had been responsible for keeping Richards safe in the vehicle. They'd continued up Highway 8 to a crossroads that was serving as the headquarters for one of the brigades in 3rd Infantry, headed west. The drive had taken them along a fairly rural-looking road for five miles or so. Then the convoy had come to an exit ramp—a cloverleaf, just like in the United States, who'd have thought?—and headed north on a two-lane highway.

The area had been well cleared by coalition troops during the past couple of days. They passed through a checkpoint, and the buildings became administrative rather than residential. It was shortly after driving past a flock of scraggly sheep, huddled together for the night, that Rodriguez realized they were indeed inside the airport complex.

The convoy drove through areas where different units had taken possession of airport buildings to use as their work space. He couldn't tell much in the dark, as the military was keeping "light discipline" so as to not make themselves a target for anyone thinking of attacking with a mortar or other firepower from a distance.

The convoy stopped in a field about two hundred meters south of a large cement bunker where the Corps Support Battalion had set up. CSB vehicles were parked along the short paved entry road leading up to the bunker. Soldiers had set up cots or tents near their vehicles.

It wasn't hard to find Chaplain Troy Henderson. His vehicle was parked with the others by the side of the road. He had a two-person hex tent set up behind his Humvee. Even though Rodriguez had finally rolled in near 2300, Henderson was still up. He was young for a chaplain, maybe 27 or 28, a newly minted captain. He was a good man and an earnest chaplain. His hair was blond, cut in a high-and-tight, and he wore glasses. He'd been hit hard by the deaths in his unit. It was clear he'd been looking forward to support from Chaplain Richards.

Instead, Rodriguez found himself the bearer of more bad news. He sounded more optimistic than he actually felt in recounting that the CIA was hot on the trail of the perpetrators, and Rodriguez even stated his hope that

Richards would be found before Captain Sapp's Serious Incident Report had spurred the Army to mount a major search-and-rescue mission in Al Hillah.

Rodriguez sat with Henderson then and just let him talk. It seemed he needed to sort through his own feelings and felt freer to talk to Rodriguez than perhaps he did with his own chaplain assistant. Finally, the two men had prayed together, for the families of the fallen soldiers, for the members of the unit affected by the deaths, for strength in the days to come. And now, for Jaime Richards.

Then each had repaired to his own cot to wait out the sleepless night.

That was where the staff sergeant was, lying beside his vehicle and studying the vast dome of sky over Baghdad, when a figure of a man approached him silently out of the darkness. He didn't notice anyone was there until he heard the whisper.

"Rodriguez."

He sat bolt upright and swung his legs over the side of his cot, hand on his weapon.

The newcomer had two fingers against his lips, requesting silence. It was the contractor who'd ridden up with them.

He came and knelt beside the cot in the darkness. He took something out of his pocket and cradled it in his hands, showing it to Rodriguez. It was a small screen, with a pair of flashing green dots in the bottom right corner.

"I know where she is," the newcomer said. "Will you help me?"

It was a strawberry.

The most noticeable thing in the dimly lit storeroom, once the door was closed, was the incessant ticking of a timer. Dorothy in *The Wizard of Oz* was given a huge hourglass to watch the final minutes of her life tick by. Obviously, when Coleman Satis had demanded that his assistant get Jaime a clock or timing device, Blonheim had gone to their kitchen and brought her the timer.

It was shaped like a strawberry. The remainder of her life was ticking away on a red plastic strawberry.

She sat down on the linoleum floor and looked around the empty room. There was nothing except a two-tier white freestanding plastic storage shelf from which everything had been removed. She scooted back to lean against the wall to the left side of the door. And then she did what she dreaded doing, what she had forced herself not to do in the presence of Coleman Satis. She reached up to her neck and felt under the open collar of her tunic.

Her dog tags were missing.

Her wedding ring was gone.

Her last connection to the man she'd loved, who had

taught her how to live in a broken, hating world and still
have hope.

Stolen.

Somehow, that was what did it.

She put her head down to her knees, and she wept. The
tears began to flow harder, and she crumpled to the floor,
unable to control the sobs that wracked her body.

She wept again for Paul, for her parents, and for Adara.
She wept in anger at a stranger who had looked at her with
such triumph and hate as he had murdered her friend. She
wept with fury that he had been able to drug, kidnap, and
strip her of her clothing and her identity, and with frustration that she had been dumped in a room, in a building
whose location she did not know—hungry, sick, and tired.
As broken as she could be.

And then, as that energy was released, a surprising
thing happened. She again felt Paul close to her. She remembered thinking in the Humvee how much he would
love this adventure, chasing the mythical sword. Well,
she'd found it. She'd held it in her hands. Maybe it was her
imagination, but she again felt Paul's smile. *You know our
connection was far more than a physical ring,* flashed
through her mind. *No one can sever the bond we had. No
one can change what we were to each other, what we
learned from each other. Love is never-ending.*

An unexplained warmth coursed through her exhausted
body. And she felt in it another wordless Presence giving
her strength. It lasted only a moment, but it left a residue of
power and courage. *You are not forsaken,* this voice spoke
without words. It was another voice that she recognized but
had not heard for a very long time.

She sat up and leaned back against the wall.

She looked at the strawberry. She had just given away
six minutes. But they were minutes that she had needed to
realign her thinking and to now analyze her situation from
a new perspective.

The U.S. Army and Yani—whoever he was and

whomever he was representing—now had someone on the inside, within feet of Coleman Satis's office and the stolen sword. She did want to show Adara's irksome brother that she had a head on her shoulders, that she could be of some use. However it had happened, she had ended up at the epicenter of the night's events. It was up to her to make the most of it.

And she would do just that.

"Where is she?" Staff Sergeant Rodriguez asked, trying to interpret the electronic colors on the handheld device before him.

"This screen shows the airport where we are, here." He pointed at the left side of the diagram before them. "That's the airstrip. The perimeter wall is about here. And she's over here . . . within a lake resort compound whose walls are only five hundred meters from that perimeter." The newcomer was standing, facing north, and he used his right hand to point off, straight east from where they stood.

"She's that close?"

He nodded.

"What's over there?" Rodriguez asked.

"Obviously, more than anyone suspected," said Yani.

"How do you get there?"

"Normally, you'd drive out the front entrance of the airport, then take a road running along the perimeter wall to the entrance of the resort compound. However, what the military is just now discovering is that Saddam Hussein loved tunnels. There are miles and miles of tunnels under the airport, and, I'm willing to bet, under the opulent homes and palaces of the resort."

Rodriguez considered. "If the military doesn't know about the tunnels, it seems fair to say they haven't cleared them," he said. "Sergeant Adkins told me that the CIA is involved in finding the kidnappers. Maybe we should report this to them."

The burden of command is one not easily set aside, for sleep or any other diversion, especially during war. Colonel Abraham Derry lay sleepless on the cot in his tent. He stared into the darkness, listening to the ever-present buzz from a 15K generator as problems from the unit ran through his mind. On a typical night, it was well past 1:00 A.M. before his body would succumb to exhaustion and he could fall asleep. This night was no different.

So he was fully aware of the footsteps running up the path and anticipated the knock on his tent door before it came.

"Come," he said quickly, encouraging the messenger to enter his personal space. Captain Whittaker slipped through the tent flap, face illuminated by an eerie red glow from the flashlight he carried.

"Sir, the XO needs you in the TOC right now. We have just received an SIR from Baghdad."

"This must be a good one." He sat on the edge of his cot, rubbing his eyes. "The XO usually prides himself on handling Serious Incident Reports without 'disturbing me,' as he puts it."

"It's the chaplain, sir. . . ."

Abe Derry came immediately alert. His eyes had adjusted to the darkness, and he could see the anxiety on the battle captain's face. "What's happened?" He threw on his pants and grabbed for his boots. His mind immediately went to the worst-case scenario.

"I don't know. The commo NCO took the report straight to the XO, who screamed something like, 'Damn that chaplain!' and then he yelled for me to come get you."

"Tell him I'm on my way."

He relaxed a bit as he finished lacing his boots. *If Ray is pissed at the chaplain,* he thought, smiling slightly, *at least she isn't dead*. He grabbed his battle gear and headed for the TOC.

April 9, 2003, 1:40 A.M.
Logbase Rock
Tallil Airfield
Southern Iraq

Lieutenant Colonel Ray Jenkins was having a very ani-
mated conversation on an iridium phone when his group
commander parted the flaps to enter the Operations Center.

"Attention in the TOC!" shouted the TOC guard, jump-
ing up from his seat behind a small desk.

"Carry on," replied Colonel Derry, putting his hand on
the young man's shoulder to gently press him back down
into his seat as he reached behind him for a cup of coffee
from a coffeemaker.

"I don't care if she outranks you!" The executive officer's phone conversation could easily be heard throughout
the tent. "You were the convoy commander; you should
never have let her go! So tell me again what this Sergeant
Adkins said about the situation. . . ."

He paused, obviously not happy with the other half of
the conversation. "That's ridiculous! I can't believe . . . !"
Another pause. "OK, Brian, just get your ass back here tomorrow. Let us worry about Richards." He turned the
phone off, looked as if he would throw it across the room,
then thought better of the potential destruction of government property.

Colonel Derry had been quietly sipping his coffee, leaning against the TOC guard's desk. The private first class was looking straight ahead, trying very hard not to betray his thoughts about the conversation they were overhearing.

"Guess I'd better go sort this out," said the commander. He set down his coffee cup and, with a conspiratorial wink toward the guard, headed to the back of the tent. "Ray, let's go in my office," he said to his executive officer as he slipped into a side compartment set off for private meetings.

Abe Derry flipped a folding chair around and straddled it, leaning his elbows on the backrest. Ray Jenkins, face flushed and body taut with nervous energy, chose to pace back and forth in front of his commander.

"What have you got?" asked the colonel.

"Richards is missing. She may have been kidnapped, but we cannot confirm this. According to Captain Sapp, she and her assistant took a side trip to Babylon while waiting on the fuel tanker testing. A master sergeant from 101st returned with some cock-and-bull story about Frank McMillan—that CIA station chief who was bivouacked here—chasing a terrorist and claiming that he may have taken prisoners." He handed a copy of the official report to his CO, who began to read it intently.

"The commanding general is going to shit a brick when he hears this!" continued Jenkins. "And if this hits the media—" He stopped mid-sentence, noting the look on his colonel's face.

"We have an officer who is missing." The colonel's anger was evident in the intensity of his words. "She may be injured, or even dead. And you're worried about the corps commander? How about a little concern for what we tell her next of kin? Or better yet, how we go about finding her?"

Ray Jenkins was speechless. He had never seen the colonel so angry.

"Here's what I want you to do." Abe Derry was all business now, looking through the facts listed in the report. "First, contact Corps and find out who our interagency liaison is. We need someone who can link us up with the people working this terrorist issue. Second, have the S3 contact the brigade at Al Hillah. Find out what the status is of the area search of Babylon. Finally, alert Public Affairs that we may need help keeping a lid on this thing. I agree that media should not get involved. That could endanger Jaime. I will call the general myself to let him know about the incident. Any questions?"

"No, sir," was Jenkins's subdued answer. He spun 180 degrees and headed into the TOC, a man on a mission.

Colonel Derry sighed and looked back to the Serious Incident Report, hoping to find some clue as to the whereabouts of his chaplain.

April 9, 2003, 1:44 A.M.
South Tunnel entrance to Satis's Headquarters
16 kilometers west of Baghdad
Central Iraq

The tunnel that entered Satis's headquarters from the south was whitewashed. Electric wiring ran the center of the rounded ceilings and stopped for a bulb just once per hundred feet or so. There were guards posted at each corner turn.

No one besides the very top echelons knew of the tunnels, so the men were there more for ceremonial purposes than doing actual guard duty. They were Gerik Schroeder's men and had been chosen for their devotion to the cause and for their ability to follow commands. Although they were the elite of his corps, each was known simply as a "foot soldier."

The Commander was not fond of Gerik, but he liked the term "foot soldier." Simple. Elegant. Said it all. Along with Grosskomtur Gerik Schroeder and Coleman Satis, the Commander expected complete, unquestioning adherence to his orders. He was not often disappointed. In fact, it was the Commander who had originally seen the potential for using Gerik's men and had put together the seemingly unlikely alliance.

As the Commander approached the first corner, dragging a prisoner whose hands were zip-tied, he saw the guard stand and squint at them, not with apprehension, but with interest.

As he entered the pool of light, the guard snapped to attention. "Commander!" he said, with eager respect.

"No unexpected guests tonight?" the Commander asked.

"No, sir!" the guard reported. "You have a prisoner?"

The Commander didn't feel a need to answer the obvious. Instead, he let the cord with which he had been leading his hostage go slack for a moment.

"Foot soldier, face the wall," he said.

The guard did so, without surprise and without question. No sooner had he turned away than the Commander took the Beretta Cheetah .380 pistol from the waistband at the small of his back, put it at the base of the foot soldier's skull, and fired. The man slumped to the ground.

The Commander pulled the cord to his prisoner tight again, but he did not move. When the Commander turned back, he saw the old man looking at him calmly, sorrow reflected in his eyes.

"That was not necessary," the old man said.

"Ah, that's where we differ. I felt it was. And I hold the gun."

"Nothing is worth such an act."

"Again, our opinions diverge. I stand to gain quite a bit this very night."

"What does it profit a man if he gains the whole world—"

"But loses his own soul?" the Commander finished, and he chuckled. "Tell you what. You keep the souls. I'll take the whole world."

He laughed again and proceeded on, heading down the damp hallway, where soon the bodies of three more foot soldiers would mark the direction toward the Iraqi headquarters of Coleman Satis.

There was a door, with a silver lock in the circular handle.
There was a floor, covered with dark gray linoleum. There
were four walls painted industrial green. There was a ceiling painted gray. There was a vent near the top of one wall
and a grate cover held in place by four large screws. When
she'd seen that, Jaime had moved the plastic bookshelf beneath it and climbed up. The screws were tight.

She had two pieces of paper with rubbings of the
cuneiform tablets. She had a short pencil, with one end
sharpened, no eraser on the other end. She had a blank
piece of paper. She had a mug with an inch of tea still luke-
warm on the bottom. There was a plastic ticking strawberry, and one 25-watt lightbulb above her.

On her person, she still had her own underwear and now
a tunic, pants, and head scarf and a light, open pair of sandals. That was it. Everything she had brought with her for
situations such as this was gone.

Jaime stood for a moment, replaying the inventory again
through her mind. Then she decided to take a minute and
look at the cuneiform that was supposedly so important.
She sat cross-legged on the floor against the right-hand
wall, so that the papers would be under the light. The rub-

bing had been done with a dark crayon and was fairly easy
to see. She was surprised to find it contained mostly numbers. Brief descriptions were interspersed among the numbers. Some of the numbers apparently pertained to
grassland, some to a mountain, some to a lake district. And
then there were seasonal divides for planting season, grow-
ing season, harvest. The numbers were graphed according
to which season and location you were looking at.

As she contemplated this, her fingernails ran through
the dirt where the linoleum met the wall. There was a gap
where the tiles should have been caulked. The storeroom
either had been a low priority or had been done in a hurry.
In fact, there was a dirt strip all the way around the room,
and the linoleum was curling up slightly and pulling away
from where the floor met the walls.

It occurred to her that they hadn't been planning to use
this storeroom as a prison. The bookshelf was still against
the wall under the vent. She climbed it again. The vent and
the screws that held it were sturdy. She grabbed the vent
cover itself and pulled as hard as she could. She lost her
balance and caught herself as she stepped backward off the
shelf. The grate cover had jangled slightly. It seemed possible that while the grate was firm, the wall was not finished
the way it should be.

She stood looking up at it for a minute. Then she picked
up the brown mug, gulped the last splash of tea, and hurled
the mug onto the floor as hard as she could. It chipped but
did not break.

She climbed back up onto the bookshelf and sent the
mug earthward with as much force as possible.

This time, it shattered.

She climbed down and examined the pieces. It was hard
to believe her luck.

The handle lay, still attached to a two-inch-by-one-inch
portion of the side of the mug. She picked it up and smiled.

Once again she quickly climbed atop the shelf. She began digging at the wall where it met the side of the vent

cover. It brushed away in small spits of powder.

The head scarf, the *hijab,* was getting in her face as she worked. She grabbed it off her head, folded it, and jumped down to put it safely on the first shelf.

She had worn a *hijab* before. It had seemed romantic, then. As she scraped diligently away at the wall, she allowed herself to remember her sophomore year in high school, when her father had taken a year's leave of absence from his surgical practice and her mother had renewed her credential as a nurse to go to a refugee camp in Pakistan. They'd asked her, Susan, and Joey if any of them would like to accompany them. Jaime had been the only one to say yes. Susan had not wanted to miss out on her senior year in high school, and Joey did not want to miss his long-anticipated freshman year.

Jaime went. It had profoundly changed her life. She found that far from being alienated by the vastly different culture, she felt a bond with these people whose will to survive was so strong. She especially enjoyed the company of the women and girls and didn't mind wearing a *hijab* when she was with them. As she came to respect their faith, she discovered new depths of her own Christian faith. She began talking to God on a daily basis. She became close friends with an 11-year-old girl named Ali who disappeared one day. After days of tenacious searching, Jaime was finally told that her family had given the girl in marriage and there was nothing to be done about it. The law was on the side of the parents. For the first time, Jaime wondered if she should become a lawyer.

She also fell in love with a boy named Raïf, the son of one of the Muslim doctors. There was a Romeo and Juliet quality to the relationship, which was as emotionally intense as two 15-year-olds could imagine.

Once their relationship was discovered, Jaime had immediately been called into the tent her father used as his office. In her eyes, her father, Dr. James Richards, was perfect. He held himself a bit aloof, even from their family, but she always assumed he had loftier things on his mind. He'd seemed only bemused when their mother had reported youthful misbehaviors to him through the years. Jaime's parents had assumed that their second child was their last—because they'd decided to stop at two or for some medical reason Jaime didn't know—so even though she was another girl, they had named her after her father. Apparently it was a great surprise when her little brother, Joseph, had joined them the next year.

Jaime had been proud to be named after her father, the great doctor and humanitarian. It didn't mean that he noticed her any more than he noticed the others, but it was a tangible link.

So she had been floored that day in his office-tent at the rage he'd directed at her. *"Don't you understand you could ruin everything, all the work we've done? You selfish girl! If the other doctors, if the camp directors, found out you were seeing this boy, we could be kicked out. Told to leave! I haven't come this far and worked this hard to be thwarted by a juvenile crush! Do you understand me?"*

"But Daddy—"

"No buts. You promise me right here, right now, that you will never see him again. I want your word."

She'd stood her ground. She'd stared him down. She had her principles, too.

"No," she said. "I love him. I won't let us be separated by the prejudice of our elders."

Her father had grabbed her, shaken her. He was tall and lanky, but his grip was iron. His face was red, livid with rage. She'd never seen him like that, never known he was capable of such intense anger. *"It has nothing to do with prejudice. It has to do with an international situation of which you obviously have no grasp. It has to do with hundreds of thousands of lives that can be saved if I can finish my work. . . ."*

She'd stood her ground.

Her mother, who traditionally had acted as the liaison

between father and children, had packed Jaime's things. She'd been sent home.

It had been unnecessary. Raïf had apparently seen reason more easily than she had and had told her, diffidently, that he was already engaged and he could no longer speak to her.

The plaster was breaking off easily around her fingers as she chipped away at it with her makeshift tool.

Jaime understood now that her father was right. She had been 15. It was not a life match. It was not worth causing an incident. She knew her father had been working on a way to bind proteins that could save starving people from death, far past the point when they could traditionally be saved.

But she had loved Raïf.

She grimaced to herself at the self-importance of 15-year-olds.

She reached up and grabbed the grate cover again with both hands. She pulled on it. This time, there was movement.

She picked up the cup handle again and continued chipping, now focusing on the other side.

Another foot soldier facing the wall. Another bullet to the back of the skull.

Another body slumped lifeless on the floor.

Coleman Satis had the strange experience of watching his video monitors as the Commander, the man he had long counted a colleague, walked purposefully through the tunnel entrance to Satis's headquarters, murdering their guards.

What was going on?

Satis pulled his own gun from the side drawer of his desk and held it in his lap, releasing the safety. The knock that finally came on his door was curt and hurried, and the newcomer did not wait for an answer before the door burst open and his form filled the door frame.

"I've been expecting you," Coleman Satis said. "You've had me curious since Gerik reported your surprise appearance at Babylon."

"It's time for us to talk, Satis. Things need to be clarified," said Commander Frank McMillan, letting his gun hand drop to his side, pointing the Beretta casually at the floor.

"By all means, come in and close the door," said Satis. He did not take his hand off his own weapon.

Frank took a step back, pulled the old man to stand in front of him, and pushed him through the door. He kicked it shut and shoved Kristof Remen, letting him trip backward onto the couch.

"It seems clear that our ultimate goals have diverged," said Frank. "Best to come to an understanding now, don't you agree?"

Satis looked at the CIA station chief before him. Frank McMillan was one of those men who had succeeded by making himself the linchpin that held disparate pieces of the operation together. A Knight of Eugenia highly placed in the CIA—as more than a few of them were—he had been assigned to infiltrate the Ancestral Heritage Society two decades earlier and instead had found like minds to his own and a robust organization of usable foot soldiers. While the CIA had been impressed by the depth of his infiltration, he had risen quickly through the ranks of the Society.

Yet Satis had always assumed that if Frank would betray one master, he'd betray two just as easily. The lifeless bodies slumped in the tunnel hallways and displayed on the video monitors to the side of his desk underscored that assumption.

"What is it you're offering?" Satis asked. Part of him enjoyed having elements of surprise introduced by colleagues. It kept him on his toes. Part of him was ready to kill Frank McMillan—who had disposed of several perfectly suitable foot soldiers—and have done with it.

Frank strode over to the desk. "It seems clear that what you're really interested in is Eden," he said. "While I'm interested in more . . . worldly power."

"You prefer being indispensable to the Agency and to our men on Capitol Hill. And to the new American empire."

"Exactly. I will help you find, and conquer, Eden—and to keep as many troops there as are needed. If your information is correct, it is a society without a military force to protect it, so the acquisition should be relatively easy.

You rule Eden, and I manage the rulers of this outside world."

Satis couldn't help but smile. "You doubt Eden exists."

"And you have no doubt that it does," agreed Frank. "So we each think we stand to gain more than the other."

"Our compatriots think I'm crazy, don't they?"

"Everyone thinks you're crazy, Satis. It's part of why no one wants to get in your way."

The businessman asked, "So you think I'm delusional, yet you're willing to plunder Eden should it actually exist. You didn't need to come here in person to say that. What is it you want?"

"Proof that I have the power to possess anything I want from any country in the world. The ultimate gift for Eulogia."

Frank gestured toward Kristof Remen. "You were right about releasing the old man. He did just as you hoped he would, went straight to the museum in Mosul and acquired the missing elements you needed to chart your way to the entrance to Eden. But I think you realized too late that all these things put together are only a secondary source. Even if you succeed in translating the cuneiform, how long will it take you to decipher how the information should be used? And how hard will it be to match the ancient maps to modern topography? It really would be a pity to get this close and miss the opportunity because you needed another day of code breaking."

Satis still had one hand on his leg near the handle of his own Beretta. In the other he held a black Sharpie, which he drummed on the cusp of his desk in irritation.

"Come to the point."

"I think you've realized you let a primary source go in exchange for a secondary source. You claim Remen was your mother's guide from Eden. *He* is the primary source. *He* is the one who knows the way in."

"Until you showed up in Babylon, my actual plan was to

have Gerik recover both the primary and secondary source," said Satis dryly.

"So, instead, you'll have to choose," answered Frank. "I want the sword. In exchange, I give you the guide."

The two men turned as one to look at Kristof Remen, where he sat on the sofa. He met their gazes but said nothing.

"And if I don't agree?"

"I know you have a gun under there, Satis," said Frank. As he turned he raised his own weapon and aimed it point-blank at Remen's forehead. "What happens, if I don't get the sword, is that the only man who knows how to get you to your destination dies. Here. Now. And you don't have all day to decide. In fact, you have thirty seconds. Or there's blood on your couch."

He turned the gun sideways and brought the barrel closer to the old man's forehead. Remen didn't seem to notice or mind.

But Coleman Satis did mind, and he couldn't pretend he didn't.

He went to the steel drawer of his credenza and inserted the key. Then he slowly, dramatically, removed the heavy velvet bag.

"Remove the sword, and show it to me," said Frank.

Coleman Satis had not gotten where he was without learning how to add drama to a demonstration. The hush in the room as he removed the sheathed sword and then, in one long, quick movement, drew the sword from its sheath was replaced by an audible gasp. It seemed the only appropriate reaction.

"So, you, with the foot soldiers and the U.S. military, will still support us in the taking of Eden?"

"Absolutely. We're here awaiting your call."

"And tomorrow, I will rule Eden. . . ."

"And I will guide the leaders outside. Our power will still be joined."

Coleman Satis stepped forward, waited for CIA Station Chief Frank McMillan to holster his firearm, and handed him the soft brown bag. "For Eulogia," he said.

Frank wasted no time. He turned on the balls of his feet and swung out into the passageway with his prize.

Satis turned to the guest newly arrived in his office. "Ah, Mr. Remen," he said calmly. "I had hoped we'd meet again."

It was sadly helpful that the tunnel entrance to Jaime and Kristof's location was punctuated with dead guards. Yani noticed the video surveillance early on and had wondered why there had been no response to his presence. The answer had become clear upon the discovery of the first body. Someone else unfriendly had been down the path before him. He didn't know what was happening up ahead, but he hoped he wasn't too late.

The hardest part of his night had been watching the screen of his handheld and waiting until both Richards and Remen had "landed." It was a relief, and somewhat of a surprise, that they had ended up at the same location, although they had been brought there separately. It gave him the indication that this location was an important one.

A corpse at every corner. Very disheartening.

He rounded a final turn and found a gray metal door. Again, he didn't know if he should be relieved or chilled that it stood open. The opened locks on it were substantial and would have cost him some time had they still been in use.

A quick look at his handheld showed that both his objectives were just ahead, in close proximity to each other, but down different halls. Which to go for first?

Circumstances might force the matter, but if possible, he'd go for Richards first. She seemed more likely to be able to help with the recovery of Remen than the other way around.

He paused by the opened door and listened for sounds of any fighting. He heard none. But he did hear the low talking of two men, possibly guards, in the distance, coming closer.

He moved quickly forward to the juncture of several passageways and used his mirror to look around the corners. Both halls were momentarily empty. He saw doors in both directions and breathed a prayer that he choose the right one to give him somewhere to hide on this, the right side of the gray metal door.

April 9, 2003, 2:16 A.M.
Satis's headquarters
16 kilometers west of Baghdad
Central Iraq

"Kristof Remen. I do thank you for your expertise in choosing the items from the museum in Mosul. The tablets, the atlas . . . all very helpful."

Coleman Satis placed the two ancient tablets on his desktop to illustrate that he was indeed in possession of the treasures that Remen had left in Hammurabi's ruins at Babylon. "And, you see, even though Commander McMillan chose to leave with the actual sword, I do have a tracing of it here—the exact shape and size, if it somehow points to something in the atlas. Obviously, if you knew which items to grab, you know how they interact with each other. I have very little patience at the moment, so I'm hoping you'll be willing to enlighten me?"

Kristof Remen sat, his arms bound behind him, looking benignly at the powerful businessman before him. He didn't speak.

Satis expelled a deep breath. This was exactly how the old man had responded ever since being brought here from his home in a small Swiss village.

The man was irritating.

But Satis had known this about Remen and had planned accordingly. There was too much at stake.

"I have spent my entire adult life tracking you, Mr. Re-men. You were the one who brought my mother out of Eden. I'm not a member of some lunatic fringe. I am a di-rect descendant of an Edenite. And the stories she told me! When I was young, before we had money for a television, she would spend hours weaving stories, telling me of the land of her birth. The colors—she would always come back to the colors. Precious gems so abundant they're used to decorate the outside of the houses. A society of incredi-ble advanced technology. And, I may add, no army to de-fend it.

"Why was she punished so harshly for missing her ap-pointed time to return? For God's sake, she would have died if she hadn't gone into the hospital—or she would have miscarried me! What kind of society lets you never return, just because you miss your one appointment to be taken back to the door?"

His anger had turned his spoken voice to a deep growl. "You were her guide. It took years of looking for my peo-ple to find you, but here you sit. My mother, alas, is not alive to see this day. But if you think I've spent all this time and all my resources bringing you here to be trumped by your smug refusal, I suggest you think again."

Silence filled the room.

Finally the white-haired gentleman spoke. "I'm sorry you have spent so much of your life in search of some-thing, without which you feel incomplete. And I am sorry I am not able to help you," he said.

"Think again," Satis replied. He went to his intercom. "Blenheim," he said. "Please bring in our guest."

APRIL 9, 2003, 2:25 A.M.
The Grosskomtur's *home base*
Five kilometers west of Baghdad
Iraq

They didn't even go inside.

The Fedayeen liaison Gerik had arranged to meet back at his home base was waiting in the dark of the carport. The only indication that he was there as Gerik drove in without headlights was the tiny orange circular glow of a cigarette in the dark.

The night was oddly quiet. No explosions were illuminating Baghdad in the distance. If there was small-weapons fire, the sound did not travel that far.

"I am interested in your proof," the man said from the darkness as Gerik parked his car out front and sauntered to the darkness below the overhang.

"What is the word from Hussein? They're saying he and his sons were killed in this morning's attack."

"They do not yet know the kinds of 'insider misinformation' they're dealing with," the man replied. The moon had already set, which made the darkness thick. Gerik could see that the man was thin and tall. He had a large fist-shaped birthmark on his left cheek. He did not wear a beard, but his chin evidenced several days without a razor.

"So, Uncle Saddam is alive?"

"Who else would have this kind of available cash?" the

man asked irritably. As he did, a second man in black robes stepped up behind him. The newcomer was meant to seem threatening, and he did. The first man reiterated, "I said I was interested in proof."

"You don't have the luxury of demanding proof. Your people double-crossed us," Gerik growled.

"You were not moving quickly enough."

How's the war going? Was the invasion quick enough for you? Gerik wanted to say. But this was a business meeting.

"Whatever your reasons, we are successful. You are not. The price has doubled. We have a man who spent his boyhood in Eden," Gerik continued, referring to Coleman Satis. "He has led us to the guide who knows the way in."

Gerik handed him a computer-generated aged photo of Kristof Remen and then a Polaroid photograph of the actual man.

"The door opens tonight, and we will be there. I don't have to tell you it is the ultimate hiding place. People disappear into Eden as if they've disappeared off the face of the earth. And so they have.

"As further insurance," Gerik continued, "in case anything untoward befalls our guide, we now have our own map to the entrance." This time Gerik handed him a photograph of the sword and sheath, another of the cuneiform tablets, and finally a small square photo of the atlases.

"You may recognize them as items missing from the museums yesterday morning. They were gathered by a team of specialists. We are confident of our location, and we are happy to share our information with you, although you were not so forthcoming with us. Can you meet the price?"

"We are willing to pay if your information is accurate."

"You yourself know that Mr. Hussein has gotten very close to the entrance himself. It has certainly taken years of searching and hundreds of thousands of acres of marshes drained. He perhaps doesn't even know how close he's come. But I can't think of a more fortuitous time for him to find out. He needs a place to hide. We can supply him with one. Assuming you have the cash."

Gerik was now so accustomed to making deals that he might or might not live through that he was beginning to feel impatient. He was doing his best to disguise the fact that it made him tremendously impatient to deal with men who weren't even Aryans. Civilization destroyers, at best, these two. But who cared, as long as they had the cash that would help further the Cause?

"I have the bank account number," said the *Grosskomtur*. "You have the apparatus to make it happen?"

The first man said, "You will give that number to me. I shall make a phone call; then we shall wait here until someone who has access to your account calls to tell you it is suddenly richer."

"Agreed," said Gerik. "And, by the way, if our 'uncle' is not currently somewhere south and east of Baghdad, he will want to be heading in that direction. The rendezvous is eight P.M. I shall return to headquarters so kindly furnished by our uncle, and will call you when we are leaving with the guide."

"Very well."

And both men went to place their separate calls.

April 9, 2003, 2:27 A.M.
Satis's headquarters
Central Iraq

The floor of the storeroom was covered with chalky dust
before Jaime was able to forcibly pull the grate out of the
wall above her. Her arms were tired from working so diligently above her head, and the site of her old baseball injury throbbed. Now that the grate was open to her, she had
to figure out what to do. Yes, the opening was probably
large enough for her to squeeze into. But how could she
possibly get up far enough to hoist herself in?

She climbed down and looked at the incessantly ticking
strawberry. She had twelve minutes before someone came
for her—assuming they were also keeping track of the
hour Satis had given her. They would not be pleased with
the use she'd made of her time. She had to be gone by then.

How to get up to the open grate? When she surveyed her
options, it became clear that the bookshelf was her only
choice. She'd been standing on it for 40 minutes, and obviously it was too low. Unless . . . she wedged her shoulder
against it and pushed it upright, so that it was standing on
its side, lengthwise rather than horizontally. Her *hijab* fell
to the floor, and she scooped it up.

It took three tries to hoist herself up on top of the
shelves. Once she did, she could see into the ventilation

shaft. It seemed she could barely fit into it, if at all. And it was dark.

Two strikes against it. She certainly didn't want to get wedged in, stuck in the oblivion of a dark duct.

But there was no other choice.

She struggled to pull herself up. There was nothing to grab hold of. She finally was able to wedge her shoulders into the rectangular opening of the duct, then push against the wall with her feet to propel herself farther in. Once her weight was on the floor of the duct, she almost lost her nerve. She had never thought of herself as frightened of confined spaces, but the walls and ceiling closed in tight around her.

She would have given up, except as her eyes adjusted to the cloying darkness, she saw the barest hint of light ahead of her down the shaft.

Jaime headed for the light.

She worked her way forward, arms outstretched. She looked at the dim bars of light ahead and cleared her mind of any other objective.

Slowly she crept. At one point she looked ahead and was surprised to find she still carried her head scarf in her hand. Her hair had been released from the French braid, and it swung free at shoulder length. She wasn't used to having it in the way. It kept falling into her eyes as she moved. Of all the times she had wished her hair to be free of confining Army regulations, this wasn't one of them.

She wondered how many minutes she had now before someone came for her and noticed she was missing.

Her whole world became the dark rectangle of space that stretched before her.

Finally, she arrived at a spot parallel to the shafts of light, finding they shone through a grate identical to the one she'd removed. She pushed at it with her hands, but it was fastened tightly enough that it didn't move. She remembered how shoddily the wall itself had been finished alongside the other grate, and she pulled herself forward down the shaft past the grate until her feet were even with the metal. Slowly and deliberately she started kicking one side with her heels. She longed for her Army boots instead of the sandals she'd been given. After what seemed like several minutes, she finally felt movement. Emboldened, she kicked with renewed vigor.

Her kicks became more aggressive, and eventually her heel hit metal and kept going. The grate had come free from one side of the wall. This gave her confidence and she bashed at it with both feet at once. After a dozen strikes her feet hit nothing when she kicked. It had swung open.

She didn't know what kind of room it opened into. But at the moment the room was unoccupied. That was as much as she could ask.

Jaime lowered herself feet first. She was afraid at any moment she would be discovered missing. If anyone fired a gun through the shaft, there was no way she wouldn't be hit. So she slithered out as quickly as she could. Once her waist was through, she dropped to the floor.

She was in another storeroom. This one had not been cleared. Boxes and building supplies lined the walls. Obviously the building they occupied was not yet complete.

She didn't have much time. She had to be out before they came for her and found her gone. She didn't want to put her head scarf on, but she might need it to complete her costume when she emerged. She tied it around her neck, the ivory material hanging down her back.

This door opened easily from inside. The hall matched the only other one she'd seen. The walls were lined with mottled white marble, as were the floors. Doorways were outlined by black marble, coming to a rounded peak above the portal. A decorative balustrade railing of raised marble protruded about four feet from the floor and ran the length of the walls. She knew she was in Coleman Satis's headquarters, but again, she couldn't figure out where or why there were no windows.

This corridor was vacant. She heard voices to her left,

so she went right. She reached a right-hand turn. She stopped and looked quickly around the corner, wishing she had one of Yani's mirrors. There was a short hall with one closed door. Another hallway crossed it, maybe 25 feet ahead, and then it continued on, becoming flanked with doors. It seemed straight ahead would take her into the heart of the headquarters. The hall ended in a T-turn to another corridor. She thought she saw the backs of a few guards there, but their focus was on the hallway in front of them, which likely contained Satis's office.

Which way led out? She needed to get to the next corner to see if there were any clues.

What was her plan? Should she flee, or should she try to rescue the sword?

Since she was without crucial information, alone and unarmed, it seemed the height of hubris to think she could rescue the sword herself. No. Best plan was to get out and alert the authorities to its whereabouts. That was mission enough.

Her first objective was to get to the next intersection and see if there was any indication of which way might be the exit. Her hour was surely up. There was no time to waste.

She took the calculated risk and ran up the right-hand corridor to the only doorway. As she'd hoped, there was just enough room in the door frame for her to push herself back and be hidden from sight.

She slowed her breathing. She peered around the corner and saw that the two guards at the far end of her hall were still talking. One suddenly stepped backward. She flattened herself back. As she did, two things happened. She heard the flick of a cigarette lighter as the guard turned away from his cohort to light his cigarette.

And she saw a flash of movement as someone dashed across the intersection just in front of her.

The guard with the cigarette obviously saw the same thing. He mustn't have been sure what he'd seen, because he didn't shout and run. But he did say something to his partner, who came around the corner to look down the hall and picked up a walkie-talkie. Then the two men started in her direction.

Her only hope was that they would turn before they reached her, down the hallway where the person had disappeared. Unfortunately, the guardroom they'd alerted was behind her. Voices approached from the direction she'd just come.

What now?

If it had been three minutes earlier, she still would have been hidden in the second storeroom. As it was, she had nowhere to run. Her heartbeat accelerated. The guards from behind rounded the corner and nodded to the guards coming the other way, who indicated that the intruder had turned at the corner. All the men drew their firearms at the same moment.

The two additional guards had nearly passed Jaime before the closer one saw her in his peripheral vision.

Startled, he stopped and stared at her blankly for a couple of seconds. And then he took a step back and pointed the barrel of his Beretta at the center of her forehead. His friend started yelling something in French.

The guard walked her out into the middle of the hall and indicated he wanted her hands on her head.

She obliged, her injured shoulder burning.

The first two guards, dressed in black pants, white golf shirts, and black vests, led the way around the corner with their guns. Apparently, that hall was now empty.

The four conferred, gesturing at Jaime.

Along with the adrenaline pumping through her veins, there was also anger. Who had spoiled her hard-won escape?

One of the men pointed to the second door up the hallway where the intruder had run. It looked to Jaime to be the storeroom where she'd been kept. Two of the men approached it, guns high, and pushed on the handle. It opened easily. The locks had been undone from outside. They kicked the door fully open and dropped into firing stance, yelling something in French.

"All right, all right. Ya got me. Don't shoot," came a voice she remembered all too well. It was Bill Burton's Texas drawl.

And Yani came walking out the door, hands on his head, two guns pointed at his heart, one at his head.

As they brought him down the hallway toward Jaime, his face lit up. "Hi, darlin'," he said. "I'm mighty relieved to see you."

It was as though he were sauntering through an air-conditioned office building in Dallas. When he reached the spot where she stood, hands still on her head, four guards surrounding them with loaded, cocked weapons, Yani stepped up to her, put his right hand on her shoulder, his thumb tilting her chin, leaned down, and kissed her.

It was an openmouthed, proprietary kiss. He was tall and made of steel, and everything in his demeanor said he knew what he was doing. Jaime fought to hide the fact that even in this most unlikely of circumstances, her body had ignited like a brushfire.

The guards, who had been trained to expect most things, did not expect this.

Yani turned to them, his hand still on her shoulder. "I suppose you want to know who I am," he said. "Bill Burton." He extended his hand as if expecting a handshake.

"You're with the U.S. Army?" said one of the four. He had extra pins on his shirt, which Jaime took to signify rank.

"Army? Lord, no. If I was Army, you'd be hearing helicopters and bullhorns, don't you think? Just me. I promised my ladylove here that I'd always be there for her. I admit you gents gave me something of a challenge to make good on that."

They were all still staring at him. He stood, half-grinning, his hand now draped around her shoulder.

"You're alone?" said a second man.

"Yes. Came alone. Followed my girl."

It had been a while since Chaplain Major Richards had

been referred to as a girl. "Hands on your head!" It was the
senior guard, getting his sea legs back.

Yani obeyed. The top man again pulled out his two-way
radio. He spoke back and forth to someone Jaime thought
she recognized as Blenheim, again in French. Jaime's only
French had been in high school, but she did her best to understand important snatches of the conversation. Apparently, they bought Yani's assertion that he was alone and
not military. Blenheim was perturbed that Jaime had been
able to escape. The guard asked if he should bring Jaime
and the intruder directly to Satis's office, but Blenheim, beginning to sound distracted, said not now, something more
important was going on. Blenheim then said irritably that
the prisoners should be locked in the most secure room
available until they could be dealt with. There was a pause;
then he gave instructions for which room that should be.
The guard's eyebrows registered surprise.

The conversation over, the leader, whom Jaime began
calling Bruno in her own mind, seemed at first a bit non-
plussed that something was happening that could be more
important than the escape of a prisoner and the entry of her
intruder boyfriend. But as Bruno realized that both Satis
and Blenheim now were otherwise urgently occupied, a
sense of his own power settled on him like a mantle. He
waved his gun, indicating that they should move down the
hall that led into the center of the headquarters. He exuded
authority over the other men and his captives.

When they reached the far corner, Jaime found she had
been right. It was the hall that held Satis's office. They kept
walking, past four other closed doors, to the end of the corridor, where they drew up, all together, before one single
locked door. It was different from the others. Instead of
having a gracefully curved Arabic design over it, it was
flanked by rigid Doric columns, supporting a triangular
Greco-Roman carving over a black steel door. The door
simply bore the three numbers 322.

The leader took out a ring of keys, unlocked two dead

bolts, and finally opened the lock under the door handle. It reminded her of Paul and her small Manhattan pied-à-terre, which they used when he taught late classes at Union Theological Seminary—except this one had the locks on the outside of the door, instead of the inside.

The door swung open. A light switch was thrown. But the dim illumination that came on was red. Surprised, Jaime looked up to find a skull and crossbones above the inside of the door frame. The red light shone out of the eye sockets of the skull.

Would wonders never cease?

The room before them was like nothing Jaime had ever seen before. On the floor at her feet, the number 322 was spelled out in mosaic tile. In the middle of the room was a square table, with what looked to be a skull on a pillow, next to a five-minute hourglass. Dark wood wainscoting rose halfway up the wall. Directly across from the door was a large fireplace, with a small coffin in front of it. Above the mantel hung a full skeleton. It looked to be child sized. She shivered. Below the skeleton was a gold frame. She couldn't tell what was in the frame. The only other light came from a long glass case on that same wall. Inside hung another full skeleton, this one adult sized.

What was this place?

"Cuff her," Bruno said to his compatriot. Two men roughly turned Jaime around, pulling her arms behind her and fastening the zip-tie cuffs around her wrists. They were tight enough that they irritated her shoulder and bit into her skin. She wondered if Satis purchased them by the gross.

Bruno and a second guard were patting Yani down. They took everything out of his pants pockets, including his small handheld screen, and made him take off his tennis shoes. She was fairly certain their best escape aids were being removed.

The guards stood him up, roughly pulled his arms back, and cuffed his hands behind him as well.

"Wait. I have an idea for the lovebirds," said Bruno,

whom Jaime was liking less all the time. He was certainly milking his temporary power status for all it was worth.

He brought Yani over to the square wooden table that sat in the center of the room with the skull on it and sat him down with his back against the table leg. Bruno then cut off Yani's cuffs and recuffed his hands behind the leg of the table. He cuffed Yani's ankles as well and instructed another guard to bind his legs together with a thick nylon cord. Yani seemed unperturbed by all this, as if they were serving his meal at a nice restaurant in Dallas, instead of trussing him up to await execution.

Her turn. Dear God.

Bruno grabbed her and steered her over to Yani by the bindings on her hands behind her back. "Sit on his lap," Bruno demanded.

"What?" she asked, confused.

He pushed her down, roughly, so she was indeed sitting astride Yani's lap, facing him. Bruno used the sharp shears he carried to cut off the cuffs behind her. Then he pushed her into Yani's chest. He shoved her arms forward, grabbed her wrists on the other side of the table leg, and cuffed them again. Her arms felt like they were being wrenched from their sockets. Pain screamed through her injured right shoulder, and she exhaled heavily to keep from crying out.

To make matters worse, he instructed another guard to pull her legs around the wooden table leg as well, and they cuffed her ankles.

She could barely move. In fact, pulled tight against Yani's black knit polo shirt, she could hardly breathe.

What a fine way to spend the final minutes of her life.

"You did a bad thing, trying to escape," Bruno said. "I'll see to it that it doesn't happen again. *Ladylove*," he said with a snarl.

And the guards left the room, chortling with laughter.

Andy Blenheim proudly led the young boy through the hallway to Mr. Satis's office. This was the meeting Blenheim had been waiting for and wondering about—when Satis sent for the boy.

"The young master," Blenheim said. The old man was still seated on the divan, arms bound behind him.

"Another job for you, Blenheim," Satis said, motioning his assistant over to him. Andy approached at once, and Satis pointed at the monitors in front of him, which received feed from the cameras in the tunnels. He gestured distractedly toward the square screens that showed the lifeless bodies of the murdered guards.

"Tell the remaining foot soldiers that we need cleanup," he said.

Andy Blenheim looked at the monitors, speechless.

"The Commander did leave a mess," Satis said. "See to it."

"Yes, sir." Andy made a small bow toward his boss and left the room.

The boy didn't even look at Satis. "Uncle!" he said instead, his face igniting with hope. He ran to the gentleman and fell on his knees, throwing his arms around him and burying his face at Kristof Remen's waist.

"Uncle Kristof, why are we here?"

"Such a touching scene!" Coleman Satis sat back in his desk chair. "Let me answer that question for you, boy. You're here because your great-uncle has been very unhelpful. He will not respond to threats of any kind against himself. He has had a good life. He would not mind a little pain. He is even ready to die, should the need arise. But even such an evolved man as he must have some feelings. Especially for a child. The only son of his only niece. How much pain will it cause your mother—both your parents—to lose you? Certainly there is no secret worth watching a young life be wasted?"

Kristof wished he could put a hand reassuringly on the boy's thick brown hair, which had a slight natural curl. He wondered how long ago the boy had been kidnapped from his parents' home in Geneva. Kristof's niece, Annaliese, the college professor, must indeed be wild with worry. And Stefan, with his sense of humor and his imagination, was a favorite child of everyone.

"Let's get something straight, Mr. Satis," Remen said. "Your mother did not lose her way back to Eden because she was hospitalized to save her unborn child. She was 'cast out,' because it became clear her values and priorities were no longer in concert with those of her neighbors. She was not abandoned. She was brought out, taken to her country of choice, which was the United States. A home and a job were found for her. She left with blessings in her ears. If she told you anything different, it was embellishment for her own purposes. But she lived a life of power and acquisition. It was her own choice; it was what she wanted. You have been successful in the same life. Trust me when I say that you are happier here, now, than you ever would be if you found what you think of as Eden."

"I'd like that decision to be up to me," said Satis. "My mother did tell me stories of her home. I would like to visit. And I believe you can show me the way."

"I've told you, I can't. I was a guide at one time. But when I retired, I chose a simple life. It has been decades since I knew the way to your mother's home. I can be of no help to you, no matter what you threaten. So please do not debase yourself this way."

"Let me show you something. It's an eloquent statement of what I believe." Coleman Satis turned back to the locked cabinet where he had kept the sword and that now held the original cuneiform tablets from the museum. He dialed in a combination and opened a back compartment.

He brought out a beautiful candelabrum. It was gold filigree and fitted with the same six precious stones that had been in Adara's bracelet: ruby, carnelian, turquoise, lapis, jade, mother-of-pearl. And there was an inscription. It was in a foreign tongue; even the writing looked ancient.

"What does it say?" asked the lad.

"Would you like to translate?" Satis asked Remen.

The old man replied, "It says: 'Who Rules Eden Rules the World.'"

"Exactly," said Satis. "And I do plan on that being me."

April 9, 2003, 2:52 A.M.
Satis's headquarters
Central Iraq

Andy Blenheim was becoming consternated. Things were not going as he expected. The Commander, the *Grosskomtur,* Satis. They were three strands of an unbreakable rope. What was happening?

Satis said the Commander had committed murder. But why? None of these murdered men would have stopped him from entering; in fact, they would have given their lives for him without questioning.

More distressing yet was that Mr. Satis was deviating from his oft-stated beliefs. Andy couldn't believe that the Commander had demanded the sword from him—and he had handed it over. Just like that. No argument, no struggle. The Sword of Life, which they had each sworn to give their lives to obtain and protect. And when Satis spoke to Remen, and the Commander, of the coming night, he did not mention Aryans, or the Society, at all.

"What's up, then, Andy?" asked a soothing voice, a female voice. He turned and found one of the people he revered more than anyone: one of the Adepts. The Adepts were Aryans whose spirits had become so transparent that they could experience life on a much higher level. It was said that these Aryans, who were specially anointed, taught, and trained when they were discovered, were developing the extrasensory abilities that once belonged to all Aryans. He believed it to be true.

He had seen this young woman, at a meeting in South Carolina, explain things about the universe no one had ever envisioned before, yet they made perfect sense. She also intuitively knew things about Andy that he had never told anyone.

She was intelligent, compassionate, freethinking, and only a bit spooky. He liked her very much. To his mind, she was the perfect example of the New Society, of the promised future.

"I'm glad you're here, Miss," he said. "I don't know what's happening."

"What do you mean?" she asked. "What is happening?"

"The Commander was here earlier. He took the Sword of Life with him. Mr. Satis let it go, just like that. And guards are dead in the south tunnel—Mr. Satis knows about it and is not upset in the least. But his whole life has been the Society, leading and preserving its members. I don't know what's going on. And now, of all times. This is the Time. Our time. What is he doing?"

As he spoke, he made an important decision.

"I have brought the young guest to Mr. Satis. You know of the young guest? I wish you could meet him. He's a boy, but he has a quality about him. He's important to the cause; I'm sure of it.

"Come. I want to show you something." He turned and led her down the hall, away from Satis's office.

She looked at him with guarded curiosity but followed behind.

He took her to the small, bunkerlike room he had been slipping into often tonight. As soon as she was inside, he closed the door behind them.

Now her expression was one of amused interest. "What is this place? Why have you brought me here?" she asked.

"I want you to—that is, I think you should—see what is happening in Mr. Satis's office tonight."

He brought her over to the small fish-cye view of the next room as it was encoded into files. Coleman Satis stood up and moved angrily from behind his desk.

"Come here, boy," he was saying.

And with that, Liv Nelsson came to stand beside Andy Blenheim to watch the proceedings.

"I just want to thank you so much," Jaime said through clenched teeth, "for ruining my chances at escape. Your timing isn't the greatest, is it? Fifteen minutes earlier, you could have saved me the whole crawling-through-the-vent thing. Two minutes later, you could have led me out. But noooo. You had to show up just in time to make sure guards come running down my escape hall. How did you do it?"

"Hey," he said. "If you could have escaped five minutes quicker, I would have been right there in the tunnel, waiting to be your guide. Ten minutes later, I would have been in your room, helping you get out. But no, you've gotta run just in time for them to spot you and guess exactly where I'm hidden. Bravo."

"Yeah, and thanks for the 'ladylove' thing. That was real helpful." He didn't know how lucky he was that her hands were not free.

"Sure, sweet potata," he said in Bill-Burton-speak. "Anytime."

Then he dropped the accent and the swagger. His posture relaxed and he said quietly, "The truth is, if they believed I was military, we'd both be dead right now."

"Yeah. And here is pretty great." She looked around the

cerie crypt in which they sat. "What is this place? It's like . . . a tomb in the red-light district."

"Memento mori," Yani said simply. "Remember that you must die."

"I would have liked to forget that fact for maybe five minutes today. Any five minutes. That doesn't explain where we are."

"We're in an incredibly good re-creation of 'I.T.'—the Inner Temple of the tomb that stands on Yale's campus," he said, looking around. "Even a copy of the grandfather's clock. Satis spared no expense."

"What are you talking about? There's a tomb on the Yale campus?"

"It's not an actual tomb—although there are allegedly real mummies and skeletons inside. The skull of Geronimo, and the skeleton of Madame Pompadour, the French socialite. I'm not sure who the child's skeleton is supposed to be. Or the mummy for that matter. It's the headquarters for a secret society called Skull and Bones." Yani said this as if it explained everything.

"You mean that Yale fraternity? Coleman Satis is so carried away with a fraternity that he's replicated their frat house basement in the Middle East?"

"It's not actually an undergraduate fraternity, although members are 'tapped,' or chosen, at the end of their junior year. It exists mostly to foster relationships among the members after they leave school. And it's been very successful, especially in United States politics, in all three branches of government, in the intelligence community, in publishing, banking, and big business—but the reason you should know about the Skull and Bones is that if it weren't for several highly placed Bonesmen, you probably wouldn't be here in Iraq at all."

"You're going to have to explain that one."

"The Knights are really into philosophy. And the CIA. Joining the Agency is thought of as a default career for any Knights that can't find a better job."

"Knights? What Knights?"

"They call themselves the Knights of Eulogia. The story goes that when the Greek orator Demosthenes died, Eulogia, the Goddess of Eloquence, ascended back into the heavens—in mourning, I guess. Anyhow, she stayed there from 322 B.C., when Demosthenes died, until the founding of Skull and Bones. At which point she descended again to take up residence with the fellows in New Haven. Hence they're each dubbed a Knight of Eulogia."

"And what does this have to do with U.S. troops being over here?"

"I'll tell you—because you do have a right to know why you're chained up in a tomb—but, Jaime, we've got to work while we talk. We don't have much time. Next time they come for us, I cannot guarantee such a happy outcome."

She said, "I hope you have a plan that doesn't involve any gadgets they took from you. Or cyanide capsules."

"No, nothing so drastic. You seem to be in pain, though. Are you all right?"

"Old sports injury. Shoulder. I'm OK; it just hurts." *Incredibly* went unsaid.

"You're a trouper. Now. We're going to talk through this before we do anything. OK. Are you listening carefully?" he said. And she realized his muscles were relaxed and his tone was reassuring.

"Yes," she said.

"What I will need you to do is to get the sunglasses out of my shirt pocket. Then the two of us together are going to figure out how to take the plastic cover off the ends of one of the wires. We're going to need to do this carefully, because underneath is a razor-sharp knife. Then, we're going to drop it so that one of us can reach it and cut through a handcuff. Once we have one hand free, the rest of the process will go much more quickly.

"Now. Once you have the glasses, I suggest you hold them in your teeth while I remove the plastic cover with mine. And please, remember to be careful. Once the razor is uncovered, it will slash through skin with incredible ease, so don't go swinging the glasses around in triumph."

"Got it," she said.

"My hands are below yours," Yani said. "So it seems most likely I'll be able to pick up the sunglasses from the floor. And with any luck, I can angle them to cut through my cuffs."

Jaime gave a sigh of relief. "Sounds good."

"Ready to do this?" he asked.

She felt his words through his chest, where her head was resting. She could also feel his heartbeat, strong and steady, and for a fleeting moment she thought, *I wouldn't mind staying like this for a bit.* She remembered many quiet Saturday afternoons lying on the bed with Paul, her head on his chest. He would have one arm wrapped around her shoulders as he read to her. Occasionally he would pause in his reading, lean down to kiss her forehead or cheek, then return to his reading. Jaime had so loved those quiet, intimate moments. The warmth of their bodies lounging closely together. His scent. Yani smelled different, a mixture of earth and sweat, strong and comforting. *What am I, nuts? They could return any minute and put a bullet through my head, and all I can think about is comparing this mysterious, arrogant, infuriating man to Paul? Get a grip, Richards. Focus!*

"Ready."

She went for it. The sunglasses protruded just slightly above his pocket. The hardest part was getting a firm enough grasp to actually pull them up and out of the pocket. As she did, they unfolded and she found she was holding the ear wire up, as needed. It was tricky to pull her head back so that he could reach it, but he finally grasped the plastic cover with his teeth.

It was nerve-racking as she tried to hold the glasses steady and he tried to pull the casing off. If either of them dropped the glasses, they'd be stuck.

But he was able to pull the plastic off slowly, between

his teeth. She gripped the glasses as tightly as she could. There would be a dangerous moment when he ended up with the revealed knife in his mouth. She stayed perfectly still, without flinching.

Finally, the casing came free. He looked at her and said, "You hold them," through his teeth.

She did.

"OK," he said. "So far, so good. It seems our best bet will be if I take them from you, then drop them back over my shoulder to the ground."

She nodded.

They passed the glasses from her mouth to his. He took the glasses, turned his head where he could look over his left shoulder, and dropped them, adding a slight propulsion to the toss. They fell soundlessly onto the carpet.

He turned back and let his fingers search for them.

"So are you all right?" he asked. "Did they hurt you?"

His conversational tone caught her off-guard and it took her a moment to realize he was talking about her captors, not the sunglasses. A million retorts came to mind. "I'm OK."

"You weren't raped?"

The question felt uncomfortably intimate, intensified, perhaps, by the way they were bound, as well as the taste of his recent kiss. She was glad she was not looking him in the eye. "No," she said truthfully, "I'm pretty sure not."

"Good," he said. "If you were, I would have had to have words with this Gerik Schroeder."

The absurdity of the situation hit her. Unexpectedly, she started to giggle.

"What?" he asked.

"So if I'm drugged, it's OK; kidnapped, why not? Stripped, threatened, bound, not a problem. But if he raped me . . . I suppose killing me would have merited a real talking-to."

"A stern one, you can rest assured. Ah. Found them."

His arms strained behind him. "But can't reach them. We're going to have to try to move an inch closer."

Together they tried to get traction to pull themselves closer. "The drug he used was chloroform," Yani said. "Used it on Rodriguez, too."

"He's got Rodriguez?" She tried to sit, startled, but was abruptly pulled back to Yani's chest by her bindings.

"No. Gerik left him at Babylon. He's fine."

"Who's Gerik?"

"Grosskomtur Gerik Schroeder. The man who killed Adara. And kidnapped you."

"Violet eyes?"

"So I've heard. Never actually met him. Ah. Got them. Hmm. Thing is, I can't maneuver them to reach my own cuffs. But I think I can hit yours with the knife. You willing I should try? I'll do my best not to open any major arteries."

"Go for it," she said. "So, where are we? Still in Iraq?"

"We're in a partially finished palace in what was to be a gated lake community just outside Baghdad Airport. For some reason, the upper, unfinished floors were bombed. While this quite nicely finished basement remains untouched."

"We're by *Baghdad Airport*?"

"Yes. Try to bring your hands farther down. OK. That's better."

"So we're in a basement. That explains the absence of windows. And this is a tomb fashioned by members of a Yale secret society, to which Coleman Satis belongs."

"Yes. Along with three presidents, dozens of congressmen and senators, at least two members of the Supreme Court, many people in the State and Defense Departments— and your friend Frank McMillan, the CIA station chief who was bivouacked at Tallil."

"*Frank McMillan?*"

"Class of '78."

"So what does it matter if a lot of Bonesmen are CIA?" Jaime asked. "What does that have to do with why we're at war with Iraq? We're here because Saddam Hussein has weapons of mass destruction that he is capable of using against the United States."

"Supposing he doesn't."

"But he does."

"Supposing."

"I can't suppose," she said. "Why would we possibly risk the lives of American soldiers—American kids—if not to defuse an imminent threat?"

"You've studied philosophy. What do you know about Hegel?"

"Hegel? German. Believed in the good of the state over the individual. Right?"

"Skull and Bones is an offshoot of a German university club that agrees with Hegel on many points. You're right. The state is pure Reason. 'The march of God in the world.' Everyone's highest calling is to sacrifice him- or herself to the good of the state."

"You're telling me our kids are dying for the glory of the state?" She sounded as angry as she was.

"Hegel believed it. Both the kaiser and Nazi Germany believed it—and Hegel's theories, by the way, were supported by the upper classes of many countries, including Britain and the United States. And yes, American money, including some Bones money, financed Hitler.

"But Hitler lost, and now he's labeled evil, and the theories have morphed. Bonesmen are patriotic. They believe Hegel's New World Order should be an American World Order, for the good of the rest of the world. Hegel did believe, as many do today, in 'controlled conflict' to bring about a necessary synthesis. Which in this case means that America needs an ally they can control in the midst of the Middle East. So they're creating one."

"I don't believe you. Americans don't believe in empire building."

"I think they'd quibble with you over the wording. But they believe in increasing the military presence of the

United States to take up 'global responsibilities,' to 'challenge' hostile regimes such as Hussein's, to 'extend an international order' friendly to the United States. I'm not making this up. It's published for public consumption, and displayed proudly on the Internet."

"But America doesn't believe in world domination, which is what it sounds like you're talking about!"

"I'm sure they mean it with the best of intentions."

"So we've gone to war simply to 'challenge' a regime we felt to be hostile. To forcefully plant a new ally in the Middle East. And Bonesmen have led the charge." Jaime's tone was incredulous. "And Frank McMillan set up the ambush, and the robbing of the museum?"

"It's likely, yes. Pull your wrists as far apart as possible. Have I got it? Can you feel the knife pushing on your cuffs?"

"Yes."

"Hold very still. I've got to exert some pressure."

She did as he asked and pulled her cuffs to make the plastic taut, glad the guards had used a double restraint that was made from the same nylon material through both loops and the center.

"The sword that was stolen this morning, they had it here," Jaime said. "I held it."

"It's gone now, though," Yani said. "One more thing you might want to know about your friend Frank. Besides being a CIA agent and a Bonesman, he's also Commander of the Ancestral Heritage Society. He is playing all three sides against the middle. He is working with Satis, and with Gerik. Well, he *was* working with Satis. He stopped in earlier this evening, killed several guards, and took the sword you held. He passed me on the way out."

Jaime gasped. "Frank McMillan is in this with Satis and Gerik Schroeder?"

"At least now we know who's giving them inside government and military information," Yani said. "As well as supplying information to the Agency and likely the executive branch—although I doubt his friends high up in the U.S. shadow government would approve of his extracurricular activities. And—we know who bugged you."

"Well, if we know who bugged me, we can all certainly sleep well tonight. So you came here just to fetch me?"

"Yes and no. I'm also here for the man who knew your parents. Kristof Remen. We've got to get him and get out of here. We've got to ensure he reaches the site first."

"The site?"

"Yes. The site of tonight's rendezvous."

"And what is your part in all this?" Jaime asked.

"I'm basically the driver," he said.

Then, he did the last thing she expected. He stopped what he was doing and rested his chin on the top of her head. They were both still. For a magic moment, there was peace. She felt safe.

Then the moment passed.

"Here we go," he said.

With that, he pushed hard with the knife against the center of her cuffs, and she heard the plastic rip apart. She pulled her hands free in triumph. Each still had a loop around it, but she didn't take time to slice them off. She reached back again and carefully took the sunglasses-knife from Yani's hands.

The rest of the job still was not easy. Even with her hands no longer bound around the table leg, it was difficult to reach the cuffs that held her feet bound tightly. Finally she managed to cut them apart. With a huge sigh of relief, she climbed off Yani's lap. She stood for a moment, massaging her shoulder and the blood back into her limbs, looking at the skull on the table below her, wondering if it was real and, if so, who it had been.

"Alas, poor Yorick," she said. Couldn't help it.

Then Jaime knelt and sliced Yani's hands free, and handed him the knife to do the ropes around his legs.

He stood, also flexing his feet and hands to get the blood flowing. Together they went to the hallway door.

The series of locks were flush with the door from the inside. She remembered the thickness of the dead bolts on the other side when they'd been brought in.

"Would have been easier with your gadgets, huh?" she asked.

"It presents a bit of a challenge," Yani replied.

They both sat for a moment, taking a breather, wondering how they were going to get out of that room.

"Memento mori. Are we dead?" asked Jaime, finding no reason to sugarcoat the situation.

"Not as long as we're alive," he answered. "But it does present a challenge."

April 9, 2003, 2:54 A.M.
Satis's headquarters
Central Iraq

"Come here, boy," Coleman Satis said, his patience sizzling to an end. "And hurry. I can call guards in to bring you forcefully, but I don't want to hurt you before I have to."

Stefan turned to Kristof, his eyes questioning.

"Yes. Your uncle has the answer to your plight. The sooner he decides to help, the sooner you will be free. Meanwhile, if you'd prefer not to be dragged by angry guards, come on over here."

Stefan stood. He walked over to join the media mogul by his desk.

"Take this and put it on your friend's lap," he said. He handed the child a small pile that included folded fabric, a roll of gauze bandages, and a short length of plastic tubing that could be tied as a tourniquet. Stefan walked across and balanced it on Kristof's legs, since his hands were still bound behind him. He gave Stefan an encouraging wink. Stefan turned back with a bit more confidence.

This time, there was a leather office armchair awaiting him in the middle of the floor. Satis patted it, and Stefan sat.

Satis presented Stefan with a large stainless-steel bowl, the size of a large salad mixing bowl, and rested it in his lap. Then he crouched behind the boy and ran his hands up and down the boy's arms.

"Let me tell you what's going to happen," Satis said. "Within the next few moments, I will use this long razor to slice open the young man's left wrist." Satis had opened a shaving razor, which had a sharp blade, six inches long. As he spoke, he ran the flat side of it against the flesh of Stefan's arm. "Only the left. His life's blood will begin to run out into this bowl. It will take a while for him to lose enough blood to pass out, and a while after that for him to lose enough blood that he will die. If it takes too long, we will slash his right wrist as well." He stared at Remen, trying to see a flicker of response.

"Don't worry, boy," Satis continued. "It will only sting for a second. But once your wrist is cut, don't think of trying to fight or run. That would only cause your blood to pump harder, for the end to come more quickly.

"But you, Remen. You may stop the bleeding at any time. You tell me how to get back to Eden, and we immediately free your hands so that you may bind the boy's cut and stop the bleeding. He will stay here, of course, while you come along to show us the way. If we come to a bogus end, the boy is dead. When we reach the real site, he's sent back to his parents. His fate rests completely in your hands."

The nine-year-old looked at the older man with wild, frightened eyes.

"Be brave, Stefan," Kristof said quietly. "I am praying that God will give you extra, unexpected courage. It is not so bad to die. I will die soon, myself. And what is on the other side is . . . wonderful."

"Oh, for God's sake, Remen!" Satis snapped. "The boy should be terrified! And he should be mad as hell at you, his killer!"

With a deft, quick move, Coleman Satis pressed the razor's sharp blade down and drew it across Stefan's exposed left wrist. Blood spurted out, missing the bowl altogether. Stefan whimpered and tried to raise his arm, but Satis held it down and positioned it over the bowl.

"Go ahead, Remen. Go ahead and tell him how great it's going to be to die. Tell him how his mother will be lost in grief for the rest of her days. Tell him it's because of your stubborn adherence to a cause long lost!"

"Stefan," Remen said again, his voice strong. "Have courage."

As he spoke, the door burst open, and Andy Blenheim and Liv Nelsson burst through.

"Satis, what are you doing?" demanded Liv. "This has nothing to do with the cause! A true Aryan would never do such a thing—never think in such a way!"

"You stupid girl," Satis snarled. "Get on board, or get out of the way!"

In that split second, the boy leapt up from the chair, instinctively pulling his arm up against his chest. As the adults squared off against each other, he darted between them and out the door, leaving a trail of blood behind him.

Coleman Satis stared openmouthed for only a split second as the youngster disappeared out the door. "Blenheim!" Satis yelled. "Send the guards after him!"

"They're removing the bodies from the south tunnel, on your orders," said Blenheim.

"Well then, you help me catch him!" bellowed the mogul. Expecting total and immediate obedience, he rushed out the door after Remen's idiotic grandnephew.

Thus Satis did not see Liv pick up the razor from where it sat on the floor beneath the boy's chair. She went over to Kristof and quickly cut through the center of his handcuffs. As she helped the white-haired man to his feet, Blenheim came forward, pulling a long ring of keys from off his belt. He handed it to her, with one long, ornate key extended.

"Room 322," was all he said.

April 9, 2003, 3:09 A.M.
Satis's headquarters
Central Iraq

They'd known something was going to happen, and likely soon, so when they heard the running and shouting in the hallway, they weren't surprised.

Jaime and Yani stopped work on the third lock, and they both stood silently at the door. "Here we go," said Jaime.

"Remember. The minute the door opens, I take their attention. You run. They won't expect us to be free."

She nodded and moved back to stand against the wall, waiting. And sure enough, here it came: the sound of someone undoing the top lock with a jangling ring of keys.

Jaime closed her eyes. The guards had to have noticed that the three bottom locks were not locked. She told herself to keep focused on her escape route. The element of surprise wouldn't last for long.

But when the door swung open, it was the two of them who were in for the surprise. Liv Nelsson stood there. "Follow me, quickly," she said. "We've got to save the boy."

As she spoke, an old man rounded the corner. He carried bandages in his hand. He wasn't running, but his walk was unexpectedly quick and spry.

He nodded at Yani and motioned after Liv, who began to run.

"Follow the blood," he said.

Confused, Jaime looked down to see a trail of blood heading in front of Liv, up the hallway. Here and there someone had stepped directly on it and it had been flattened into a partial shoe print.

"Hurry!" Liv urged as she rounded the corner ahead.

Yani took off running behind her. Jaime looked back at the old man, clear now that he was the old man. He gave her a gentle smile and urged her to follow Yani. And so she did, as quickly as her sandals would let her go.

April 9, 2003, 3:19 A.M.
Satis's headquarters
Central Iraq

Satis was not a man used to being crossed. He would catch
the youngster, and he would hurt him in some way that
would make Kristof Remen crack. There was no way he
was getting this close and giving up. He would get the information by sheer willpower.

The boy was running quickly, down the hallway that led
past the bedroom where he'd been kept captive. He
wheeled around the next corner. It was a dead-end hall,
which led only one place: to an iron door that closed off
the basement from the upper palace, a door to which only
Satis and Blenheim had the key. The boy would have no
way out. Which was why Satis was stunned to find the iron
door standing open, the boy having disappeared up the
wide stairs into the darkness above.

Satis roared with anger at this latest development. He
was furious at Blenheim for his obvious carelessness—
carelessness that could lead to disaster, should the boy
somehow escape and raise the alarm.

But the boy didn't know his way around upstairs. Satis
did.

He heard footsteps behind him and looked back to see
Andy Blenheim. Where was that girl, that Adept? Why

wasn't she with him? Certainly she would help as well.
The staircase made a square turn and came up behind a
hidden door to the upper level. The boy had already pushed
through, with all the strength he had. Once Satis was
through the movable wall, cool air hit his face. He hadn't
actually been outside in a fortnight. The night was silent
but still hung with an acrid smell of lingering smoke. He
cursed the fact that he had been holding the boy and the razor and had put his gun back into the credenza. He needed
a damn gun.

The moon had set, and the stars in the clear sky above
did not provide much light through the large empty marble
window holes. Saddam's workers had completed the basement headquarters before they had finished the five upper
floors of the palace. The walls were built, but scaffolding
still stood outside. In what was perhaps a smarter move
than they'd realized, the Americans had bombed the upper
floors of the empty residence. Stefan had found the wide
mouth of the staircase to the second floor, and he scrambled up it. It was odd that while the workmen had already
carved a relief of a marble banister into the walls of the
grand foyer, they had not yet installed actual marble banis-
ters on the staircases themselves. It didn't matter on the
stairs to the main floor, because the inside wall was intact
and the stairs themselves were clear.

But the grand staircases above that entry floor were now
covered with rubble from the bombing. Surely the boy, injured as he was, could not make it any farther up.

But the boy was running for his life. Nimbly, like a
mountain goat, he picked his way up through the rubble to
the next floor.

"Damn you!" roared Satis, following behind him. He
wanted to order Blenheim to light the way, but there was no
way he was going to give away their location now, with the
"coalition" parked right across the lake.

Satis had to pick his way more slowly up the stairs. He
knew that the light of day revealed the Hussein legacy—

allow shoddy workmanship beneath, then cover everything with marble. It was the same with the staircases. Even had they not been bombed, he would not have wanted to count on them being safe in 20 years.

He came up to the third-floor landing and heard the boy crying softly before he saw him. He was standing, pale and small in the darkness, in the corner near where the staircase continued up. He was holding his arm bent up at the elbow, trying to hold his hand across his wrist to stem the flow of blood. By now he must have known that Satis was right: Running made the blood pump faster. He was killing himself.

In the center of the five flights of circular marble stairs was a gaping hole that led straight down to the basement. It was as if the boy knew it would not be safe to continue up, with all the rubble, when there was no handrail or banister to separate him from the chasm beyond the edge.

But he saw the outline of Satis, the man who didn't know him but who was killing him anyway. He turned and ran.

Satis ran, too.

Now it was more than a matter of killing the boy. It was not letting him get out onto the roof of the palace, to make any noise, to give away the location. The last thing Coleman Satis needed at this moment was to be discovered on the very brink of success. He'd be more than willing to toss the kid off the roof just to get rid of him.

It was hard to pick through the large chunks of bombed concrete, stone, and marble that covered the stairs, especially in the dark, and Satis slipped twice, cutting his upper arm through his silk turtleneck. Damn! He was sorrier about ripping one of his favorite shirts than he was about the surface cut.

They were on the fourth floor now. He turned to look behind him, but there was no sign of help.

"Blenheim!" he spat. He was sure by now that his trusted lieutenant had secured Kristof Remen.

"Yes?" came the answer from below.

The entirety of the fourth floor was rubble. Apparently the targeted missile had hit high. There were gaping holes in the roof. Satis didn't even stop to think how he was going to get the boy back down. Stefan seemed to be slowing. But he caught his breath as he saw Coleman Satis picking his way through the debris toward him. He turned to the final flight of stairs and started to climb.

It was taking Stefan a long time to find his footing to get up the stairs. With each step, he sent a footfall's worth of debris showering down behind him. His slower pace, however, gave Satis a sense of hope. He was closing in on the boy.

The two of them pressed forward, straining to find safe footholds as they climbed. There were none. The staircase was a moving mélange of destroyed building and roofing materials. Stefan was trying to pull himself up, choosing the larger chunks of debris as clinging points. He chose one that didn't hold, and he slipped backward down three or four stairs.

Satis gave a roar and lunged up for him.

It was a bad move.

The debris Satis grasped held, but when he put his foot down, the concrete chunk gave way. Satis tried again. Nothing.

He pushed himself to the side, but the debris gave way in a downward shower. With both hands, he reached up for something solid to grab onto. There was nothing. He was slipping, and he could not stop himself.

It was hard to see in the dark, but he knew he was sliding sideways. He kicked backward, waiting to catch a foothold.

With his next try, his foot hit air.

Panicking, he used both hands to grasp something, anything heavy enough just to stop him. Just to stop him so he could reposition himself to slide down the steps. But there was nothing. And now his other foot hit air, and he was screwed. He tumbled down into space, into the center of the stairwell, with nothing to stop him, nothing but air . . . nothing at all.

He looked up. Through a gaping hole in the roof he saw the stars in the sky. But they grew fainter and farther away and then he hit, on his back, something hard under the center of his back, and then the back of his head hit marble.

"Blenheim," he whispered, nearly inaudibly. Andy Blenheim's face appeared above him.

"Where's Stefan?" Andy asked, bending down to hear Satis's words.

"Roof," said Satis. "Help me!"

But Blenheim was up. "The boy is on the roof," he said, and he moved off with the others.

"Help," said Satis, his voice failing him now.

Three other people ran by him, none even stopping to look. "Take these," he heard the voice of Kristof Remen saying, and one of the others returned to Remen briefly.

Then the old man knelt by the side of the dying Coleman Satis. He looked with sadness upon this broken man, whose life had been lived in opposition to all that Kristof held to be good and true. Yet he could not hate Satis, in spite of the harm he had caused to those Kristof loved. He could only pity him.

"I forgive you," Kristof said.

Satis tried to rally enough to spit in defiance. How could it be that this man, who had betrayed his mother, was there to torment him now? But he did not even have the strength to show his disdain.

Kristof Remen sat beside him and took his hand and said, "Then let me pray for you."

Those were the last words Coleman Satis ever heard on this earth.

Jaime and Yani found the climb slow going once they reached the third floor. But they continued up together, hurrying through the darkness, staying pressed against the outside wall of the staircase. Yani held the small bundle of bandages Kristof had given him.

Once they reached the fourth floor, the two of them stood staring at what were the remains of the final staircase. Even if they could find a path sturdy enough to climb, there seemed no way they would be able to find their footing to get back down.

"Stefan?" Yani called up.

"I am here," he said in French.

"We are friends of your uncle," Yani returned fluently, also in French. "We are coming for you. Are you safe? Are you sitting down?"

"I am lying down," said the boy. "I am not feeling well and I'm scared!"

Jaime looked behind them, out the huge, paneless window set into the wall of the stairs they'd just come up. She thought she saw the shadow of something outside, and she turned and carefully picked her way downstairs.

"Yani!" she said, and he turned his attention from where

he was trying to clear the stairs to the roof.

She motioned, and he came back down. "Look."

On the outside of the building still stood a large scaffolding, stretching from ground to roof. "Is it solid?" Yani asked. But he was already on the window ledge, trying his weight on the metal crossbars. They seemed sturdy enough that he was soon out the window, scaling the scaffolding above. Jaime gave him a moment's head start, marveling at his ability to negotiate the scaffold with only the thin light of the stars, and headed up after him.

There was a four-and-a-half-foot difference between the top of the scaffolding, which had three planks across it as a floor, and the rooftop. Yani hoisted himself up with ease and clambered over. Jaime spent a moment consciously not looking down before she grabbed for the roof ledge and propelled herself up. It helped that she couldn't see the ground through the darkness. The long tunic hampered her range of motion.

Once she was safely on the roof, she made her way over to where Yani knelt over Stefan.

Yani had already used the rubber tubing as a tourniquet on the boy's upper arm. He was talking to Stefan quietly, soothingly, in French. "This is Jaime," Yani said. But he said it in French and, perhaps without realizing it, did not translate her name to the English, with a hard *J*. He had transliterated her name, *jaime*. Love.

"Allô, Stefan," she said, giving him a smile.

"Jaime, could I have you here, on this side?" Yani asked.

Jaime was more startled than she expected to be, hearing Yani use her given name, and in such a friendly, off-hand way. She knew he was doing it for the sake of the boy, but still, it was . . . different.

She knelt beside Yani. He had unfolded the bandages and was pressing one gauze bandage down, hard, inside the boy's wrist. "I need you to hold pressure on his wrist while I prepare another bandage," Yani said.

She nodded. The boy's wrist was so small, so thin around. How could anyone just slash it?

Yani unrolled a length of cloth bandage. He indicated that he was going to wrap it around, and Jaime lifted her hands and replaced them over each layer of cloth, keeping the pressure constant. Satis had even provided a small, round metal container of adhesive tape, which Yani quickly opened. He cut off half a dozen pieces with his teeth; then he and Jaime together applied them tightly to the bandage.

As they did, they heard Liv's voice from below them. "If you can just get him to the fourth floor," she said, "I can get us down from there."

"All right," said Yani.

He scooped the boy up easily, as if he were a doll, and headed back toward the scaffolding. "You go first," Yani instructed Jaime. He said it with such easy authority that it never occurred to her to ask how she was supposed to make that first dangerous drop. She lowered herself onto her stomach, looked back to gauge her distance, and went back over, feet first. She landed safely on the planks. "I'm handing him down," he said, again conversationally.

Where the heck do you go to school to learn how to sound outrageously calm while holding a dying boy on the roof of a bombed palace in Iraq, knowing there's a five-story drop beneath you? she wondered. *What do you do, role-play? "This time, you be the megalomaniac, I'll be the mysterious driver . . ."*

She realized she'd heard Yani take this tone of reassurance and respect several times today—whenever he needed help from a normal person who might reasonably be expected to panic. She herself had gotten "the tone" several times.

He already had Stefan lying on his stomach, legs over the side. Jaime was able to reach them and maneuver the boy safely to the small platform. Yani was quickly down with them. He scoped out the piping that led down to the single board outside of the window through which they'd exited.

"Stefan, you're in for some fun," he said, once again lapsing into French, punctuating with a smile. He picked up the boy and positioned him over both shoulders, like a shepherd with a lamb. "Can you grab around my neck?" Yani asked. "Do you feel like you're safely on board?"

"Oui," said the boy. And before Stefan had time to either look down or rethink, Yani had swung down off the boards onto the bars that ran down the side, and presto, he was on the lower board. "You coming?" he said jovially to Jaime.

By the time she had a grasp of the scaffold, he and the boy were already back inside. They were waiting for her, with Liv, on the fourth floor.

"You're not going to believe this," Liv said, "but the elevator still works. I just tried it out to make certain." She took them over to the glassed-in passenger elevator that ran alongside the dangerous staircase. Four people were certainly the maximum, but they were all more than happy to pile in, Yani holding Stefan.

Kristof Remen was waiting for them when the elevator reached the main floor.

"How is he?" he asked Yani.

"He's weak, but if we can get him to help soon, he'll be all right. Satis?"

Remen shook his head.

Yani then turned to Liv. "Where's your friend?"

"You mean Andy Blenheim?" she asked. "He's ordering the foot soldiers out of the south tunnel. He's also cleared them out of the hallways we've just come through. He assumes that's the way we need to escape."

"Can we trust him?" Jaime asked.

"If it weren't for him, you'd still be locked up, and the boy would be dying in Mr. Satis's office," she said. "Besides, I don't think we have a choice. I know the best way out."

"I'll meet you in a moment," said Yani, and he slipped off by himself.

The others followed behind her, moving as quickly as Kristof Remen could. True to her word, she led them through a small back hallway that circumvented the main office hall, and let them out of a small door next to the tunnel entrance.

There they waited for several minutes until Yani reappeared. He looked at Kristof and shook his head. "The tablets have disappeared," he said. "Someone has taken them. But there's no time for anyone to use them now."

Blenheim had done as he had promised. There were still splotches of blood along the floors from the bodies of the fallen foot soldiers. But there were no signs of guards, living or dead.

They moved quickly and quietly through the semidark tunnels. Richards had no idea how she'd gotten into the basement headquarters, so nothing looked familiar to her. After 10 minutes, they came to a fork. The small group stopped.

"The airport complex is this way," said Liv, indicating the right-hand route.

Yani turned and handed her the little boy. "Take him back to the airport, to coalition troops, and hurry. He needs help quickly."

"But . . ." she sputtered.

"Thank you," said Yani.

"No," said Liv. "Please. I want to come with you." She was looking at Kristof pleadingly as she spoke. "Please. I've waited so long to talk to you. Just to talk to you."

"You've done us a great service," said Yani. "Now our paths diverge. Please help the boy."

"But, sir . . ." This was addressed to Yani.

He looked at her, really seeing her, but shook his head.

"Mr. Remen, please," she said, unwilling to give up. "Why can't I come? What would it hurt? Aren't I ready?"

Kristof went to her. "No," he said in a kind but firm voice. "You must remove yourself from the company of those who hate. You must divorce yourself from those emotions, as well." Then he put his hand on Stefan's head and gave the boy a kiss on his cheek. "Go back to your parents. Give them my love. I won't see them again. Grow into a fine man. Make them, and me, proud. Remember this adventure, and how much courage you had."

Remen pointed Liv down the other passageway. Then he turned, and he and Yani walked quickly straight ahead.

Jaime stood, dumbstruck, at the intersection. She looked down the hallway that led to Baghdad Airport. Obviously, that was where she should go. She was "whereabouts unknown"—missing in action. She needed to return. Soldiers would be put in jeopardy just looking for her. But how could she leave without talking to the old man? And Yani . . . you'd think he would at least say good-bye.

As she looked at Liv, now disappearing down the hall carrying the boy, Jaime felt an iron grasp on her forearm and turned to find Yani. This time his tone was not reassuring at all. "Sorry," he said. "Not yet."

"But—the airport . . ."

"Jaime, there's no way I can let you go yet. There is too much at stake, and it all has to happen too quickly. I'll do everything in my power to guarantee your safety."

"I think I've heard that before, when was it? Oh yes, just before we went to Babylon."

"Get moving."

"No. Not unless you start talking. Telling me the whole truth about what's going on."

"Come," said Kristof Remen, with total authority. "We've got a long car ride. Plenty of time to talk."

She stood, stock-still, at the crossroads.

Yani said, "I know you're a dedicated soldier. If you need me to incapacitate you to relieve you of guilt about not going back, I will. You know I can. But hey—let's not and say we did, OK?"

She did know he could incapacitate her. And he would if need be. But the most compelling reason for coming along was standing next to him. The man she'd come this far to meet. The man who knew about her parents.

Jaime looked Yani straight in the eye. And she said, "Kiss me again and you're dead."

This unexpectedly caused Kristof to chuckle as the three of them headed back down the tunnel to the left.

After another eight minutes of jogging through the underground maze, the threesome came to a small antechamber.
It was clear this was the door to the outside.

Kristof Remen was slightly out of breath, but not really
what you'd expect from a man who looked to be in his
mid- to late eighties. Yani was not winded at all. He turned
to Jaime and said, "This might be a good time for you to
put on your *hijab.*"

To her surprise, it was still wrapped around her neck,
where she'd tied it in the storeroom. It was a one-piece
scarf, in a plain, older style, not unlike the simple ones
she'd worn back in the relief camps, although it did have
lace at the edges. It was long and would fall a couple feet
down her back.

She felt the men watching her, probably waiting for her
to ask for help. But she untied and smoothed the cloth and
expertly fit it around her face and over her loosened hair. If
she wanted to melt into the local population, she knew, the
blond hair would not help.

Yani indeed seemed impressed at her skill. She gave no
word of explanation, only smiled under her *hijab*; she

smiled even more when she realized they couldn't see her smirking at them.

"Ready?"

She nodded. Yani opened the door and motioned them to stay back. He went out first, alone, then came back and motioned Jaime and Remen out.

It was a relief to move out into the night. The tunnel entrance came out through the side of a small berm by a narrow dirt road. Two palm trees were directly in front of the door. They had to squeeze through one by one.

Jaime stood, grateful to be alive, in the night air.

It was quickly apparent that neither of her companions had stopped, even for an instant. They both headed up the road, Yani in the lead.

So much for her moment of profound gratitude. They were walking with purpose, and it wasn't until she was nearly upon it that she was able to see the outline of a car under the shadow of a stand of trees. It was an old, beat-up car. As they arrived, someone got out of the driver's seat and opened the back door for Kristof to climb in.

Yani motioned Richards around the car before taking the driver's seat. The man who'd been waiting opened the other rear door for her. Apparently she was to sit in the backseat next to Remen. That suited her fine.

It was as she sat on the old bench seat and looked up to thank her helper that she got the shock of the night. Smiling back down at her was Staff Sergeant Alejandro Rodriguez.

The second car, waiting a half mile up the road, sat dark and silent until the rattletrap driven by Yani was out of sight. Gerik was in no hurry. He'd give them a mile head start, at least. If they entered any kind of urban setting, he'd move in closer.

It was all he could do to make himself pick up the radio and call the Commander. "They're out and moving," he said. "No sign of Satis or any foot soldiers. It's only Richards, Remen, a driver, and a guard."

"Do they seem apprehensive about being followed?"

"Looks like they have no clue. Not a care in the world." Oh, how he hated Frank McMillan. Gerik had always been wary of the man. But today the man had shown his true colors, as a traitor and a destroyer.

Frank claimed the scene he'd created at Babylon was to prove how far undercover he was. Bullshit. You don't betray an ally without warning. And he claimed the taking of Remen, the killing of the guards, and the taking of the sword were all to position the Ancestral Heritage Society in a place of power over Satis. But those had been perfectly good foot soldiers he had killed, purebloods each one, hand chosen by Gerik for work at this important location.

He knew their families. He knew their wives. He knew their bloodlines.

As far as Gerik was concerned, Frank's place in the Ancestral Heritage Society had ceased to exist. Once this night's mission was complete, Frank was out.

Actually, he was too dangerous to have on the loose. Correction: After tonight, after he had played his role by orchestrating the disparate bands of soldiers, Frank would be dead.

"Excellent. So you think they're really heading for the Objective?" the traitor asked now.

"Where else would you be heading at four in the morning in a country at war? If they pull into a safe house and hunker down, we're out of luck. But that would happen quickly. I don't think they will. They seem ready for a road trip," Gerik replied.

Neither man said what both were thinking: *It's come down to this.* Either they were about to hit pay dirt or their years of preparation would be for naught.

"Keep me apprised," said the Commander, and he signed off.

—PART FOUR—

*The Sword
of Eden*

When Jaime came to, it was full daylight. After they'd reached the car and she'd felt among allies, she hadn't so much fallen asleep as passed out. It had been over 48 hours since she'd slept, except in a drug-induced haze, and her body's Herculean effort to stay alert and functioning had taken its toll.

When she opened her eyes six hours later, she had no idea where she was. She slowly realized she was in the back of a car, lying across the seat, her head resting on someone's thigh. She put a hand down on the seat and pushed herself up.

"Hello," said Kristof Remen. "Did you have a good rest?"

"Yes, I think so. Thanks."

As she spoke, Rodriguez turned around from where he sat in the passenger seat and handed her a canteen. She took it and drank, gratefully.

"What are you doing here?" she asked him.

"I was kidnapped, too," he said, pointing over at Yani, who drove. "My bad luck."

None of this was making any sense. "Alejandro," she

said, pointedly using his given name, as she sat forward. *"Why are you here?"*

"My job is to protect you."

She noticed that he was no longer wearing his uniform. He did have his M-16 resting against the seat, however. Jeez. How often were you kidnapped and asked to bring your weapon?

She sat back and looked out the window. They were on a one-lane road, traveling at a pretty good clip. Local people were out walking, children in colorful tunics, women in black veils. Even wearing her *hijab,* she felt underdressed.

"Where are we?" she asked.

"South," said Yani, "in between coalition forces at the moment."

"What time is it?"

"A little after ten," said Rodriguez.

She realized that with him also in civilian clothes, they looked as much like a car full of locals as they possibly could.

"Seriously? I slept that long? Where are we headed? Are we almost there?"

"We've still got a couple of hours to go," said Yani.

"I told you we'd have time to talk," Kristof said. "I hear you're Jaime Lynn Richards. And you want to know about your parents."

"Yes, I am. And yes, I would."

The old man sat back and began talking softly. Those in the front seat would really have to listen hard to catch even snatches of what he was saying. "I met your parents only once, briefly, at the relief camp in Pakistan. I take it you know about your father's work? The breakthrough he was working toward?"

"I know he was working with enzymes. And ways to bring people back from the brink of starvation, with many fewer physical problems than they normally would have had."

"Yes. That's the crux of the matter. His work had come

to the attention of those who understood its importance and had the means to bring it to fruition. I met with your mother and father to make arrangements for such a meeting. It was a rendezvous at a location only I knew.

"Unfortunately, others who did not have such pure motives heard about this meeting. Someone followed your parents on their way. When they realized they were being followed, they immediately began to backtrack. They'd come a circuitous route—flown from India to London to Jordan—since it wasn't safe to come through Afghanistan and Iran at the time. But backtracking by car, they only got as far as a hotel room in Jordan when they were found. They would not give the location where they were to meet me, even under threat of torture." Kristof shook his head. "It was a terrible crime, whoever committed murder that day. I have been told it was a young man, a member of an Aryan organization. One who had violet eyes."

"Wait a minute. Are you saying . . . could it be . . . the same man who killed Yani's sister, Adara?"

"As I said, I was not there. But it seems likely."

Jaime sat up straight to clear her head and noticed how hungry she was. Partly to assuage her hunger and partly to buy a little time, she leaned forward. "Rodriguez, you don't have anything to eat up there, do you?" she asked.

He rummaged around on the floor at his feet and pulled up two brown rectangular plastic sacks of MREs. "Chicken stew or cheese ravioli?"

"Throw the ravioli back here," she said. She tore it open and fished around for the side dishes, because she wasn't in the mood to heat anything. Fortunately, there was peanut butter and a slice of bread. She folded the bread to made a sandwich.

"Excuse me if I'm confused, but I need to back up a few steps here. So, someone was following Mom and Dad to something secret, something worth killing for. Which was that, the location or the investors?"

"For thousands of years, there has been a rendezvous

point that many people would like to find. What makes it difficult for them is that usually there's nothing there. Only at the appointed time. The violet-eyed man knew the time was approaching and that your parents were invited to the rendezvous. I was to be their guide."

"And we're heading for that same rendezvous point now."

"Yes," said Kristof, "we're heading in that direction."

"Again, all due respect," said Jaime, "but given the current political climate, couldn't you have chosen a different location? Like, I don't know, the lobby of the Barclay Hotel in London?"

The old man chuckled. "That would have made my life easier, certainly."

Jaime turned again to Yani, in the front seat. "I thought you told me my parents died protecting that famous sword," she said.

Yani glanced back in the rearview mirror. "Jaime, I'd like you to meet Kristof Remen. He is the lost Sword we were looking for."

Kristof took over the story. "That's true," he said. "I am a member of an organization whose history goes back many thousands of years. The organization is called the Sword, and each member is also known as a sword."

"Thousands of years old?" Jaime asked.

"Yes. Information about us appears in hundreds of millions of homes around the world. It's right under most people's noses, in their Bible, and they don't realize it. 'And at the east of the Garden of Eden he placed the cherubim and a Sword flaming and turning to guard the way to the tree of life,'" he quoted Genesis. "The Sword it speaks of is a secret society made up of the chosen few who know their way to the site of the Garden of Eden."

"That's exciting, that there's an actual site," Jaime said carefully. "But please answer the question I've been asking all along. If my parents died protecting you because you know where the Garden of Eden was, well, why? Why is everyone so determined to find the site? What's there that's so precious, anyway?"

"Ah," Kristof said. "You ask the question at the crux of the matter. The idea of a Garden of Eden is like a Rorschach test. Ask people what they expect to find in

Eden, and their answers tell you more about them than about Eden. For example, race separatists like our friends in the Ancestral Heritage Society or the Aryan Nation are sure those who rendezvous there are 'purebloods.' For them, the Garden of Eden is a parable of life before 'the Fall'—or the intermarriage of races.

"Our well-meaning friend Liv is sure that those who gather there are a transcendent people who have sharpened spirits and quickened intuitions.

"Coleman Satis, on the other hand, was sure he would find power and riches." Remen shook his head. "Whereas, at this moment, you probably would say that paradise is a hot shower and a cold beer."

"Possibly," Jaime admitted, slightly irked that he would sum her up in such a surface manner, even in jest. "Yet you're telling me that my parents thought if they accompanied you to the rendezvous at the Garden site they'd find medical research investors? None of this still makes any sense. Who actually does meet there?" She was getting annoyed.

"I'm sorry," Kristof said gently. "I can't tell you."

"Then why am I here?" Jaime asked, her frustration clearly in her voice.

Yani heard the question. He locked eyes with her for a moment and looked back to the road, where other cars and larger groups of pedestrians were beginning to appear. "The short answer is, because Adara trusted you. Because, God help you, you were in the right place at the right time. You did a great service by bringing me the information chip. It warned me to find and deliver Kristof. And to make another pickup as well."

"Another pickup?" She was aghast. "You're serious, aren't you, Yani? You're a glorified taxi driver. You're picking up fares all over a country at war, and you're taking me and Rodriguez with you!"

"There is a purpose greater than our individual lives at work here," he replied.

"I'm willing to listen to your larger reason," she said. "I'm all ears."

"You have to trust me," Yani said simply.

She wanted to thump him, yet again. But they were entering a town. A town full of people who may or may not be thrilled to see American soldiers.

A man with a wooden cart and two women in black veils turned to look at the car. For while all its occupants had done their best to look like Iraqis, they were obviously not locals.

The hairs on the back of Jaime's neck bristled. She saw Rodriguez's hands tighten around his lowered weapon.

"Where are we?" she asked.

"Al Qurnah," Yani said. "We'll only be a minute."

"I've heard that one before," Jaime whispered under her breath.

"Yes," Kristof agreed with a smile. "Me, too."

April 9, 2003, 11:04 A.M.
Al Qurnah
Southern Iraq

It felt great to get out of the car, if even for a moment. Yani said simply that he needed to make a pickup, and he disappeared across the concrete square. "This is a park," said Kristof as he also got out and stretched.

"A park?" Jaime asked, incredulous.

"See that tree over there?" he asked. "That's the Adam Tree."

"Wait—did you say we're in Al Qurnah?"

Kristof nodded. Jaime turned and looked more closely at the tree. It was tall, gaunt, gray, and as dead as could be in the late-morning sun. But she knew from her studies that the town of Al Qurnah stood at the current confluence of the Tigris and Euphrates rivers. Since the biblical accounts of Eden said that the Garden was at the meeting place of four rivers, two being the Tigris and Euphrates, when flooding rerouted the Euphrates in the 1950s, Al Qurnah had taken advantage of its new location and turned itself into a tourist Mecca. They'd found a suitable old tree, called it the Adam Tree, and built this park and several hotels around it. Never mind the tree had been planted in the twentieth century and had never borne fruit. Anyone hoping for a taste of fruit from the Tree of the Knowledge of

Good and Evil would apparently have to keep looking.

But Jaime was thrilled to be here. "So, the river that is beyond that wall is the Euphrates?" she asked. Remen nodded again. "Wow. The place is . . . dried up," she said.

The remaining one-story hotel behind the tree was boarded up. She had heard of the great tragedy—how Saddam Hussein had drained the wetlands of Southern Iraq, turning eight thousand square miles of marshes and wetlands into only four hundred. The Marsh Arabs who had lived—and made a living—there for five thousand years were displaced. Many went and built their bamboo and mud huts on the outskirts of local cities. A small number stayed where they were, suddenly desperately poor, and prayed that someone would reflood the marshes and return their livelihoods.

Hussein had done it to punish the Marsh Arabs—mostly Shiites—for fighting against his regime in the decade-long war with Iran. The Shiites had also hidden enemy guerillas in the marshes, where those unacquainted with the local landscape could never find them.

So Hussein had drained the marshes, thus perpetuating one of the greatest human-caused environmental tragedies of all time. Some said that punishing the Marsh Arabs was in reality a cover for Hussein's search for the entry to Eden.

It was clear that entry wasn't here. It couldn't be, could it? But why did Yani bring them all this way, to park near a dead tree?

Curious, she started across the park. Rodriguez had gotten out of the car, his weapon casually behind him. Kristof strolled beside her.

It was as if a smoke signal must have gone up. Suddenly a large group of children appeared from nowhere, encircling them, laughing. The children wore mostly bright colors, and the little girls were young enough to wear short jumpers and tights, without any head covering. The boys wore long robes yet were incredibly nimble at climbing the few live trees that survived in the park.

One little girl wore a ruby red jumper over a striped shirt. She looked up at Jaime almost shyly.

"They are so happy, so hopeful, aren't they?" spoke a low voice behind her, in English, with an accent.

Jaime turned to find Gerik standing at her shoulder, his Beretta resting in the small of her back.

How did he get here? This man who had ambushed her convoy, murdered her friend, drugged and kidnapped her—and possibly killed her parents? Her stomach lurched and she felt like she might be sick. How did he turn up wherever she was? Was he the incarnation of evil itself?

"We meet again, Remen," Gerik growled to Jaime's companion. Gerik waved his gun just enough to show Kristof Remen that he meant business. "Move back to the car, both of you," he ordered.

Jaime looked back over at the car surreptitiously. To her surprise, Rodriguez was gone.

She and Remen moved back in that direction. The group of children dispersed from around them, aware that something disconcerting was going on. They were obviously children whose survival depended on reading adult situations quickly and acting on that information. They moved away. The little girl in the red jumper and striped shirt looked back at Jaime, leaving reluctantly.

They were almost back to the car when Yani appeared behind it, followed by two men, both dressed in robes. One had the sun-colored skin of a local, but the other was plainly white, with white hair and a salt-and-pepper beard. His face looked familiar to Jaime, but she couldn't place him.

Then Yani saw Gerik.

The park went silent. Insects stopped their buzzing; birds in the trees hushed mid-song. The only sounds came from the children who still played six yards away, unalarmed.

Gerik spoke. "You give me Remen. Or you take me with you."

"I don't think so," said Yani.

"You don't seem to understand," Gerik said, still in English. "You don't have a choice."

"There is always a choice," Yani replied calmly.

"Get into the car!" Gerik commanded in a hiss. But Jaime, Kristof, Yani, and his guests stood, unmoving.

"Put your gun down, and your hands on your head!" came Rodriguez's voice from where he appeared, two yards behind Gerik.

Jaime watched as Gerik's shoulders tightened. He did return his Beretta to its holster. But instead of placing his hands on his head, in one swift move he took a hand grenade from his belt, removed the pin with his mouth, and lobbed it into the center of the group of children.

Everything that passed through Jaime's mind did so within a splinter of a second. She saw that Yani was on the far side of the car. Rodriguez had lowered his gun and was on the move but was yards away in the opposite direction. She was by far the closest to the children and the only one capable of reaching the grenade before it went off.

As she dove toward it, she wondered if she still had time to grab it and throw it clear or if she should just jump on top of it to absorb as much of the impact as possible.

It was unexploded when she reached it. "Run!" she screamed to the little girl in red, and the children saw what she was grabbing. They turned to flee—except the little girl, who stood in shock. Jaime took a precious second to pull her arm and the grenade back to lob it.

Jaime let it fly in the direction of the river wall, and then she turned and pushed the child to the ground and fell on top of her.

The grenade was over the wall but not yet in the water when it exploded. The shock of it rocked the entire park, and the children fell to the ground, protecting their heads with their hands in a familiar move as shrapnel flew through the air.

Jaime looked up again, toward the car.

Gerik had redrawn his firearm. It was cocked and pointing directly at her.

She stood up, raised her hands, and stepped slowly away from the little girl.

His fury was white-hot. Through the years, Gerik had trained himself to make use of his anger, to use it to help him think more clearly. And now, clearly, he knew that he had no further use for this hated woman. He was here for Remen.

He could murder her. Finally.

The electricity that ran through his arm to his trigger finger in that moment before firing a fatal shot was the rarest, most intense pleasure he knew.

He had her directly in his sight.

He squeezed the trigger.

He shot to kill.

As he did, a rush of movement came from her left. Someone had jumped in front of her. It was a man, slightly shorter than Jaime. At the same time, Gerik heard another gun fire. In the widening expanse of seconds, Gerik saw the man take the bullet in the chest—and he felt a searing pain as a bullet tore into his own left shoulder.

Furious, he fired off four more shots directly into the man, whom he now recognized as the chaplain's assistant. All four hit their mark.

He saw Jaime where she'd fallen, on the ground behind her lackey. She had to move, soon, and he would pick her off.

But as Gerik focused on the chaplain, he saw five men moving around the outside of the square.

He forgot Jaime Richards. He forgot Kristof Remen.

He turned and ran.

April 9, 2003, 11:20 A.M.
Al Qurnah
Southern Iraq

Jaime lay expecting another round of gunfire.

She heard none.

She put out her hand to touch Rodriguez. He did not respond. She knew he was hit and at least unconscious. Every instinct told her to get up and drag him to the car. But that was what Gerik wanted. With Rodriguez injured, she was at the mercy of a ruthless killer.

This was it. She was moments from dead.

She didn't know which would be worse, getting up and getting shot as she tried to get Rodriguez to safety, or waiting there for Gerik to stroll on over and shoot her at point-blank range.

I am yours. Accept my spirit, was all she knew to pray.

And then—footfalls. Moving fast. In the opposite direction. She raised her head, and to her amazement, she saw Gerik Schroeder running away.

Surprised, she drew herself up to kneel over Rodriguez. And she saw.

She saw the gaping hole in his chest, where several bullets had hit home, tearing him apart.

She was kneeling in a pool of his warm blood.

Jaime was shaking too hard to take his pulse. Instead,

she put a hand over his mouth and nose. She could discern no breath.

A low scream, a keening cry, roared up from the center of her being. She looked around the square for help.

The children had scattered and run. The murderer had fled also.

And then she saw them—five members of the Fedayeen. They did not even look at her. They were chasing Gerik Schroeder.

She felt a pressure on her shoulder and looked up to see Yani looking down at her. "Jaime," he said. "I'm sorry. But we've got to go."

"Help me! We've got to get him to help!" she said.

"It wouldn't matter. He's dead. It's no longer safe here. We must move quickly."

She stared at him. He was using *the tone*.

She looked down at Rodriguez, who had done as he had promised he would and had taken a bullet meant for her. Five bullets meant for her.

"He died so you can live. Come quickly, so he didn't do it for nothing!"

Yani was pulling her arm.

"Maybe he's not dead. Maybe we can save him!"

Yani dropped to one knee beside her and spoke quietly but firmly. "Look at him. You know he's gone. You know he can't be saved."

Oh, God! she thought, clutching her chest. *Maybe he can't be saved . . . but the alternative can't be right, either! That he is dead because of me. That my friend sacrificed himself purposely, willingly. That Rodriguez is dead.*

She threw herself on top of him, as if to still shield him somehow. If it was true that he was dead, she would stay here with him.

"I'm sorry. I must take you." Yani wasn't asking; he was telling.

She felt his strong hands again at her neck. She gave a deep cry from the center of her being: "No!"

She was paralyzed in Yani's grip, and he was carrying her across the square with wide strides.

"Wait!" she said, suddenly, then fiercely: *"Wait!"*

Yani looked at her, surprised. He set her down. She ran back to Rodriguez and tenderly lifted his head, tugging off his hidden dog tags. She knew that doing so meant his body might never be identified. But she was more afraid of what would happen to him if he was discovered to be American military.

Not willing to wait any longer, Yani again approached her. She clutched the silver chain as he drew her quickly back to the car.

The local man was gone. The man with the salt-and-pepper beard was in the front passenger seat. Yani practically threw her into the backseat next to Kristof and slammed the door.

Then he leapt into the front seat, hit the gas, and headed out of town in what he guessed was the opposite direction of that Gerik was using for his own getaway.

April 9, 2003, 11:22 A.M.
Al Qurnah
Southern Iraq

What were these destroyers of civilization doing here?
Gerik had happily taken the money from the Fedayeen for
disclosing to them—and their deposed leader—directions
to the site of the Garden of Eden, a place where it was said
a man could "disappear off the face of the earth." The ne-
gotiation had been Satis's idea.

Gerik, of course, had no intention of letting those men
anywhere near the dwelling of the purebloods. He had
given them a bogus rendezvous point; obviously they had
been tailing him and discovered he had not been square in
dealing with them.

But if they slowed him down now, he could lose Remen.
He could lose his chance. Damn these destroyers!

"Did you forget something?" asked the leader of the
band of Fedayeen. He was the one who'd done the talking
at their farmhouse meeting. The one with the fist-shaped
scar. Now he strode purposefully toward Gerik. "And after
all that money . . . double the price, wasn't it? It occurs to
me that you would not be engaged in a gun battle in the
middle of the square in dusty, remote Al Qurnah if you had
the slightest idea where you were supposed to be going."

Gerik had reached his car. Once behind it, he again

aimed his gun and squeezed the trigger. This at least stopped the men of the Fedayeen from advancing farther. The others looked toward the leader, who, with a blazing look of disgust at Gerik, gave a curt hand signal. This could not be good.

Gerik threw his gun onto the front seat and climbed into the car. He turned the key in the ignition and frantically tried to put the car into reverse.

As he did, another of the Fedayeen lifted a rocket-propelled grenade launcher to his shoulder and dropped to his knee. The leader stepped left, gave a second signal, and the man took careful aim. Gerik looked up to see the man preparing the weapon to fire.

"I'd be remiss if I allowed you to leave without paying what is due," said the Fedayeen captain.

He nodded, and the man pulled the trigger. The weapon fired, sending a blast of exhaust 15 meters behind and launching the grenade in the opposite direction. Large fins sprang out as it spiraled toward its target.

Gerik had no time to react, hide his face, or even throw up his arms in a futile attempt to ward off the attack. All he could do was watch helplessly as the warhead, with its tell-tale trail of blue-gray smoke, zeroed in on his car. The grenade detonated on impact, engulfing the vehicle in fire.

The *Grosskomtur* was able to open the driver's side door and stagger out into the street. There he was met by the bullets of two Fedayeen AK-47s.

He gasped for air. He couldn't believe it. Done in by the henchmen of Saddam Hussein, the men for whom he had total contempt.

They were destroyers of civilizations.

And they had destroyed him.

April 9, 2003, 7:45 P.M.
Former Hawr al Hammār Marsh
Southern Iraq

Jaime sat at a small table in a mud-walled house. It was the home of a Ma'adan family, residents of a now-poor village, where verdant marshes had once been. Even though a shallow canal ran through the town, most of the ground surrounding the row of mud houses was parched and cracked.

No one would tell her the name of the town. It wouldn't be safe for the locals, Kristof said. That was OK with her. She was leaving soon, and she wasn't planning on coming back.

She cradled a cup of cocoa that she'd heated on the fire in the corner. The packet had been in one of the MREs Rodriguez had brought along. The woman of the house had given Jaime a robe—the only other robe she had—Jaime suspected it was her best one. It was a bright floral print on a dark background, with a long skirt, long sleeves and a high collar. Jaime had been loath to accept it, but she could no longer wear the bloody tunic in which she'd arrived. The woman had cheerfully provided her with a basin of water in which to wash. After she did, Jaime had put on Rodriguez's dog tags in place of her own missing ones. And she drank from his canteen cup.

She was too tired to think about what version of the story she would give her superiors upon her return. Her mother had asked her to help Yani, and she had. She had prayed for guidance and protection. Now Rodriguez was dead, and here she sat, in a mud hut at the far end of the world.

Yani had given her no time to go catatonic when they left Al Qurnah. He had immediately instructed her to help Kristof find the tracking device that was on him. How it had not occurred to them after Babylon that Kristof was being tracked was perplexing. It had taken Jaime and Kristof five minutes to find the small circular GPS dot hidden in his collar, just where the tab was. They'd pulled it out and thrown it from the car. Yani then made a U-turn and gunned the car for the real route to their destination.

Then she'd allowed herself to go catatonic. They passed palm trees and water buffalo, as well as countless herds of sheep, and had driven along a river for a while. When they reached this small village, life did not stop. Apparently the locals were used to battered old cars pulling up and strange people getting out.

The house that served as their home base was the largest in the town, which won the distinction by having a small alcove for the kitchen, separate from the rest of the one-room house. It was the room where Jaime had changed her clothes. It was the room where she now sat.

She hadn't seen Yani, Kristof, or their new "fare" since they'd arrived. Jaime assumed they were making rendezvous preparations. She was glad Kristof was safe. She was glad she'd been able to do as her mother asked and help Yani have a successful trip, making his important pickup.

Other than repeating those thoughts, she kept her mind blank, her head covered, and drank cocoa out of Rodriguez's canteen cup. She could not yet bring herself to count the cost.

She clung with every fiber of her being to the idea that

some people remained who would not give their loyalty and allegiance in exchange for power and wealth. That there was something more, something better, something higher than the rich elite of the world, who could decide to initiate "controlled conflicts" and let men like Rodriguez die.

The woman of the house and her teenage daughter had prepared a simple dinner a couple of hours before, and the family had eaten it outdoors. They had asked Jaime to join them, but she had politely declined.

Her mind occasionally returned to wondering what version of the story she'd give when she got back to base. But she was too tired to even begin to hammer it out.

Certainly Yani would drive her back. But she hadn't seen him since their arrival. Suddenly it occurred to her that he might already be gone. That the plan might be for her host family to tell her in the morning that the others had left and it was up to her to find her way back. . . .

But Yani couldn't be gone. They had reached no resolution. He was the only one who had been there from the beginning of this perilous journey. He knew what she had risked, what she had lost. Whether he admitted it or not, even to himself, he had lost something precious, too. He had lost Adara.

He couldn't be gone.

Panicked, Jaime leapt to her feet and ran to the reed door that led outdoors. She didn't have time to push it before someone pulled it open from outside.

It was Yani. His frame easily filled the doorway. He wore a tunic and looked much like he had when she'd first met him back in Ur, except he wore no hat. His black hair was again tousled, with a slight curl. He was alone.

"Hi," he said. "It's time for us to talk."

As Yani entered the hut's kitchen, Jaime had a sudden vision of him stalking over to her, forcefully picking her up, pinning her against the back wall, and kissing her again, as he had outside Baghdad.

Of course, he did not. He was his job. And she was hers. But with that brief vision came the realization that what she had really feared was missing the chance to say good-bye to Yani. Yani, a man she had met only, what, two days ago? Impossible. What had this man done to her?

He strode to the only other chair in the room where it sat beside the small fire. He pulled it to the table and sat down across from her. She noticed he carried a duffel bag. He was obviously ready to move on.

"There are some things I need to tell you," he said. "Some things that still need to be explained."

They'd been through too much, and she was too tired, to mince words.

"What's really at the Eden site?" she asked. "What is everyone really after? Oil? Certainly there can't be that many undiscovered precious jewels. Or is bdellium secretly necessary for modern satellite weapon systems?"

He sat for a moment, leaning back in his chair, and

looked at her, really looked at her. She returned the favor. It was as if through his eyes she saw a replay of their whole journey, their whole relationship.

He put the front legs of his chair back on the dirt floor and asked simply, "Do you trust me?"

She held his gaze a long time. She remembered every time he'd answered an important question with the dismissive, *You'll have to trust me.* Now he was asking if she did.

"Yes," she said.

"That's why you're here," he said softly. "It's because you're grounded in reality—yet able to believe in the unseen—that helped Adara choose you as a backup. And," he added simply, "you've earned my trust as well."

Those simple words were worth more than any other accolades she'd ever won, any public words of praise she'd ever been given. She was still basking in the glow of them when he said conversationally, "Here's the thing. Eden still exists."

The world again crashed in around her. *Oh no. He is delusional, too, after all.*

"What the world calls Eden," he continued, "Is the one place on earth that exists for the good of its neighbors. There is not much coming and going, but former Edenites are at work quietly bringing peace and healing throughout the world. It also is very technologically advanced, because many of the world's great thinkers, teachers, and scientists have come to lend support to this altruistic society. One must be invited to enter the society, and must be willing to leave everything behind."

He looked like he meant everything he said—though it also seemed like a memorized speech that he'd given before.

"Yeah, right," she said, her cynical self happily resurrected to the surface. "Like Shangri-la or Atlantis."

"Over the centuries the legend has grown. People like Satis and Liv have pursued the reality and have gotten close."

She felt a deflation—as if there were anything left in her

to deflate—the kind you feel after the fourth date with the perfect guy, who turns out to have a wife on the side.

She had trusted Yani. Even worse, she had felt her heart begin to stir for the first time since Paul. Jaime had actually begun to think, *Maybe, just maybe, this is someone who could make me feel alive once again . . .*

And now this.

"And it doesn't show up on any satellite pictures because—"

"Look, I can't give you precise information, but your favorite archeologist, Dr. Zaruf, was correct about one thing. The Garden currently exists *under* the Gulf. I know what you're thinking. It's not some magical place. The only thing that can be considered even remotely miraculous was the original oxygen bubble and the placement of the land shelf when the Garden and surrounding countries flooded back during that famous Flandrian Transgression you spoke of. Now the daily running of the country can be quite easily explained by physics and math.

"The only real pain—as you've noticed—is that absolutely no traceable communication transmissions are allowed between Eden and the outside world. That's why we must rely on 'messengers,' like Adara, to bring us necessary information."

"Like computer chips."

"Sometimes on electronic chips. The fact is there is no free passage between the two worlds. Even the Edenites themselves don't know the way in and out. If they feel called to go out into the wider world, they are approved for a 'door opening'—which happens only at certain times. The most it ever happens is twice a year. Then, there are times when the entrance to Eden is imperiled, as it is now. After tonight's opening, the door will remain closed until it's deemed safe to reopen it. So, if I didn't get Kristof here tonight, he would have been at the mercy of Satis's cronies for the foreseeable future."

"So, if even Edenites don't know the way in and out,

how do they know how to find the door?" As if any of this made any sense to begin with.

"They're given a knockout drug before the trip. They wake up in an accepted safe house on the outside. Only the dozen members of the Sword know how to come and go at any given time. It's a great honor to be chosen to be a member of the Sword, as Kristof was, but it requires total sacrifice. The usual term is for thirty active years. When Kristof's niece chose to leave Eden and live in Geneva as a professor, he also chose to live in the world he had moved through so freely for decades. He is not currently an active member of the Sword.

"But I am."

Jaime squeezed Rodriguez's tin cup so hard that the handle bent slightly. "So you're it. You're actually the Sword that everyone's been chasing after."

"Kristof was the missing Sword I had to bring home," Yani said. "But yes. The Sword has been with you the whole time."

"So," said Jaime. "Will Frank McMillan, who now has the physical sword, and possibly the ancient atlases and the cuneiform tablets, be able to decipher them to find the door?"

"There are two answers to that question. First, the sword that Frank has isn't the real one. The actual Dagger of Ur—and its sheath—is currently in a flooded underground bank vault in Baghdad. We do keep track of it. However, whoever had the replica made paid top dollar. It's probably close enough to do the job. But what Frank doesn't know is that the sword itself doesn't give the answer. Instead, finding the location depends on how you position the filigree of the sheath on one of the old atlases. The tablets only tell the positioning, not what to position. Not to mention, I think Frank has other, more worldly, pursuits uppermost in his mind."

"So, then, was Gerik right? Are Edenites the pure-blooded Master Race he was looking for?"

Jaime realized she had never seen Yani laugh before. It transformed his face. Made him look much younger.

"No. In that way, I guess you'd call it the greatest mixed-breed society on earth. People are invited for their inner qualities with complete disregard for the outward."

"So. Besides the whole underwater thing, how is Eden actually different from the rest of the world?"

He looked at her without a trace of guile and said, "We still walk with God in the cool of the day. And we believe, as you do, who rules Eden rules the world. We just happen to be clearer about Who that is."

She stared at him, and she thought, *If only.* Here he was, calmly describing the most incredible things. Yani's strong hands rested quietly on his thighs, no sign of tension or nervous activity. His steady, unwavering gaze seemed to penetrate her soul, as if he was willing her to believe him.

If only. What a great bedtime story. Frankly, it was no threat to her. Let him be as crazy as he wanted. She just hadn't expected it. She couldn't let herself dwell on yet another loss—the loss of who she thought he was. Who she'd so desperately needed him to be.

None of this was going to help her with a plausible explanation back at base.

Yani looked at his watch. It was a new, different one, with an illuminated dial, much information, and many gizmos on it. "It's nearly time for me to go," he said.

"OK." She was beyond exhaustion. None of this made any sense. Perhaps she'd wake up tomorrow, in her tent back in Tallil, and find it was all a dream. But his next words shattered her illusion and pulled her as violently awake as if he'd tossed her suddenly into a snowbank.

"I have one more thing to tell you," he said. "Your parents did not both die in that hotel room in Jordan. Your mother is in Eden."

In that instant, Jaime went from enjoying his quaint tale to despising him for telling such a personal lie.

He watched her stiffen.

"When our people reached your parents, shortly after Gerik Schroeder had, your father was dead, and your mother was critically wounded. Since her identity was compromised, it was no longer safe for her in the *terris* world. The decision was made to bring her in to try to save her."

"And she never sent us word? Us, her own children? My mother would never do that. You don't know how awful it was!"

"Jaime, she couldn't. You were being watched. Any word from her would have put your lives in jeopardy." He continued in a low, steady voice, "Your mother's grandmother was also an Edenite. You have family there."

She could do nothing but stare at him.

He continued, gently. "The reason all that information about you—your family, your husband—was in the necklace device I showed you in Ur is that you're being invited to come, as well."

He picked up his duffel bag. As he continued to talk, he brought out three silver wine goblets and a bottle of French Merlot. Not the contents she had guessed.

"This is what is going to happen. I will offer you two goblets of wine so that we may have a farewell drink together," As he spoke, he uncorked the bottle and poured wine into all three cups. He pulled his back.

"One of the goblets will have hydrochloride in it. One will not. The choice is yours. If you choose the spiked drink, you will wake up in Eden, but will not be permitted to tell anyone outside where you have gone. If you choose the regular goblet, you will remain here until the other three of us have gone. Then you will be taken a safe distance from this village and given means to contact the nearest Army base."

He matter-of-factly pulled a small vial of powder out of the duffel. He opened it, poured it into the cup on the left, and stirred it briefly with the long cork. He put the cork down in front of that cup, lest there be any mistake about which was which.

Her breathing was ragged.

He was obviously crazy. She stared at the dosed drink. This was obviously some nutty Jim-Jones-drink-the-Kool-Aid thing.

And yet . . . everything Yani had told her so far had turned out to be true.

What did he call her? A rational person with faith. Faith in what? In extraordinary things. In life beyond this one. In a God who ruled Eden—who ruled the world. In spite of everything.

She wanted to believe. She wanted to know that the temptation to believe him was based on more than Yani's incredible good looks or the electricity she felt every time he touched her.

Yani pushed the two goblets forward to her. Then he picked up his goblet of wine and raised it to her for a final toast.

So much raced through her mind. Even if it was true, could she do this to her brother and sister, who had lost so much family already? Could she leave the soldiers she had come to serve? Could she endanger those who would be sent to search for her?

She looked again at Yani. He met her gaze. And, to her astonishment, she realized he really believed this crazy thing.

Trust me. How many times had he required that of her?

To her further astonishment, Jaime Richards also realized that she was not the same woman she had been, just a day earlier. She did not want to live in a world devoid of the possibility of something beyond. She did not want to live in a world of fighting and death, of Schroeders, McMillans, and Satises, and not have a Yani, who stood for something true.

She couldn't have lost Rodriguez for no reason.

She could not stand that.

She had to believe.

She picked up the cork, and the goblet behind it.

Yani braided the fingers of her left hand with the fingers of his right. Their palms locked in fervent prayer, as if to say, *Together, we can take on the world.*

In that moment, Jaime knew she believed.

She met his steady gaze, raised the goblet in a toast, and together they drank.

EPILOGUE

DEPARTMENT OF THE ARMY
HEADQUARTERS, 57TH CORPS SUPPORT GROUP
UNIT #93404
APO, AE 09303-3404

April 14, 2003

Mr. Joseph Richards
234 Garden Street
Terre Haute, IN

Dear Mr. Richards,

I wish to express my heartfelt concern to you and your family for the deep distress you must feel as you wait for news of your sister Chaplain (Major) Jaime L. Richards. I know you must be very frustrated, and I promise that I will keep you informed as we continue to search for her.

Jaime was last seen in the ruins of Babylon near Al Hillah, Iraq. Evidence collected to date indicates she was kidnapped by someone working with the Fedayeen, and taken to a farmhouse on the outskirts of Baghdad. A member of the Central Intelligence Agency was able to follow her captor's trail to that point, and his search of the house uncovered many of her personal effects. Those items will be returned to you as soon as our forensic experts have completed their analysis. There were no signs of struggle, or any other indication that she has been harmed. Unfortunately, there were also no further clues as to her whereabouts.

When I deployed, I vowed to bring home every member of my command. I do not plan to break that vow. Jaime is a valued member of my staff, and loved by all the soldiers. We miss her dearly, and will not rest until she is found.

I know that there is little I can say to ease your mind as you wait for information about your sister. If there is anything I or any member of my command can do to assist you, please do not hesitate to ask.

                    Sincerely,

                    Abraham M. Derry
                    Colonel, Quartormaster
                    Commanding

ACKNOWLEDGMENTS

No book is ever the work of only one—or in this case, two—persons. We owe a great debt of gratitude to many others, including the following people:

Our editor Jennifer Enderlin for her unsurpassed vision and insight; Susan Cohen for many years of agenting and friendship; Kimberly Cardascia for keeping the world running with humor and aplomb; Noel Lewke for ready help with information about military logistics systems and stable design; Kathie Sakenfeld for helping us find the perfect Akkadian translator, and J.J.M. Roberts for accepting the challenge; James Shanahan, A, D.O., for free medical advice—seemingly, the more nefarious, the better—as well as for general snowblowing; Craig Johnson, who may have seen more dusty corners of Ur than Lord Wooley himself; Gary Kessler, who made the manuscript all it could be; Dr. Juris Zarins, who convincingly places Eden in southern Sumeria; Carole King and Barbara Wild, who wrestled so much more than serial commas; Bill DeSmedt, author of *Singularity*, who always knows a little too much to be just what he seems; Christian Fuenfhausen, an unending fountain of creative ideas; Jerry Todd, who knows how to make art pop; our favorite spook—you know who you are—we hereby acknowledge in writing that in its day the Farm did indeed field a decent football team.

Thanks also to our manuscript readers who added so much at each phase of development: Johanna Skilling, a great friend and colleague; Mary Ann O'Roark, a true professional and one of life's best gifts; Nancy Moore, a font of unending knowledge about great mysteries; Colleen Larsen, a good friend, colleague, and smart reader; Tom Mattingly—in a way, we've gone on this perilous journey together—thanks for the friendship as well as the sage advice; Chris and Deb Holton-Smith, for your unflagging support and enthusiasm; Ernie and Polly VanderKruik for insights and advice; Julie Edens, who was always there when help was needed; Ryan Edens, for giving a teen perspective and not crashing B. K.'s truck while learning to drive a stick shift; Janet Horton and Donna Weddle, as steadfast pioneers and great mentors; Paul Weddle, whom B. K. would trust with her own—and Derry's—life; and finally, Ian "Red" Natkin, who not only gave spirited commentary on the book, but also years ago accepted a chaplain of a different faith, drew her into the staff inner circle, and taught her how to be an effective staff officer.

Thanks also to Robin Davis Miller at the Author's Guild, for sharing her knowledge and wondering why authors don't have longer acknowledgments. Obviously, we listened.

From Sharon: My love and thanks first to Robert Owens Scott. One way to ensure a life of adventure is to have a husband who is a 3rd degree black belt, both in Tae Kwon Do and in life. (We're not getting older, we're getting more dangerous!) To Jonathan and Linnéa, two fine human beings who happen to be my children—it's no fun going away without you to come home to. As always, to my father and mother, William and Marilynn Webber, who gave me a firm foundation and set me on this unpredictable course. To my brother, Stephen Webber, and his wife, Susan: Thanks for doing the genius musician thing so I don't have to. To my nieces, Aubrey and Angela Webber, both so creative that I expect to be best known to the ages as a footnote in their biographies. And, of course, to B. K.: We may have been the only girls in Springfield, Missouri, playing French Underground and living to write the stories about it—and writing plays, and making movies. You always called out the bravest in me and challenged me to be my best. Please keep taking the hard path, but please—keep living to tell the tales.

From B. K.: First, I give thanks to God, for blessing me with great family and friends, and making every day such an adventure. For the unlikely partnership that began with two girls in Mrs. Conard's sixth-grade class and grew into a friendship for life. For James R. Struthers, who showed me how to be a pastor. For Steve Fairbanks and Lindsey Arnold, who started me down that camouflage path. For the "Brown Hall Gang" and the wild adventures that kept seminary life from bogging down with academics. For Kris Gerling, always keeping me grounded in reality; Joann Mann, Karen Diefendorf, and Mark Jones for never being afraid to share what you have learned with others; and Doug Swift for your zeal for ministry and great intellect. For Chris Wallace and Andi Jansen, for great supervision and support both before and after my sidetrip to the desert. For all of my chaplain assistants over the years: you are great soldiers and true professionals.

For my family: my stepmother, Maxine; sister, Linda; sister-in-law, Lynda; niece, Deanna; and "international" sister, Kati: The care packages have made every deployment a little easier. For Randy, who may never fully understand how much it meant to return to American soil after spending months in a combat zone and to find my big brother standing there waving the flag to welcome me home. And for my mom and dad. I know you are here in spirit, and in many ways, you are responsible for the completion of this book.

From both of us: Thanks to everyone who has shown us, in word and deed, that a life of faith is the grandest adventure.

Read on for an excerpt from S. L. Linnea's next book

Beyond EDEN

Coming soon from St. Martin's Paperbacks

PROLOGUE

Monday, December 5, 2005, 7:05 A.M.
London, England

On the morning of the day on which he would be kidnapped, Jimi Afzal cut himself while shaving. It was a small nick, but it bled, and he was unhappy because he didn't want anything to serve as a distraction to the proposal he was pitching at his nine a.m. meeting.

He'd worked hard to earn this meeting. He was an associate editor at one of the few mid-sized independent publishing houses left in London. He had long wanted to do a series of nonfiction books with a brilliant man who had been nominated for a Nobel prize in physics and was a friend of his parents. When the gentleman was over for dinner, as he had often been at the Afzal family flat, he got to talking about physics, and life, in a way that was compelling and accessible. Jimi just knew there was the potential for a series of classic books. After careful wrangling, he had gotten the agreement of the friend, the support of his mentor editor, and an appointment with the executive editor of the company, whose approval would be needed for such an ambitious project. An appointment that day, December 5, 2006, at nine a.m.

He dressed in his best suit, skipped breakfast, pulled on

his grey wool coat, and left his flat on Westbourne Gardens a half hour early.

The street noise, the people, the winter chill were all nothing more than backdrop to the presentation he was running again and again on a loop in his head. He was momentarily pleased that he'd reached the platform in the Queensway tube station of the Central Line just as a train was arriving—perhaps the augur of good things to come.

So lost was he in his own thoughts that it took him seconds to realize the air had somehow turned orange. That his eyes were tearing. His throat burning.

Everyone else turning, coughing. Panicking, even, in an oh-so-British, excuse-me-my-good-man, let-me-off-the-train-and-up-the-bloody-elevator kind of way.

His eyes were burning now, but he was in the flow of people heading towards the exits. Emergency services were arriving. A voice of authority over the speaker system. *Stay calm, exit in an orderly fashion.*

A young woman next to him was crying. *I can't breathe, I can't breathe*, she was sobbing. He put his arm around her shoulder and said, "Don't panic, you'll suck in more bad air."

But all he was thinking was, *Nine a.m. This can't make me late. Damn terrorists.*

Then he was up and back outside. Ambulances, stretchers, constables, arriving news crews.

He dropped off the girl, still sobbing, to emergency personnel and walked through the crowd of terrified people.

Can't be late.

He started walking east on Bayswater, wondering if life were normal a street over.

Behind him, blaring horns, snarled traffic, shrieking people, chaos.

"Are you all right? What's going on?" A woman's face leaned forward.

He looked up to see a black limousine beside him, the back passenger window rolled down.

"Terrorists, I suppose. Chemical attack."

"Horrid! So sorry! You all right?"

"What? Yes, don't know about the others, but I'm fine. Eyes sting, that's the worst, really."

"So sorry!"

"Right. Thanks."

"You need any help?"

"I just need to get to work."

"Well, there I can help." The limo door popped open. "Climb in, then."

"Oh, no, don't want to bother . . ."

"Come on. I'll feel I've done my part." The limo's passenger was also dressed for work. Power dressed, black designer suit, black-rimmed sunglasses.

All right. Maybe the day was saved, after all.

"If you really mean it, thanks so much."

He climbed in, and the car snaked forward. It had been past the tube entrance when the evacuation began, and now it was inching out of the area. Seemed it would be free of the mess fairly shortly.

"Where to?"

"Sorry?"

"Where to?" the woman asked, extending a hot cup of tea.

"Golden Rachmann Publishing. It's . . ."

"I know it," she said, and smiled. She picked up the telephone handset and had a brief discourse with the driver.

"It's not far past my stop," she said. "Not a problem."

"Thanks so much."

Even given the favor the woman was doing him, and the tea he was now holding, he again retreated into his head, into the midst of his presentation.

The tea was in a real cup, with a saucer. It was heaven in his throat, which still burned. The woman finished her own tea, put the cup on the small table where the hot pot was, leaned across him, and said, "This is me."

The car rolled to a halt, and she climbed out in front of a chic building.

"Thanks so much," he said again as the car began to move.

Thank you for seeing me, Mr. Rachmann. I believe we have an extraordinary opportunity before us . . .

The words played again and again in his mind.

They were beginning to make less sense.

His tea was gone. He set his cup down next to the woman's empty cup.

He looked out the window and was shocked to see countryside. He was confused. So confused. His head was spinning.

"Driver, you've got to let me out," he said, banging on the window. "Driver, we've missed my stop."

But the car kept going. He swayed, and lurched back towards the long bench seat. No, this wasn't right. This wasn't right at all. Through the worsening haze in his mind, he tried to open the back door, even though the car was moving. But it was locked. It wouldn't open.

Let me out! Nine o'clock. I must, really . . . he said. And he passed out on the backseat without fully comprehending that he wouldn't make anymore nine a.m. meetings for a very, very long time.

Sunday, December 18, 2005, 6:50 P.M.
Warwick, New York

Nutmeg and ginger. No matter how many pine-scented candles were sold as part of the Christmas season, for Juliet Kettner, it was the aroma of baking with nutmeg and ginger that would forever signal to her that the season had truly arrived. She hummed along with the radio station that was playing Christmas songs, and peeked in at the gingerbread men in the oven. The kids would be back soon, and she knew they'd all prefer the chocolate chip cookies, but now they, too, would have ginger-scented memories of the season.

What a great day. The first large snowfall of the season had blanketed Warwick on Friday, canceling school and warming hearts everywhere. By today, Sunday, when the kids from church had planned to go Christmas caroling, the roads were clear, yet the ground was still white. How perfect was that?

The kids had a blast caroling, both at the homes of targeted "shut-ins," as well as up and down blocks where friends and families resided. Finally a group of a dozen or so had come back to the Kettner house for pizza and snow play, ending with hot chocolate and warm cookies by the fire.

The Kettner house was a block from Stanley Deming Park, a large village park that had a classic sledding hill. The remaining middle-schoolers had grabbed saucers and sleds and headed out, promising to be back by seven p.m., since it was a school night. Parents would start arriving soon to pick up their offspring.

Juliet tossed another log on the fire in the great room and headed to the front door. She could see the outlines of the kids trudging back up the final hill from the park. Right on time. They were singing as they approached, another old standard: "Grandma got run over by a reindeer . . ."

She grinned and opened the door, reminding them to stomp their boots before coming in and shedding snow clothes. Their breath was white, their cheeks were crimson from the cold, but they were in high spirits.

"Everyone into the great room! Popcorn is out, grab a cup of cocoa as you pass through the kitchen. Half have marshmallows, half do not, take your pick! Cookies coming in right away!"

The gingerbread was ready. She used a spatula to scoop them onto a Christmas angel–shaped platter, and waded into the great room. Christmas tree lighted and glowing in the corner, room now stuffed with kids, laughing, dropping to the floor, arguing over television channels.

She put down the trays of chocolate chip cookies first, and then looked for her son's friend whom she knew particularly liked gingerbread. Didn't see him first time through.

"Anyone seen Ryan S.?" she asked. They had multiple Ryans, and went along the school habit of differentiating them by first initial of last name.

"Probably in the bathroom," said Ian T.

But a few minutes later, he hadn't re-emerged.

"Seriously, guys, where's Ryan?" she asked again.

"He was with us, Mrs. K. He was racing with Jonathan and Kevin."

"He wiped out big time, twice!" added Jonathan, enthusiastically.

Juliet had done a sweep of the entire first floor, to no avail. She called her own two kids out of the crowd to see if Ryan's snow clothes were in the pile by the door. They didn't seem to be.

"Guys, stay here. I'm going to check the park. I'll be right back," she said. She pulled on boots over her stockinged feet, wrapped a coat around herself, and went out.

In contrast to the house, the outdoors was eerily still. There were no streetlights in the hilly part of the park where the sledding had taken place, so the snow was grey, and shadows loomed large. All the sledders were now gone. The park was entirely empty.

"Ryan?" she yelled. "Ryan S.?" she yelled louder. The whistling wind was the only reply.

She trudged by herself along the abandoned hill, seeing the various sledding tracks cut into the snow banks, worn flat by multiple uses. There were no huddled children, left with an unnoticed broken ankle or broken back.

There was nobody.

Maybe a friend from Ryan's neighborhood had offered him a ride home, and he had neglected to tell anyone?

That had to be it.

Juliet turned around and headed home. As she got to the top of the hill, she saw the first three parent-cars turning onto her block. The second car, a white Prius, was Ryan's mom. And she was in the car alone.

Juliet Kettner's heart sank.

Forever after, she would think of this as the day that had ruined the warm comfort of nutmeg and ginger for her, forever.

February 23, 2006, 10:00 A.M.
40 km SE of Ad Diwaniyah, along MSR Tampa
Iraq

Command Sergeant Major Zack DeCamp was not having a good day. He commanded a five-vehicle convoy that served as the Personal Security Detachment for the 5th COSCOM Commanding General who was based in Balad, Iraq. If the CG, the Commanding General, had to get somewhere by ground, it was DeCamp's responsibility. Most American soldiers in Iraq prayed they didn't have to ride in a convoy very often during their deployment. But convoys were DeCamp's way of life.

Today the five vehicles had done a test run along the road from the COSCOM headquarters in Balad, an hour north of Baghdad, down to Tallil, which was four hours south of Baghdad. It hadn't been easy. Waiting on the engineers to defuse two improvised explosive devices, coping with small arms fire, and a plain old flat tire had put the convoy three hours behind schedule. And now, he was monitoring a very interesting conversation on his SIN-GARS radio that threatened to delay him even more.

"Checkmate, this is Earthpig Five, over," came the initial call over his headset.

"Go ahead, Earthpig, this is Checkmate." DeCamp knew that "Checkmate" was the quick reaction force that patrolled this portion of the route between Scania and Tallil. He figured that "Earthpig" must be the large convoy that had just passed them on the other side of the divided highway.

"Checkmate, there is an LN female who just tried to flag down our convoy. She was right along the shoulder waving and signaling to us. It looked very suspicious." "LN" was the term for "local national." DeCamp knew the convoy commander was concerned that she might be a suicide bomber, or trying to set them up for a trap farther down the road. "She is currently located one kilometer north of checkpoint Delta. Over."

Command Sergeant Major DeCamp looked at his map and clenched his teeth around the unlit cigar stub dangling from his lips. Guess who would be coming up to the position in a matter of minutes? He sighed heavily, then spoke into his radio. "Checkmate, this is Outlaw Seven."

"Go ahead, Outlaw Seven."

"We are one klick from location reported by Earthpig Five. Will check it out."

"Roger Outlaw Seven. Call if you need backup."

"We ain't gonna need any," he growled to himself. His Personal Security Detachment was its own damn backup. It consisted of five fully up-armored Humvees, each with a rotating turret and gunner with automatic weapon. Compared to the old canvas-sided humvees, these machines looked like Brinks trucks.

If Earthpig, barreling in the opposite direction, had just passed the woman, she should be right about here . . . and indeed, it wasn't long before he spotted her, standing alone on the opposite side of the highway. Her head was covered with an ivory-colored scarf, and she wore a long green tunic and matching pants. She waved at them as she had the convoy before.

Speaking over the convoy's internal communication system, DeCamp laid out the plan of attack. "Outlaw One-One and One-Three, cover my right and left. I'm going straight up the middle. Outlaw Eight and Five, take up blocking positions on the highway."

His driver cut the wheel to the left and bounded across the median, heading straight for the woman. He skidded to a halt twenty-five meters directly in front of her, kicking up an immense cloud of dust that sent her into a coughing fit. The next truck pulled off to his right about thirty meters, as if to cut off her escape path to the south. The third did the same to the north. The last two held back to stop any traffic that might approach along the highway. Every turret had a large automatic weapon trained directly at her.

The only feature DeCamp could make out were her eyes, and they were understandably wide open and fearful. It seemed she grasped her disadvantage in the current situation. She slowly raised her hands in the air as if to say, "I surrender." He muscled open his door, drew his nine-millimeter pistol from its holster and took a few steps in her direction. He knew he painted a very imposing figure, despite his short five-foot-nine-inch stature. His swarthy skin and stocky frame, combined with a tanker's helmet and body armor which included extra shoulder protection as well as knee and elbow pads, gave the impression of a Storm Trooper from *Star Wars*.

The woman was of medium build, slim, and an inch or two shorter than he. He motioned for her to put her hands behind her head, and she followed his directions. He then waved his 9mm toward the ground, and she dropped to her knees.

By now, the Command Sergeant Major was close enough to tell that she was carrying no weapons. Nor could she be hiding any bombs. He decided to take a chance and approach her. He dug into his pocket and pulled out a special card written in Farsi that the Civil Affairs team had given him to help communicate with the Iraqis. He held it before her eyes, and saw her brow furrow.

"What is this supposed to be?" she blurted out.

He jumped back, startled. "You speak English!"

"Of course I speak English. I'm an American!"

"What do you mean, 'of course'? What the fuck are you doing standing along the side of the road in local garb waving at convoys?"

The woman struggled to suppress a smile at his rather crass answer. "It's a long story, and one I will gladly share with you, but do you suppose that we could first point all these weapons in some other direction?"

"Oh yeah, sorry." He holstered his 9mm and reached down to help her stand. "I'm Sergeant Major Zack De-Camp, Fifth COSCOM. Who are you, some sort of reporter working with the locals?"

"No, I'm an American soldier. My name is Jaime Richards. I was with Fifty-seventh CSG under V Corps. I may be listed as MIA." She reached up and removed the head scarf, allowing her blonde hair to fall freely to her shoulders.

DISCUSSION QUESTIONS FOR
CHASING EDEN

1. Do you identify with Jaime Richards—her spirit, courage, loyalty? Why or why not? Do you identify more with another character? When you read, how often do you identify with a character? Does that affect your enjoyment of a book?

2. Jaime is a woman working in a profession that is usually reserved for males. Do you think women should serve in the military or as ministers? Why or why not?

3. Jaime was in the middle of a combat zone and not carrying a weapon. Do you think that was crazy? Do you understand why she said that under immediate threat she prayed she'd "have the courage" not to pick up a gun? Would you make the same decision if you were in her shoes?

4. How has Jaime been shaped by the loss of loved ones in her life? Do you believe she coped with the losses honestly? Did these losses bring her strength? Can you identify with her journey through loss and the beginnings of healing?

5. No matter what your religion, can you identify wit Jaime's struggle with her beliefs? Do doubt and ques tioning weaken or strengthen faith?

6. Are there thoughts or actions of Jaime's that surpris you because she is a minister?

7. In what ways was Yani like Jaime's husband Paul? I what ways were the two men different? Do you under stand how Jaime could be attracted to each? Do yo believe Jaime and Yani could ever have a real relation ship?

8. Jaime Richards, Coleman Satis and Gerik Schroede each lived according to what they believed was mos important in life. How did their values dictate thei actions?

9. Do you believe Coleman Satis's lust for power was in stilled in him by his mother, or was it born of his ow choices?

10. Gerik Schroeder honestly felt he was building an en lightened society. Did his beliefs give you any insigh into the Nazi mindset? Could you understand how h could feel his quest was a noble one?

11. How did the actions of Gerik and Jaime in the squar at Al Qurnah illustrate the values and character o each?

12. Do you agree with Frank McMillan when he said tha most wars were fundamentally religious wars?

13. Kristof said that what people would expect to find i Eden tells a lot about the person. What would yo hope/expect to find in a perfect world?

14. Would you have made the same choice Jaime did at the
    end of the book? If so, why? Would you have been
    looking for escape? Adventure? Spiritual fulfillment?
    To help advance civilization?

AN INTERVIEW WITH
SHARON LINNÉA AND
B.K. SHERER

What was the genesis (pardon the pun) of the plot?

Sharon: All mysteries for me start with "what ifs?" Obviously, I was closely watching the beginning of the Iraq War back in 2003. When it came out that the Iraq Museum and the museum in Mosul had been robbed simultaneously, by pros who knew exactly what they wanted, the questions were immediate: Who did it? What did they want? Why? How did they have access? How did they know when? Why were there no guards? How powerful were the men who made it possible for this robbery to take place? Powerful enough to make sure the museums were unguarded? Powerful enough to start a war?

Also, for centuries, humankind has told stories about, and been intrigued by, the idea of Eden, which was undoubtedly located in Mesopotamia—perhaps in the Iraq/Iran/Kuwait Gulf area. I love subjects where, the more you research, the more intriguing the material becomes.

Eden aside, suddenly the evening news was filled with images of the Tigris and Euphrates, talking about Ur and Babylon and Nineveh. Wow. These places are real—and we're there.

Finally, of course, B.K. was over there and I wanted to know, in some small portion, what it was like when she seemingly disappeared behind what felt like a veil of white smoke. Again, questions.

How accurate are the descriptions of the places in the book?

Sharon: We did our best to ensure the descriptions were accurate as of the date of the story. Of course, we chose many locations specifically because we had someone on the ground who had been (or was currently) there. That included larger locales such as Tallil and Baghdad Airport, but also unusual ones such as Satis's bombed-out palace. With others, we came as close as we could through interviews, maps, and photos.

How do the two of you work together? How is that complicated by Chaplain Sherer's deployments?

B.K.: We brainstorm well. One gets an idea. The other adds on, and it gets rolling until you can't really identify where anything originated. Ultimately, though, Sharon is the one who normally writes it down. I am the kinetic expression who likes to act out the motion and action of the scene. Then she can take those pictures and present them in a clear, exciting, verbal way.

Sharon: As far as working during B.K.'s deployments, of course it's easiest to spitball together in person. But it's bizarre how, in this day of the Internet, it almost doesn't matter where B.K. is. During her first deployment to Iraq, during the very first days of the war, I was lucky to get a handwritten letter, no stamp of course, turning up in the mailbox when I least expected it. By the time she went back, there was Internet and phone, and except for the time difference, she really could have been anywhere. I'm sure she appreciated coming back from a long day of facing the human cost of war to have me bugging her about going over a new scene from book two!

B.K.: Actually, I didn't feel "bugged" at all. In fact, working on the book helped me relax during my second Iraq deployment. Some people play video games to let off steam, others work out. I would return to my hooch in the evening and escape into the world of Jaime and Yani for a short while.

You have been friends since the sixth grade. As kids did you make up stories together? Were any of these adventure or mystery stories?

Sharon: We met in Mrs. Conard's sixth-grade class in Eugene Field Elementary School in Springfield, Missouri. We'd both moved there from other places: my family from the Chicago area, and hers from New York State. At first, I was ticked off with her because she was irritatingly smart and competitive and she'd purposely catch up to me and surpass me in the color-coded SRA reading folders. Drove me nuts.

B.K.: And I was absolutely amazed at the number of guys Sharon could date simultaneously. Wait . . . no . . . that was later, in high school.

Sharon: But at some point we realized that if we joined forces, we'd be unstoppable. That was probably shortly after I discovered she was not only very smart, she was also wacky. Our collaborations began immediately.

The first was a play for the sixth-grade talent show,

about the French Underground, which was to both of us the epitome of standing up in the face of tyranny, although I don't think we verbalized it that way at the time. But we also made movies together, and wrote a full-length theatrical comedy called *A (K) Night in Ruthin Castle.* We started a company when we were in junior high called "Imagining Things Enterprises." We had film festivals, and started a magazine. We used to write interviews with each other, and make up quotes if we needed to, then hand the copy to the other one and say, "Here, read this out loud." So then she really would have said it.

B.K.: Hey, Sharon, stop giving away our secrets. Now they're going to know how we did this interview!

How is Chaplain Jaime Richards like Chaplain B.K. Sherer? In what ways are they different?

Sharon: Well, they both have the same first name (Chaplain).

B.K.: (ha ha)

Sharon: Truthfully, I know that's a natural question, but a hard one to answer. Bottom line: Every character in the book contains parts of B.K., parts of me, and parts of other people we know or have heard about.

As a writer, I know a character has a life of her own when she or he starts speaking naturally in my head— when I recognize the voice, the cadence, the thought processes, the sense of humor, or lack thereof. We've joked that Jaime is the perfect woman—the best parts of each of us. But then Jaime leapt to life and became her own person.

I will say that Jaime does have a lot of B.K.'s qualities— the courage, the fierce loyalty, the vulnerability, the importance of faith in her life, and the ability to be there with people. On the other hand, Jaime has my height and hair color and is limited by my vocabulary and emotional intelligence.

But Jaime really is her own person, with her own life and her own journey that's very different from either of ours. Were Jaime real, she'd undoubtedly know B.K., since they've been in such proximity so many times.

And of course, Chaplain Sherer would never swear under any circumstances . . .

(Answer had to end as Sharon was laughing so hard she couldn't continue.)

B.K.: And don't forget that both Jaime and I were predestined to be Presbyterians!

Sharon: Hang on. I happen to be American Baptist, and I know how easily Jaime could have chosen to go a different way!

Do you ever argue?

B.K.: Never.

Sharon: Constantly.

B.K.: Define argue.

When did Sharon Linnea write her first novel? What other books has she written?

Sharon: Funny you should ask. I wrote my first novel in seventh grade. It was titled *What Are the Odds?* It was an international spy caper featuring B.K. and myself as the protagonists. We joined forces with the twin brother I'm sure Kurt Russell never knew he had.

I've known I wanted to be a storyteller since I was about nine years old, and I've been very blessed to be able to make a living as a writer and editor since before I graduated from college. Some of my books have been biographies of heroes of mine, such as Princess Ka'iulani and Raoul Wallenberg. Please see my Web site (SharonLinnea.com) for a (much) lengthier answer to that question.

Since Chaplain Sherer is still active duty, did she have to get approval for this book?

Sharon: Absolutely. We have great respect for the military and have done our best to play by the rules, which are there for good reason. The manuscripts are always cleared by the Department of the Army so that we don't give away anything vital to national security. And I adore the disclaimer they had us put in the factual notes. Seriously. It's one of my favorite sentences in the book.

When does the next Jaime Richards thriller come out?

Sharon: It comes out in October 2007, so if it's November 2007 or after, you should be ordering now and finish reading this later. Thank you.

What do you hope people get from the Eden thrillers?

Sharon: A ripping good read. The chance to ponder interesting questions. But mostly hope. Hope that in a world in which it so often seems that greed and violence hold sway and might makes right, that there is a conspiracy of the good—of the humble, the loving, the peacemakers—which has been there since time began, and in which everyone's invited to participate.

Also that being humble and loving doesn't mean you can't kick butt should the need arise.

B.K.: When ordinary people face extraordinary circumstances, they often discover strength they never knew they had. That strength comes from many sources, provided by the God who never lets us face our troubles alone. I see examples of this every day, and hope the readers will be encouraged to recognize the experience of this in their own lives.

For a more extensive interview, visit SharonLinnea.com, JaimeRichardsThrillers.com, or edenthrillers.com